"I think he's depressed," Nick said. "It happens to military dogs when they lose their handler. They lose interest in training…forget how to play."

"I've heard about that, but never treated it." Kate watched the shepherd. "Well, now that we know more about him, we can handle him better and start to rehab him. Who knows? Maybe we'll even find him a forever home."

Ben looked up at her. "A forever home?"

"That's what we call it when a dog finds people who will love it and make it a part of their f[...] r the rest of its life. A forever home."

There was a hearth[...] omes aren't forever?" Ben[...] g of that hit him. "S[...]hey don't want them[...]ed up at his dad, then ju[...]nce and headed for the sanctuary[...]

Kate stared aft[...] speechless. She would never have expected to hear such hurt from a vibrant and seemingly well-adjusted child. Had she totally misread Ben's relationship with his father?

"What was that about?" she asked Nick.

"It's not exactly a secret." Nick's tone flattened as he spoke. "Ben's mother left us after I returned from my last deployment. He had just turned four. He doesn't talk about it or about her. But sometimes…it comes out."

"So his mother is…"

"Not in the picture." He produced a tight, humorless smile. "It's just him and me."

Dear Reader,

Animals have always been a big part of our family life, especially dogs. When the last of our beloved schnauzers passed away, we felt the loss keenly, but weren't sure we wanted to go through another puppyhood. We searched online adoption sites for an older dog and found a golden retriever that touched our hearts. When we went to meet the dog, we found the "rescue" to be a very odd place that had household items stacked on upper and lower porches. But our attention went to the sweet golden girl who was to become our Gracie. After taking a short walk around the yard with us, she headed for our car and stood beside it as if to say, "Let's go home, guys."

Gracie is loving, attentive, mannerly and a world-class food mooch. But it was clear from certain behavior that she had been abused in her former life—she was frightened of human feet and cowered whenever we approached with something in our hands, even a food dish. With time and love, she has grown more confident.

Then one day we opened the local paper to find that the "rescue" where we had gotten Gracie was being investigated for animal hoarding. The stacks of household stuff were a symptom of good intentions gone terribly wrong. As the story played out, we watched on the evening news as volunteers removed animals from the place, and we could hardly believe what we saw. That experience led me to do eye-opening research. When a new shelter opened in our county, I knew I had to write about the people who give so much of themselves to make the world a better, safer place for animals. And about how rescuing an animal can sometimes rescue us.

I hope you enjoy this story of the veteran and the veterinarian!

Betina Krahn

HEARTWARMING

Soldier's Rescue

New York Times Bestselling Author

Betina Krahn

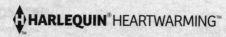
HARLEQUIN® HEARTWARMING™

Recycling programs
for this product may
not exist in your area.

ISBN-13: 978-0-373-36851-8

Soldier's Rescue

Copyright © 2017 by Betina Krahn

This edition published by arrangement with Harlequin Books S.A.

For questions and comments about the quality of this book,
please contact us at CustomerService@Harlequin.com.

® and TM are trademarks of Harlequin Enterprises Limited or its
corporate affiliates. Trademarks indicated with ® are registered in the
United States Patent and Trademark Office, the Canadian Intellectual
Property Office and in other countries.

Printed in U.S.A.

www.Harlequin.com

Bestselling author **Betina Krahn** is a mother of two and owner of two (humans and canines, respectively) and the creator of dozens of satisfying happily-ever-afters. Her historical romances have received numerous reviewer's choice and lifetime achievement awards and have appeared regularly on bestseller lists, including the *USA TODAY* and *New York Times* lists. Her books have been called sexy, warm, witty and even wise. But the description that pleases her most is "funny"—because she believes the only thing the world needs as much as it needs love is laughter. Visit her online at www.betinakrahn.com to learn more about her and her books.

For Kate and Nicholas

May each of you find a love that helps you become the person you are meant to be.

CHAPTER ONE

TO HELL WITH speed limits.

He was driving on a dry, sunlit back road without another vehicle in sight, the perfect place to open it up and make time. And he was already late.

Florida trooper Nicholas Stanton put his foot down hard on the gas and felt his senses make a corresponding shift into overdrive. He registered the wire fences along the sides of the county road, hummocks of scrub palmetto and stubborn live oaks, cattle grazing and smatterings of cowbirds and egrets around farm ponds. Heat radiated visibly off the worn macadam, and of habit, he touched the air-conditioner controls—which were already set on high. Barely five minutes went by before he spotted something in the road ahead.

"Sh—*crap.*" He was trying to work on expletives. He was a single dad with a kid who was all eyes and ears. And who was playing in his first ever soccer game in exactly— he glanced at his watch—fifteen f—*frickin* minutes. As he crested a small rise, he could see far enough to know he had to take his foot off the gas. The big engine of the cruiser whined as it slowed, and when he topped the final rise, there they were.

Dogs. One lying smack in the middle of the road with the other standing over it.

"Aw, hell." Nick slammed on the brakes and came to a jarring stop twenty feet from where they blocked the center of the narrow two-lane road. He paused for a minute, breathing hard and taking in the situation. He could probably slide around them on the berm, but he could see a drop-off into a concrete culvert just ahead—and those dogs would still be here when some local came shooting down the road at breakneck speed. With a growl, he pulled his front wheels over the centerline and flipped on his light bar.

It was his job to make sure accidents like that didn't happen.

He stepped out into the heat, his shirt sticking to his back, and donned his Florida Highway Patrol hat against the still-fierce evening sun. He stood for a moment with his legs spread and his hands on his belt.

Dogs. It would be *dogs*.

He took two steps toward them, and the standing dog—a black-and-tan German shepherd, thin and rangy—sprang in front of its companion. Its ears were up, nostrils flared, and a low growl reverberated deep in its chest. In full protection mode. The downed dog had long reddish-gold hair and a pretty face...golden retriever for sure.

Nick watched the shepherd's eyes, sensing he was being sized up even as he was assessing the dogs. He'd seen that wary body language dozens of times in Iraq and Afghanistan. Muscles weren't tensed to launch—yet—but every nerve in that lean body was firing in preparation. Closer now, he could see scars on the shepherd's face.

"Tough guy, huh." He took a deep breath, determined to get it over with. "Well, I've seen my share of action, too. You got a buddy down, and if you want me to take a look, you're going to have to back off. *Now.*"

When he moved in, a full-blown snarl came from the shepherd. But as Nick hoped, the dog backed up a step, then two, still growling, glancing fiercely between Nick and his wounded friend. They were both thin and looked like they had been on their own for a while, but the shepherd, at least, seemed to know something about humans. Not entirely feral.

Nick kept one eye on the shepherd as he knelt cautiously beside the golden and surveyed the damage. Female. There was blood on her hindquarters, and a rear leg was canted at an odd angle. A glance across the worn pavement showed spatters of blood, some not fully dried; the accident had happened here and not long ago.

Aw, damn. She didn't even have the energy to drag herself off the road.

He ran his hands gently over the golden's side, avoiding the shepherd's gaze and the blood on the injured dog's rear quarters. Her ribs were prominent but seemed intact. The dog lifted her head and opened her eyes.

"It's all right, girl. It's all right. Just checking you out." He held out his hand for her to sniff, and she gave a couple of feeble thumps with her tail before dropping her head and falling back into a half-conscious state.

She'd be dead before long unless he did

something. There was a new shelter in the east part of the next county…

If he thought about it too much, he'd make himself crazy.

"Just do it," he muttered irritably.

Instinct took over. He stalked back to his cruiser, retrieved a thick wool blanket from the trunk and opened the cruiser's back door. He covered the bloody rear of the golden with the blanket and lifted her carefully into his arms. She was fifty pounds of deadweight, but didn't protest at being moved, though it had to be painful as hell. He managed to slide both her and enough of his shoulders into the back of the vehicle to position her on the seat so that her hindquarters would be supported.

As he withdrew from the car, the shepherd shoved past him into the footwell of the back seat.

"Hey!"

The shepherd gave him only a glance before sniffing and nosing his injured companion. Nick stood braced across the door frame, watching. God knew what would happen to the dog if he was left here alone. Big, alert brown eyes searched him. The trust Nick saw—or imagined—in those eyes caused an unwelcome tightness in his chest.

Dogs. Why the hell did it have to be *dogs*?

"All right," he snapped, rationalizing the only course his troubled feelings would allow. "You go, too. The public will probably be safer with you off the streets."

He closed the back door, slid behind the wheel of the cruiser and took off. He was halfway to the county line when he remembered why he'd been flying low earlier and felt his stomach clench.

"Sorry about the game, Ben."

ALL IT TOOK was a touch.

The little balls of fur sensed something warm and good and migrated toward her, climbing sightlessly over each other, tumbling, mewling.

"It's okay, little Mama," Kate Everly, DVM, said as the dirty, matted schnauzer sat up anxiously to watch the calm, soft-spoken stranger kneeling beside her. Even if Kate hadn't had a special knack for reassuring animals, the mother dog was too depleted from whelping to do much more than worry. "I'm just going to check your babies."

With a sniff of the back of Kate's hand, the mother looked up at the humans standing around the old cardboard box and sank back with resignation. Kate picked up the puppies, one by one, and gave each a thorough examination.

She felt the pudgy little legs and soft pink pads of the feet of each of the four puppies, then she turned them over and checked their abdomens and listened to their hearts. Afterward she settled them against their mother, who sighed and lay back in the newspaper bedding as the last pup recognized her scent and began rooting for milk.

"They're in pretty good shape, actually," Kate said, rising from the floor of the makeshift surgery she and her partner, Jess Preston, had created in the kitchen of the old farmhouse that had become the headquarters of Harbor Animal Rescue. She swiped her shoulder-length hair back with her wrist as she headed for the old porcelain sink to wash her hands.

"For puppy mill escapees, you mean." Nance Everly, one of the shelter's founders and not-so-coincidentally Kate's grandmother, stood over the box with crossed arms and a scowl. Nance was a tall, straight-backed woman of seventy with silky white hair and a faced tanned and lined by years of outdoor life in Florida. "Look at the mother. She's a mess. Filthy, undernourished—it's a miracle she survived their birth."

"But she with us now. We feed 'em good," volunteer Hines Jackson said, bending stiffly beside the box and letting the mother sniff his hand before running it down her back and side. "She gonna be okay. She got good bones."

Kate finished drying her hands and leaned a hip against the worn laminate countertop stacked with jars and tins of first-aid supplies. "Who dropped them off? Anybody see this time?"

"Nope. Just opened the office door and there they were. A box full of scared-and-needy." Nance's face darkened. "Damned criminals. Breeding these dogs dry of health and hope, keeping them caged and forcing them to bear litter after litter—"

"Preachin' to the choir, Everly," Hines said with a knowing glance at Kate, who gave a rueful smile. This was one of Nance's hot buttons.

"There you are." Janice Winters, a uniformed officer from Sarasota Animal Control, stuck her head in the doorway, wearing a look of disbelief. "Got a real beaut this time." She led them out of the surgery and into the main reception room, where a russet brown heap of fur sat on an old blanket. The creature turned its head to them, and with the reference point of two dark eyes Kate was able to make out the head of a dachshund. On steroids.

Or carbs. Lots and lots of carbs.

"Good Lord," Nance said, walking around the beast. "I've seen a lot of stuff in my time, but this—"

Silence fell as they took stock individually. The dog peered anxiously from one to another of them, looking like it was trying to move, but couldn't.

"Where on earth did you find it?" Kate asked, sinking to her knees and letting the dog nose her hand before running it over the bulbous shape. The fat was appalling; it distorted every aspect of the doxie's body and all but prevented the animal from walking. The poor thing's stomach scraped the ground and, from what she could see, was scoured raw from its attempts to move.

"In an alley across from the Westfield Mall," Officer Winters said, shaking her head. "We got a call from a woman driving by and went out to investigate. I've never seen anything like it. I mean, how long would it take to feed a dog that much? He must weigh—fifty, sixty pounds?"

Kate helped Hines drag the blanket and the dachshund into the surgery and then slide him onto the scale.

"Fifty-two, actually." She shook her head. "Enough for three dachshunds. What kind of human being would do this to a dog? Let's get him up on the table and see about that belly." She motioned for Hines to help, and together they lifted the dog onto the exam table. He struggled when they rolled him, but fat-bound as he was, he was as helpless as an overturned turtle. He was indeed a male, and Hines chuckled and christened him "Moose."

"We have to put you on a diet, Moose," Kate said, cleaning and then spreading salve over his abraded belly. "And when we get you nice and healthy, we'll find you a forever home." When she finished listening to his heart and lungs, they turned him over and she took blood samples and checked his joints, which were, amazingly, intact. "He's in surprisingly good shape," she told her grandmother and the animal control officer standing in the surgery's doorway. "Except for the thirty pounds of extra lard he's hauling around." She stroked his head to reassure him, then took his head between her hands and looked him in the eye.

"We're going to take care of you, fella." Her magic worked; the dachshund relaxed, sniffed and then licked at her hand. "We'll find somebody to foster you and—"

"Me," Hines said, his dark eyes glowing and his jaw set in a way that said there was no arguing with him. "He comin' home with me."

"You sure, Hines?" Isabelle Conti, the shelter's director, glanced at the aging volunteer's arthritic hands. "He's going to take a lot of work."

"I never been afraid of work, Izzy. Old Moose here needs me. Who knows, maybe I need him, too." He moved to the head of the table and petted the dog. "I hope you like green beans, old son." He laughed as the dog eagerly nosed and licked his leathery hand. "'Cause you gonna be eating plenty of 'em."

They helped Hines put Moose and some supplies in his lovingly maintained 1987 Lincoln Continental and watched as he drove slowly out of the sanctuary's gravel parking lot.

The lowering sun was painting golden edges on the rose and purple clouds lining the western horizon, and Kate paused to appreciate the gentled light and listen to the rustle of the nearby palms. She slid her hands into her back pockets and lifted her face to the breeze.

Sometimes the magnitude of the career she had chosen seemed overwhelming. Whenever she confronted the heartbreaking ways human failings and animal vulnerability could collide, she found herself making the decision all over again to stand on the front line of decency and compassion. It was her job to treat and care for patients who could not speak for themselves, and whose trust of humans was unequivocal and often undeserved.

She was unaware of her grandmother

standing behind her until Nance hooked Kate's arm through hers and tugged. When she turned, Gran's sun-weathered face was soft with understanding. Her gran had always seemed to know what was happening with her before she knew herself.

"Come on." Gran led her back to the main office. "I know just the cure for that look."

Minutes later, they were on the puppy-room floor, ensconced with eight rambunctious balls of fur, tossing toys, stroking fuzzy new coats and avoiding sharp little milk teeth. It was impossible to dwell on human irresponsibility in the face of such a contagious love of life. The pups threw themselves wholeheartedly into learning and exploring, seeking out Kate and her grandmother and Isabelle. They chewed and licked and tumbled. They investigated toys and the room's boundaries, tracked through the water bowl and barked at the humans sitting in their play area. They attacked each other and teased their caretakers; it was enough to melt the most jaded heart.

Kate picked up one of them in her arms and cuddled him, inhaling his sweet puppy breath and laughing with delight at the way his little pink tongue licked her face.

"They're almost eight weeks old." Nance turned to Kate as if an idea had just occurred. "Hey, why don't you take one of them home with you?"

Kate rubbed noses with one of the pups, feeling her gut tighten. "Don't have time, Gran. My life is hectic enough with the practice and the new house—I haven't even finished unpacking."

"You've been *unpacking* for six danged months," Nance said.

"Exactly. I'm too busy. And, of course, there's the shelter." She shot a narrow look at Nance. "The one my grandmother keeps roping me into giving away my hard-won professional expertise to."

"Excuses, excuses." Nance gave a huff. "You can't postpone life forever, Kate. Just because *he* turned out to be a jackass—"

"Gran." Kate raised a hand to prevent a familiar argument.

"I'm just saying. You need to find someone to share your life with."

"I have more than a *someone*, I have a partner and a grandmother and a bunch of friends and this shelter and another whole farm full of rescues and strays."

"That's *my* farm. My animals," Nance said.

"Yeah? How many times have I heard you say that no one ever owns an animal? That they are all God's creatures and they're just given into our care for whatever time they're here on earth?"

"Fine. They're in *my* care. It's time you got your own to care for."

"Once again—" Kate grinned, knowing she had won "—not enough hours in the day." She nuzzled another puppy nose. "Right, Pee Wee?"

Moments later the sound of the shelter door creaking open drifted into the puppy room, followed by heavy footsteps. She looked over to find a large pair of boots—big and well polished—settling in the doorway. She followed khaki-clad legs up to a broad pair of shoulders bearing a badge, and on up to a serious pair of aviator shades. The officer stood with his hands propped on a heavy service belt, looking at them.

"Got an injured dog in the cruiser," came

a deep, authoritative voice. "Hit by a car and lost a lot of blood. I don't want to move her."

"I'll take a look." Kate was on her feet in a flash and hurrying for the makeshift surgery. Behind her she could hear Isabelle say that they didn't usually take in injured animals, but he was in luck—one of their volunteer vets was on premises.

A minute later, she emerged with her stethoscope draped around her neck, snapping on a pair of gloves. The officer, Nance, and Isabelle were already out the door, so she dashed after them. A black-and-cream highway patrol cruiser sat in the gravel drive, its engine running and light bar flashing, sweeping the area with red and blue.

The big officer opened the rear passenger-side door and hesitated a moment before waving Kate toward a blanket-wrapped form lying on the back seat. Before she could completely duck through the door, a growl set her back outside. A shepherd rose out of the shadows onto the seat beside the injured dog, ears up, every muscle taut with warning.

"Come on, you stubborn— She's going to look at your friend." The officer was around the car in a flash and opening the far door, dragging the shepherd back to clear the way for her. "He was with her when I found her," he explained as Kate took a deep breath, slid into the foot well and got busy with her stethoscope and penlight.

"Pupils reactive. Heart is slow but steady—good so far." She carefully felt the golden's prominent ribs and rear quarters and ran her hands gently over the injured leg. The scrape of bone against bone said it all. "She's got at least one fracture. I need X-rays to see how bad it is, and she needs fluids right away. I may have to do some surgery." She glanced over her shoulder at the shelter and frowned.

"I don't have all of the equipment I need here." She looked at the officer, who was half in, half out of the cruiser, restraining the unhappy shepherd. He seemed to have the big, rangy dog in hand, and the fleeting thought occurred to her that having things under control was probably his norm. At that moment, she envied him. "She'll have to go to my office," she said, popping off the gloves. "I hate to ask, but can you drive her over there? She shouldn't be moved more than necessary."

"Just tell me how to get there," he said, his voice full of certainty.

Kate inhaled sharply as if she'd been holding her breath.

"Why don't you ride with the dog?" Gran said as Kate emerged from the back seat. "I'll bring your Jeep over later, and Isabelle can pick me up."

It sounded reasonable. She nodded and handed her keys to Gran. As she slid back into the rear seat, she was aware of the officer releasing the shepherd into the front seat with a warning and then closing the rear door. The shepherd climbed over the hardware in the front—computer, radio, scanner, racked gun—not the least bit intimidated. He turned and put paws on the seat back to watch what was happening behind him. The officer slid behind the steering wheel and managed to click his seat belt and crank the wheel with the palm of his hand at the same time.

"You'll want to hang on," he called over his shoulder.

She scrambled for room beside the injured

dog and found a seat belt just as they took off, gravel flying. She jerked against the restraint as the cruiser's tires grabbed the asphalt of the county road.

Lights and sirens for an injured dog; this was a first for her. She glanced up at the officer in the front seat and caught a few more details: strong jaw with a hint of a scar beneath a Florida tan. Dark hair cut high and tight—military, for sure. Judging by his erect bearing and contained physicality, he could handle himself—probably *had* handled himself.

She gave directions, then stroked her patient and murmured quiet reassurances. When she looked up, wary eyes in a brooding shepherd face were watching her. Distrust. She'd seen that look a thousand times in animals and sensed that she'd need the officer's help at the end of this mad dash. Turning back to her patient, she carried in her mind's eye the image of the shepherd anxiously nosing her patient's head.

"Thanks for doing this, Officer…"

"Trooper. Stanton. Nick Stanton."

"Kate Everly. DVM."

"I gathered." He seemed to glance at her

in the rearview mirror; it was hard to tell where he was looking behind those shades. "Lucky you were there."

"My grandmother is on the shelter's board. She ropes me into helping regularly."

He nodded and said nothing more.

Clearly a man of few words.

CHAPTER TWO

"So, THIS IS YOURS," Trooper Stanton said, killing the siren as they pulled into the parking lot outside the darkened Lakeview Animal Clinic. The building was a stucco-covered one-story with a dozen indoor runs, two surgeries and half a dozen exam rooms; perfect for a two-vet operation.

"And the bank's," she said as she pointed to the drive at the side. "Around the back— we can take her straight into the surgery."

The minute the cruiser stopped, she jumped out and headed for the steel security door to punch in the lock code. Then she stepped inside and turn off the alarm. Seconds later, the trooper lifted the injured golden from the cruiser and carried her to the rear entrance. Kate went ahead of them, turning on lights and making sure one of the surgery tables was clear.

"We'll start a line first—get some fluids going in her—then we'll do an X-ray or two." She grabbed clippers, a bag of saline and an IV needle.

He settled the golden gently on the table and watched as Kate made a more thorough examination, then shaved one of the golden's front legs.

"I got this." He grabbed the needle pack as she reached for it, and he ripped it open. "I don't know anything about X-rays, though. That's your department."

But he *did* know about starting IVs in dogs? She was halfway around the table to protest when a growl startled her. The shepherd braced himself in a warning stance near the table, his nose up and twitching as he read the surgery's mix of urgency, animal scents and medicinal smells.

"Can it, tough guy." The trooper straightened as the dog ignored him. He barked an order to *sit*. When the dog defied that order, he made a fist and did a biceps curl, snapping the fist to his shoulder. After a tense moment, the dog lowered its rear to the floor. He stared at the dog for a minute, seeming a little surprised it had worked, then went back to starting the IV.

His take-charge attitude in *her* surgery rankled, but something stopped her from setting him straight. Maybe it was the knowledgeable way his fingers swabbed the shaved area, felt for a vein and carefully inserted the needle. Maybe it was the shepherd's obedience. Still, she didn't move until the line was established and he raised the bag, looking for a place to hang it. In the midst of starting the IV, he'd taken off his sunglasses; they were hanging from a shirt pocket.

"Where did you learn to do that?" she asked. His eyes suited his face—big and bold—an arresting light hazel color.

"Iraq." When she crossed her arms and waited for more, he looked less comfortable. "We had dogs…and…sometimes they got dehydrated."

"Interesting," she said after a moment, sensing there was a lot of story behind that terse description. His rescue of these dogs made sense in light of his military experience. Soldiers in combat got close to their canine comrades, and that experience often carried over to civilian life.

Still, this dog was a stray, and whatever

time and effort she expended would never show a positive on the practice's balance sheets. The odds of a favorable outcome were probably just south of fifty-fifty, but she had to do whatever she could to treat the dog.

Annoyed—with him or her own soft-hearted impulses?—she pulled over a pole for the IV and went for the portable X-ray.

Thankfully, this didn't take much time. Because it was just as she feared: the X-rays showed a hairline in the pelvis and a major compound fracture in the leg. She called her partner, Jess, to come in to help, but the call went straight to voice mail. It was Jess's night off, and she was probably out with her man-of-the-month.

"I'm afraid if we wait until tomorrow to do the surgery she'll be in even worse shape," she said, mostly to herself, while running a hand gently over the golden's head.

"I can help," Trooper Stanton said over his shoulder as he washed his hands in the scrub sink. When he turned and propped his hands on his service belt, spreading his elbows enough that his chest strained his shirt. She frowned, wishing he wouldn't do that and that she wasn't drawn to watch him do it. Her frown deepened.

"You ever helped with a surgery?"

"Field stuff. Stitching sometimes. Mostly wrap and run." He cocked his head, watching her decide. "I'm not a fainter."

"I would guess not," she said under her breath. Decision made, she turned to the shelves along the far wall to pull surgical supplies. Halfway there, she stopped dead, confronted by a shepherd braced for action. "Um, we may have a problem here."

Trooper Stanton scowled and then ordered the shepherd to the table where his injured companion lay. The dog approached cautiously, rose with one paw against the table and sniffed his friend.

"She's going be okay, tough guy, but you have to give the doc here room to work." He strode to a nearby door, flipped on a light inside the exam room, then shoved the shepherd in. The instant the door closed between them, there were thumps against the door and barks of protest. Stanton drew a deep breath. "It's for the best."

Jess, Kate's partner, was a big gal, but even the large gloves she used were a tight fit on the trooper. To his credit, he didn't complain, and he held the anesthetic mask properly and paid scrupulous attention to Kate's directions.

She described the damage and the basis for her decision-making at each step as they went in. There wasn't much to do with the cracked pelvis; nature would have to take care of that. But the broken leg had to be held in position while she pinned the bones, and he supplied the necessary muscle without a twitch. Twice she paused to listen to the golden's heart and pronounced it within safe limits.

More than an hour later, they finished cleaning and closing the last cuts on the dog's hindquarters. She injected antibiotics and pain meds into the IV and watched for any reaction. As she hoped, there was none.

"Well, that's it," she declared, ripping off her gloves and stuffing them, along with the bloody drapes and used instrument packs, into the garbage can. "It's up to her now. You want to help me move her?"

They picked up the blanket she lay on by the corners and transferred the dog onto a low shelf where she could be monitored while being out of the way. "Our version of the recovery room," she explained with a wry smile.

She checked the dog's heart and lungs again, then rose to find Trooper Nick Stanton staring through the window, his expression as dark as the night outside.

"Everything okay?" she asked.

"Yeah." He seemed oddly subdued as he gestured to the door of the nearby exam room where a thud and some growls reminded them there was still another problem to solve. "What about him?"

She chewed her lip as she studied the door and then looked back at her patient. "Maybe we should let him see she's all right. Then we could put him in a run for the night. I'll take him back to the shelter tomorrow."

The shepherd shot out into the surgery and followed the trooper's direction to where the golden lay recovering. He sniffed her head to toe, seemed to understand her condition was grave and began to pace. Kate snagged a leash from the rack by the waiting-room door and approached the dog in a calm manner. She managed to get the leash over his head before he bolted.

Stanton reached for the lead and ended up dragging the animal into the kennels, where they were bombarded with barking from dogs overnighting at the office. As the door to the run closed, the shepherd clawed at the leash and shook his head to remove the loop from his neck.

"I'd say he has trust issues," Kate said as she watched the dog.

"From the scars on his face, he's got reason," Trooper Stanton said, working to recover his breath.

"Could be he had a run-in with another dog." She retreated down the alley to the back room, flipping off the lights in the noisy kennel. Stanton followed, retucking his shirt and resettling his service belt.

"Could be that humans sponsored that run-in."

Out in the surgery again, she busied herself wiping down the table and equipment. He paused across the room, watched her for a minute and then looked around.

"Nice place," he said. "You and a partner?"

"And the bank," she said, pausing with a towel in one hand and disinfectant spray in the other. "Can't forget the bank." A moment later she stowed the cleaner and washed her hands. As she knelt beside her newest patient, she heard him come around the table and stop nearby.

"How is she doing?"

"Sleeping it off. I'll give her another dose of pain meds in the morning. If we can keep her comfortable, she'll heal better." Overwhelmed by his presence, she rose and stepped back.

"Okay, then. I guess I'm done here," he said, staring at her.

"I guess so." A foot or two wasn't enough space to escape awareness of his size, his body heat and the aura of control that radiated from him. Warmth slid down the back of her throat; she felt a little conspicuous as she cleared it. "Thanks for the help. You're kind of good at this, Trooper Stanton."

"Nick," he said, his voice a little deeper than moments ago.

"Nick," she said, and offered her hand. "I remember. And I'm—"

"Kate. Nice working with you, Kate." He shook her hand, careful not to look directly at her. She knew because she was being careful to avoid eye contact herself.

"You okay here? By yourself?" He glanced around the surgery.

"Yeah. I'll call Gran. She's going to drop off my car." She realized now that she could probably have driven herself over to the office. Odd that Gran insisted she ride along with the trooper and that she would bring Kate's Jeep over, but hadn't.

"Okay, then." He seemed a little uncertain, then backed toward the door. "I'll take off. Have a good night, Doc."

"Thanks, Nick. You, too."

As he exited, he turned back. "Lock this door behind me."

Control. It wasn't just the shepherd who had issues. But then she did exactly what he said, and as she did, she smiled.

It was another fifteen minutes before Gran answered her cell. There were loud voices and music in the background; her grandmother and Isabelle were *not* at the shelter anymore.

"I thought you were dropping off my Jeep. Where are you?"

"We're at Bogey's, grabbing a bite and a

beer. I figured you'd need some time to—um—I thought maybe that nice statie might give you a ride home." Gran had a hint of mischief in her voice, and two and two came together to make a sneaky four. Grandmotherly manipulation: strand her granddaughter with a hunk of a state trooper and see what developed.

"Yeah? Well, he didn't." She reddened, hoping her disappointment didn't register in her voice. "So, you owe me a burger. With the works. And a hard cider or two." She glanced at the golden. "Looks like I'll be here pretty late—maybe all night."

NICK PULLED HIS cruiser into the driveway, killed the engine and sat for a minute, looking at the lights from the living-room windows of his neatly landscaped three-bedroom ranch. He dreaded going inside. Ben's first soccer game, and he'd missed it. It was all his son had talked about for days; shin guards and footwork, free kicks and headers, strikers and defensemen. The expansion of his vocabulary alone was enough to make Nick endorse his participation.

Ben wasn't a very physical kid, at least

until now. He talked too much like an adult and spent more time with books and computers than most eight-year-old boys. The idea of him joining a team, mixing it up with other kids, and learning the basics of fair play was reassuring. And Ben had enjoyed sharing his newfound enthusiasm with his dad—recounting what happened at practices and begging for additional sessions in the backyard.

With his long hours, Nick wasn't always able to help that way, but had done his best to encourage him. And he had promised to be there for Ben's first game, cheering him on from the sidelines.

Then he'd come across the dogs.

He dragged himself out of the cruiser, locked it up and was met at the front door by a pair of warm brown eyes in a face filled with understanding. His mom stepped back to let him enter and shook her head as he silently removed his service belt and stowed his gun in the lockbox on the top shelf of the entry closet.

"How is he?" he finally asked as he turned to face her.

"Hurt. Quiet." She winced at the misery in his face. "Of all the days to be late, Nick."

"I ran into a situation…" He blew out a breath, knowing the best excuse in the world couldn't cover this failure. After a moment, he squared his shoulders. "Where is he?"

"In his room. He already finished his homework."

Nick paused and looked at his mom. Sarah Stanton's short hair was fashionably cut, graying in streaks that she augmented with highlights at the salon. She carried a few extra pounds, worked out twice a week and made sure they all ate healthily. She was a listener, a guide and a genuine and caring woman; the epitome of what a grandmother should be. It weighed on him that she had to be more mom than grandmother for another generation of Stanton men. He grieved even more that she seemed to relate to his bright, serious-minded son better than he did.

"Just talk to him, Nick. Explain. He'll understand." She read his anxiety like a book. She always had. "He needs his dad."

That came like a punch to the gut, even though he was sure she hadn't meant it that way. Ben needed his dad all the more because he didn't have a mother. Not for the last four years.

His next steps, through the family room and down the hall to his son's room, were among the hardest he had ever taken. Anxiety kept his shoulders square and his expression taut; it was only on the inside that dread softened him to a slump. Why was it that after four years he still felt like every interaction with his son was some kind of a test?

He stood in the doorway for a minute, preparing himself. It was a typical kid's room in most ways: twin bed, posters on the walls, bookcase stuffed with books, rock collection and robot models, and a huge toy box spilling action figures, vehicles and train parts onto the carpet. On the desk near the window were a crystal-growing experiment in progress, a small microscope beside an ever-expanding bug collection and a telescope. The poster on the wall beside the desk was a chart of constellations in the northern hemisphere sky. How many eight-year-olds could tell you where the Pleiades were?

Ben looked up with a frown and then back at the Tyrannosaurus rex he was assembling. Was that look concentration or disappointment?

"Hey. How did the game go?" He settled on the bed across from Ben, who sat sideways in the chair at his desk, the half-assembled T. rex skeleton on his lap. Doing something with his hands always seemed to calm him; Nick had seen him rebuild that very dinosaur a dozen times.

"Okay."

"Just okay?" Nick groaned. It was going to be one of *those* talks where every word he got out of Ben would be like pulling a tooth. "So did you play a position?"

"Yeah."

"Which one? Defenseman? Striker? Goalie?"

"Defense."

"Get any good assists in?"

"No."

"Get any good shin bruises?" He looked Ben over with a half grin.

"No."

Silence fell. This was pointless. Nick braced and changed tactics. Best to just come right out with it, a frontal assault of the problem.

"I'm sorry I didn't make it, Ben. I had a situation come up, a problem on one of the county roads—" almost as an afterthought he added the rest of it "—with some dogs. I had to take care of—"

"Dogs?" Ben's head came up, and he searched his dad's face with wary interest. "What kind of dogs?"

"Well, I think they were strays. They were thin and pretty dirty—like they'd been on their own for a while. One got hit by a car and was lying in the middle of the road. I had to stop and pick her up and take her to that new shelter on Curlew Road. It turned out the dog needed a vet."

"A hurt dog?"

"Yeah. She had a broken leg and some bad cuts."

"What kind of car hit her?" Ben set the dinosaur back on his desk.

"I don't know. I came along later. She was blocking the road, so I had to pick her up and clear the highway. She had lost a lot of blood."

"Did you get blood on you?" he asked, scanning Nick's uniform.

"I don't think so." Nick looked down and

then back at Ben, surprised to see new light in his son's eyes. "I was careful. I covered her with the blanket I carry in the cruiser, and I drove her to the shelter."

"'Cause you're a vet, and you're supposed to help people and dogs."

Nick realized the connection Ben was making and smiled. "I'm a *veteran*, that's true. But she needed a *veterinarian*—an animal doctor."

Ben nodded, digesting that and frowning at his mistake. "What color was she?" He transferred to the bed beside Nick. "Was she a big dog, or a little one?"

"Well, a golden retriever—I think—so, sort of big. The other dog was a German shepherd. He didn't want anyone to touch his friend, so I had to stare him down to get close enough to help."

"Did he try to bite you?" Ben was more fascinated than alarmed.

"No." Nick chuckled and ruffled Ben's hair, surprised by Ben's desire for every ghoulish detail. There was an eight-year-old boy in there after all. "He and I came to an understanding pretty quick."

"So, you took the hurt dog to a hospital? What did they do to her?"

"Well, it was late and the other doctor wasn't available, so I helped the vet do some surgery to fix the dog's leg and hip."

"Like a real doctor does? With blood and everything?"

"Yeah, like real surgery."

"So she's better now, and she's going to be fine?"

"The vet was good and she did her best. But the dog has a ways to go before she's really well."

Ben thought about that for a minute.

"How long before she gets well?"

"Well, when a soldier breaks a leg, it sometimes takes months for them to heal and get back to walking. It's a lot the same for dogs, so at least a couple of months." He avoided the question of how likely it was that a stray would get the weeks of care and attention she needed to fully recover.

Ben's eyes widened.

"Can we go see her?" Ben was on the very edge of the bed now, his face filled with anticipation. "At the hospital?" When Nick began to shake his head, Ben really poured it on. "Pleeeease, Dad, can we go? It's a hurt *dog*." It was a little late to remember that he had been talking a lot about dogs lately and bringing home books about them. "Maybe we can help."

"But we're not sure the dog will—"

"I'll do garbage runs every single day and make my bed all the time—honest. Can we go tomorrow, *please*?"

"You have school tomorrow." Nick clasped his son's shoulder, feeling himself softening. For some reason the idea of going back to the animal clinic made his palms sweat.

"Then, Saturday. Can we go see the hurt dog Saturday? That's two days away." He grabbed Nick's arm and held on tight, as if his very heart were in Nick's hands.

It was probably a mistake to let him get involved with those dogs on any level; there was no guarantee the golden would even survive until Saturday. But Ben didn't ask for much…whether because he was content with what he had, he didn't want to be a pest or he feared being disappointed, Nick couldn't have said. God knew he'd had more than his share of pain and disappointment in his young life. At that moment, as he looked down into his son's big, hazel eyes, Nick would have agreed to take him to the moon and back.

"Okay, I guess. If they're open. Saturday."

Whatever happened later, it was worth it just to have his son throw his arms around his waist and hold on for all he was worth.

He stroked Ben's head where it lay against him and for the thousandth time questioned if he was doing right by the boy. Would he ever feel up to the job of father and guide for the son he didn't really understand? Would he ever be able to make up to the boy for his mother's abandonment? But then, how could he help Ben understand why she'd left them when he didn't understand it himself?

Later—after he'd put Ben to bed, had some of his mom's warmed-over ziti and sunk into a chair in front of *Thursday Night Football*—he groaned privately at what he'd agreed to do. Saturday. He was going to have to see that vet again, the curvy little blonde with the big blue eyes and strong hands. Sure hands. Gentle hands. The image of her stroking the golden's head, reassuring the dog, came back to him in a rush, and on its heels came the memory of that first moment in the puppy room.

She'd been sitting on the floor being mobbed by puppies, smiling, laughing—her face, her whole being radiating vitality and pleasure. The rays of the setting sun were slanting through the windows and struck her from behind, causing her hair to glow. *Glow.* For a minute there, he'd been struck speechless and just stared.

There were other women present, and the floor was strewed with puppies, chew toys and spilled water, but Kate Everly hugging those puppies was all he saw. It had taken every bit of discipline he could command to remember his mission and tell them about the dog.

His hands curled into fists at the remembered urge to touch her.

Then he had driven like a madman to her clinic and volunteered to help with the damned surgery. After years in Iraq and the Stan, you'd think he would have had enough trauma and gore. But there he was, itching to get back into it while sneaking glances at her shape—which admittedly was pretty sweet—and watching her hands. What was it about her hands?

He groaned aloud and finished his beer in a couple of gulps. He didn't need to be thinking like this, feeling like this. But he kept going back to the end, when he'd stood close to her, watching her face. He knew he should back off and give her some room, but was unable to make himself do it. Every nerve in his body had hummed with awareness of her.

He crushed the empty can and squeezed his eyes shut, forcing his thoughts back to the problem at hand. The dog had a fifty-fifty chance. He had promised Ben they would check on her, but there was no guarantee she would still be there on Saturday. He didn't want to think about the disappointment he would see in Ben's face if something happened to the animal in the meantime. He'd gotten himself into a situation.

Man up, Stanton. For God's sake—just hope the golden makes it a few more days. And who says Kate Everly will even be there? She has a partner—maybe he'll be there instead of her. Just keep your head in the mission, your hands in your damn pockets and get it over with.

CHAPTER THREE

THE GOLDEN WAS holding her own.

Kate stood at the counter of the rear surgery at noon that Saturday, entering notes into the computer on her last patient of the day when the golden raised her head. She drank from the water bowl they had placed nearby, and Kate paused to watch, marveling at the dog's progress. The golden was still weak, but the stitches were holding and she was showing some interest in food, at least if it came from a human hand. She seemed to be comfortable around people, and Kate couldn't help wondering for the twentieth time where she had come from and why she was wandering the countryside in the company of a temperamental shepherd.

"You know," she said to the dog, "if you stay around here much longer, we're going to have to give you a name. If you have any preferences, you'd better speak up, because

Jess is dying to name some poor critter 'Ermahgerd.'"

She knelt by the dog, running hands over her silky head and soft ears. "Good girl." The dog gave a tail thump in response and Kate smiled. She checked the IV line taped to the dog's foreleg, found it secure and slid inescapably into the memory of how it was done. Those big hands—she could see them in perfect detail—neatly muscular, surprisingly agile—

"That papillon of Mrs. Richardson's is a piece of work."

Kate started and turned to see her partner exiting exam room 3.

"The old lady swears 'Poochie' picks out her own outfits every day," Jess continued, shaking her head. "Today it was blue taffeta and pearls. *Pearls*. The dog's got a better wardrobe than most women I know."

"Well, it wouldn't take much to be better than mine," Kate said with a laugh, tucking her hair behind her ears and rising. She looked down at her khakis and the faded green polo awash in animal hair and sporting a couple of damp spots she didn't want to investigate too closely.

Jess, on the other hand, looked like an ad for vintage Abercrombie & Fitch: plaid shirt and stylishly faded jeans beneath her white coat, and expensive, half-laced hiking boots. She stood six feet tall, had long, dark hair that she wore pulled back into a haphazard bun, and moved with an athletic grace Kate had always envied. Even in her most wind-blown or just awakened state, she managed to look good.

They were complete opposites, which was probably one of the reasons they had become fast friends the first semester of vet school and had always wanted to go into practice together. Short, honey-blonde Kate was the neat one, the careful planner and progress monitor, the one determined to iron out all the wrinkles in life. Jess was messy in everything but her work, spontaneous and adventuresome, and loved parties, men and changing her mind.

"How is she doing?"

"She's coming along." There was no small bit of pride in Kate's assessment. "If she keeps this up, in another few days we can move her to the shelter."

Jess came to stand beside her and look down at her patient.

"Then maybe she'll get to see her boyfriend again." She chuckled. "That dude's a handful. I can't imagine anybody scooping him up and taking him home. Not unless they live in a bunker somewhere." She shrugged out of her white coat and hung it on a hook by the waiting-room door. "Hey, maybe you ought to call that big trooper and have him come over to help move her." She brightened visibly. "You know, the one with all those muscles and the *uniform*."

Kate gave her a don't-go-there look and regretted ever mentioning Nick Stanton to her, much less describing him so thoroughly. She fished through the papers on the nearby counter for the shopping list she'd made last night. "Don't you have a supply run to make?"

"I'm just sayin'." Jess's smile was pure provocation. "I know you have a weakness for uniforms." Kate's deepening glower only incited her to continue. "You've got to live while you can, Kate. You can't let what happened with Jared ruin the rest of your life."

"My life is not ruined just because I'm

not attached to a man. I have a lot to do, and I enjoy what I do. I don't have time for… wasting my time." That last came out a little more vehemently than she intended. Jess put her hands up in surrender, then snatched the list and headed for the back door, where she paused for one more volley.

"Sex, properly done, is *never* a waste of time, sweetums."

Kate watched the door well after it closed, roundly annoyed by her partner's final salvo. Jess was fond of making one last crack and escaping before she could make a blistering comeback. Not that she usually could come up with a blistering comeback, but she at least deserved the chance to try. The *man* thing was a running argument they would likely never settle: Kate believed in stable and serious relationships, while Jess pursued fierce and spontaneous affairs of the heart.

"Doc?" LeeAnn Monroe, their spiky-haired receptionist, poked her head through the double doors that led to the waiting room. "The patients are all gone and I finished the bank deposit, but before I could lock the doors, a man walked in, asking to see you."

"What about?"

"He said it was about that golden—the one that cop brought in."

A frisson of expectation ran down her spine. "Is it a state trooper?"

The quirky receptionist shrugged. "No uniform. Big sucker, though."

"You can go, LeeAnn," she said, heading for the waiting room. "I'll see what he wants and then finish locking up." She took a deep breath, surprised at how her heart was suddenly racing. It might not even be—

Beyond the double doors stood a tall, broad-shouldered man wearing jeans, a T-shirt and cross-trainers. At the sound of her footsteps, he turned, and she stopped a few feet away, and when she looked up into his eyes, her stomach slid to her knees. She *hadn't* just imagined how big and male he was or how that affected her.

"Can I help you?" She sounded a little breathless to her own ears as she tried to take refuge in hard-won professionalism. "Trooper Stanton, right?"

Before he could respond, a young boy stepped out from behind him with widening eyes. Beautiful golden-hazel eyes, just like Nick Stanton's. The trooper laid a hand on the boy's shoulder to halt him.

"Yes. Nick Stanton. And this is my son, Ben."

"Are you the doctor who took care of the hurt dog?" Ben asked eagerly. His brown hair stuck straight up in front, and a few new teeth were fighting for space with ones he hadn't lost yet. He had on a green shirt sporting the number 7, matching shorts and shin guards beneath padded knee socks.

"Yes. I'm Dr. Everly. Nice to meet you, Ben." She covered her surprise by extending her hand. With a glance at his dad, who nodded, he gave her a very grown-up handshake.

"I told him about what happened to the dog, and he made me promise to bring him to see her." Stanton released Ben's shoulder and shoved his hand into the pocket of his jeans. "I didn't realize your Saturday hours ended at noon. He had soccer practice this morning and—I don't want to keep you—"

"It's no trouble," Kate said, focusing on Ben. "The dog is doing fairly well. Want to see?" She motioned for them to follow her through the doors and into the surgery, where she stooped in front of the boy to match his height and draw his gaze to hers. "Now you have to realize, Ben, she was hurt pretty badly. We had to shave some of her hair in places and stitch her up. And she's not exactly frisky, okay? She's still a pretty sick dog."

Ben looked thoughtful and then nodded. When they reached the shelf where the golden lay, the boy stood for a moment, taking in the dog's condition. His expression sobered, and she could see his mind working behind his eyes. Edging closer, he instinctively reached for the dog before he caught himself.

"Would it hurt her if I petted her?" He looked at Kate and then at his dad, who remained silent, deferring to the professional.

"I think she'll be fine with it." She was aware of Nick's gaze on her and slid naturally into teacher mode. "Just be gentle. I think she likes people."

He gingerly touched the dog's head with a couple of fingers, then seemed to relax and moved closer, using his whole hand. "That's where you had to do the surgery?" He pointed to the bare lines of stitches on her leg and hip. When Kate nodded, he frowned. "Did it hurt her when you cut her?"

"No," Kate said, seeing where his logic was taking him, "we wouldn't let that happen. We put her to sleep, so she wouldn't feel anything while we fixed her leg. You want to see how?"

He nodded, and she pulled over the portable gas bottle and the mask attached to it. "We put this over her muzzle, and she breathed in gas that made her go to sleep."

"What kind of gas?" he said, coming to look at the mask and touch it. "Like what they give to kids when they take out their tonsils?"

"Oh, so you know about that." Kate smiled, understanding a little more about this boy from that statement. "Did you have your tonsils out?"

"No, but Wyatt did, and he told me all about it." He headed back to the golden, more confident that he wouldn't hurt her, and gave her a careful stroke that rated a tail thump. Then she raised her head to sniff him and look around. "Look, she's smelling me!"

"I think she likes you, Ben." Kate smiled. "That's the most interest she's shown in anyone since she's been here. Try talking to her."

"What's her name?"

"Well, that's a good question. We don't know. She was a stray—no collar or tags. But that's a funny thing about dogs—if you love them and are good to them, they'll start to answer to any name you want to give them." She knelt beside the shelf to give the golden a few strokes and meet Ben's thoughtful gaze. Having him give the dog a name might be a bad idea at this point; she still had a lot of recovery ahead of her. "She's a golden retriever, so for now, why don't we just call her Goldie."

He muttered "Goldie" a couple of times, as if getting used to it. "We're going to get you well, Goldie." Then he looked up with a determined expression. "Can't we make her better faster?"

His use of "we" was not lost on her. He was a sensitive kid, and she could tell he was already invested in this dog, for good or for ill. She hoped he would take away a positive lesson from this, and then realized with a mental groan that making it positive was probably up to her.

"Okay, let's talk about healing." She sank to a seat on the edge of the shelf beside the dog she had just named Goldie. "We doctors—people doctors and animal doctors alike—can't *make* our patients well. Their bodies have their own special systems for doing that. What we do is put things back in place and give them medicines that will help their bodies heal themselves. You know how when you get a cold, it takes a couple of weeks to get better?" He nodded, so she continued. "Well, during that week or two, your body has to figure out which viruses are making you sick, then round them up and lock them away. Your body has a kind of virus police already in place. They just need time to get to work and then repair anything that got damaged."

She gestured to Goldie. "It's the same with her. We set her leg bones so her body can knit them back together in the right places, and we stitched her up so her cut will stay together while her body grows new tissue to keep it together permanently. All of that takes time." She smiled. "One of my old professors always said 'Time is the best healer there is.'"

Ben nodded earnestly and then put his face close to Goldie's.

"You take your time, Goldie. We'll be here to help you get better." Then he looked up at his dad. "Won't we, Dad?"

Kate bit her lip to keep from grinning as Nick struggled with that.

"We can check in from time to time," he conceded, "and see how she's doing."

Kate smiled at Ben, who was already on to the next topic.

"What about the other dog? What happened to him?" Ben looked around the surgery as if hoping for a glimpse.

"The shepherd?" Kate rose from the shelf and looked at Nick. "We took him over to the shelter yesterday. It was all my partner and I could do to get him into the Jeep."

"Can we go there and see him, too?" Ben said in a tone that was clearly a prelude to full-blown wheedling. Kate saw a muscle twitch in Nick's jaw and enjoyed watching this formidable man made defenseless by his son's plea. "He's probably worried about his friend."

"I don't think that would be a good idea, Ben," Nick said, visibly uncomfortable.

"Why, Dad? His friend is here, sick, and he may be scared."

"Plus, there are puppies who need to be played with and socialized," Kate said on impulse, batting away guilt at supporting Ben's begging when Nick clearly didn't want to go. "And there aren't always enough volunteers to spend time with them."

Nick paled, caught in a perfect pincer movement. He seemed to be working hard not to squirm; cords were visible in his neck.

"Okay, we can go to the shelter." He sent Ben a stern look that didn't seem to impact the boy's grin, so he added, "Just for a little while."

She smiled. "I just have to check on the dogs in the runs and then lock up. I guess I'll see you there." As the Stantons headed for the front door, she heard Nick's deep voice rumble.

"Just to be clear, we are *not* taking any puppies home."

And she grinned.

CHAPTER FOUR

THE PARKING LOT was nearly full that afternoon when Nick and Ben arrived at the Harbor Animal Rescue. Nick took in the rambling farmhouse. He could see people in the fenced side yards, playing ball with some dogs. Ben climbed out of the back seat and headed straight for the fence. His face lit like it was Christmas morning as he climbed on a fence rail and watched the dogs romping and enjoying all the attention. Nick hung back for a while, but then made his way to Ben's side and leaned on the fence to soak up his son's enthusiasm.

For the past two days, dogs were all Ben could talk about, and Nick had a bad feeling about where this "hurt dog" stuff was heading: Ben asking for a dog of his own. It wasn't that he didn't want Ben to have a dog someday. He just wasn't sure his son was ready for that level of responsibility. Caring for a living being involved a lot, and to be frank, he really didn't want to have to—

"There you are." The doc arrived at their side in the middle of his ruminations. He straightened and laid a hand on Ben's shoulder as she gave them a sunny-from-the-inside-out kind of smile that made his belly tighten. "Want to come inside and check out the puppy room?"

"Yeah, that would be great!" Ben fairly glowed with excitement as he jumped down and headed after her without even a glance at his dad.

Nick sighed and followed.

She led them in the front door of the shelter office, and he fell in behind her and Ben as she explained the rules. "Simple, really. Wash hands before and after a play session, no roughhousing, don't let the puppy chew on any part of you and if the puppy tries to get away, let it go."

Reasonable rules, he told himself as he tried to avoid looking at Kate Everly's khaki-clad hips and honey-gold hair. She was curvy and bright and a major animal lover. He watched the way she touched Ben, the way she used her hands as she talked, the purposeful ease of her gait. Grace, he thought. It sounded old-fashioned, like something his mother would say, but that was the only proper name for it. She had an open, feminine way about her that made people comfortable—probably a good thing in a doctor trusted to care for beloved animals. But those same qualities made every nerve in his body twitch with…anxiety? Expectation? *Interest?*

There were eight little bundles of fur in the puppy playroom. They were mixes—varying fuzzy shades of solid colors—long-haired dogs in the making. Ben did the obligatory hand washing with his eyes glued to the puppies. He was practically quivering with eagerness.

When the doc asked if Nick was going to join them, he gave a shake of his head and stepped back to lean a shoulder against the door frame. He watched Ben chase first one puppy, then another, trying to pet them. The pups sniffed him and bounded away to investigate other things. Kate Everly found a dry spot on the floor, sank down and patted the floor beside her. She showed Ben how to let the puppies come to him and sniff him.

Moments later he was being swarmed by curious puppies and was beaming as he petted them and told them how cute they were.

There were other people in the room, one older volunteer and a girl who looked to be about twelve. The puppies tumbled over their own paws and climbed the humans and tried to chew on their shoes, their pant legs and their fingers. And there was licking. Lots of licking.

Nick stiffened, and his hands fell from his pockets into fists at his sides.

Ben caught one little fur ball chewing on his shoelace and lifted it up to look it in the eye, saying, "No, no. That's not allowed. You better get with the program, kid."

A sound that was somewhere between a laugh and a groan came from Nick's throat, but thankfully was quiet enough to get lost in the confusion of puppy yips and human laughter. His whole body was now rigid; his breath came fast and shallow; and his vision was narrowing to a memory that mingled too intimately with present events.

There had been puppies…little mutts born in the stacks of old supply crates that edged their camp. The brood was adopted by his platoon, and when the mother disappeared—his guys fed and fostered the pups. For them, the pups became personal, something good to relate to in such foreign surroundings, something to care for and protect.

He could still see them…jumping after tennis balls somebody had sent to a war zone in a well-meaning but clueless Christmas package…sleeping sprawled on their backs or curled into sleek little balls that were slid gently into the men's packs. Some of the little buggers snored or yipped or practiced running in their sleep, which never failed to set him and his men laughing. The bomb dogs assigned to their unit seemed just as enthralled with the puppies as the men they served with were. Jax and Colo, both male shepherds, were downright respectful of the little buggers; brought them balls and shared bones, played tag in the yard, and let the puppies climb and nip—

The blood drained from his head, and suddenly he found it hard to breathe.

He did an about-face and strode out the door and out of the office.

In the parking lot he bent over to recover, taking slow, deep breaths to fight down the anxiety those memories always raised. Gradually, the tightness in his chest subsided and the darkness threatening his vision retreated.

After a few minutes, he was able to take a last, cleansing breath and let it go. It was four-plus years ago and a world away. It had nothing to do with his life now, he told himself every time, but it still weighed on him...a burden he didn't want to share, especially with Ben.

Squaring his shoulders, he sought normalcy in walking the grassy berm that led to the fenced exercise and introduction areas. There were a number of people about, considering adoption and watching as candidates played with their children. But in the farthest yard, he noticed a young man with an uncooperative dog on a lead, trying to get his charge to cooperate. He watched as the dog became a whirl of motion and the volunteer shrank back to the end of the leash, sputtering a stream of entreaties and anemic commands.

A moment later the dog yanked the lead from the volunteer's hands and began to run. Nick headed for that far exercise yard, feeling an urgency he couldn't explain. The dog managed to stop before hitting the fence, but then ran the entire perimeter, frantic for a way out. It was Goldie's friend. The shepherd. And it seemed like he was getting ready to jump.

"No!" Nick barked out, catching himself and the dog by surprise.

In another heartbeat he was climbing over the fence and standing a few yards from the headstrong shepherd, his feet spread and his fists propped on his hips. The dog hesitated as his gaze flicked between Nick and the nearby fence…ears forward, nose testing the air…escape clearly still a powerful pull on him.

"No," Nick said matter-of-factly, his tone firm and certain. "You don't want to jump that fence. You've got it good here, tough guy…plenty of food and a clean, dry place to lay your head. You don't want go back to sleeping in culverts and eating out of garbage cans."

The dog was still tense and ready to run, but he was listening to Nick's voice. Did he remember the other night? In the surgery, he'd obeyed an order to sit, and just now he stopped dead at *"No."* Maybe he had been trained somewhere along the line. If so, giving him a few familiar commands might help get him under control.

Nick dropped his arms to his sides, lowering his tension, though not his alertness. He waved the grateful volunteer back and took a couple of steps toward the dog, where he paused, making his posture relaxed and confident.

Nothing ventured, nothing gained.

First command: "Sit."

As in the surgery, the shepherd just stared at him, every muscle taut. Then he added the hand motion, the snap of a fist up against his shoulder. After what seemed like forever, the dog sank onto his rear haunches, a coiled spring ready to release at the slightest provocation.

Nick nodded, thinking of other commands they had used while on deployment. The shepherd watched him as he began to walk the perimeter of the exercise yard. Scent was the quickest way to familiarize a dog with a human, so he walked by the dog, keeping a few feet between them and not looking at him, but close enough for him to

get a good whiff. Interestingly, the shepherd
didn't move; he just watched and processed
the scent. Nick wondered if he would remember it from their contact the other night
and if he would respond.

"Stand."

If dogs could frown in confusion, this one
did. Nick glanced back and saw the hesitation. He stopped, turned and added a hand
signal for "stand": arm curled toward the
biceps and then punched straight out to the
side, where he held it for a moment. The dog
came alert and stood.

Nick smiled.

"You know your commands, tough guy.
Silent ones anyway. Let's see what else you
can do."

The shepherd did indeed know a range
of nonverbal commands: stay, down, fetch.
Every order delivered and executed helped
the shepherd relax a bit more, until one last
command—where he refused to bring the
stick back and veered toward the fence.

"Come here," Nick ordered with as much
authority as he could muster. The shepherd
caught the edge in his voice, and after a
pause brought the stick back. It took some

serious negotiation to get him to understand a "let go" command, but he finally dropped the stick and backed away.

This time, Nick picked up the stick and said, "Break." That was a nonstarter. He tried "sit" again and the dog obeyed. After a few moments of toying with the stick, Nick held it up and said, "Finished!" The dog stood, tail twitching, watching Nick. He threw the stick again and this time the shepherd retrieved it and bounded around the yard with it like a puppy with its first toy.

NANCE EVERLY HAD just pulled her old Chevy truck into the gravel parking lot of the shelter when she spotted a big man in jeans and a T-shirt bursting out the office like his hair was on fire. The guy rushed to the grassy area at the side of the exercise yards and bent over as if he were going to hurl. She bolted from her truck to see if she could help, but before she got close enough, he straightened and stood with his hands on his belt, taking deep breaths. She halted as a look of relief came over him.

This was a first: somebody getting sick over a visit to the shelter.

He seemed to be recovering. She watched as he headed down the greenway. There was something familiar about him. Shaking her head, she turned back to the office and was surprised moments later to find Kate ensconced in the puppy room with a young boy who was as cute as a bug and alive with enthusiasm.

She paused just outside the doorway to watch her granddaughter teach the boy about puppies. There was a light in Kate's eyes that Nance hadn't seen for a while. She broke into a wistful smile. Her granddaughter deserved a family of her own and a lifetime of loving and being loved. If only she would cooperate and open herself up to possibilities around her.

"We've got quite a crew today," she called as she entered the room and headed for the sink. "Who's your friend, Kate?"

"Hey, Gran." Kate's face bloomed with a 50-megawatt smile as she put a hand on the boy's shoulder. "This is Ben Stanton. His dad is the trooper who brought in those two dogs the other night. They dropped by the office to check on the golden and then came here to see about the shepherd. I twisted

Ben's arm into helping with the puppy play this afternoon." She laughed when Ben reddened and grinned.

Nance replaced the towel, then joined them in the puppy pen and stuck out a hand.

"Hey there, Ben. Nice to meet you." The boy gave her a very adult handshake, and the sense of what she'd seen outside struck her forcefully. His dad, the state trooper, had been about to empty his stomach on the grass outside.

KATE HAD OBSERVED Nick standing in the doorway watching his son with the puppies, and she'd been jolted by what she saw. Pride, tenderness and what could only be called longing had bloomed in his face, until something more haunting took over. What made him leave the puppy room with such a devastated expression? It was as if he'd closed a door on all the tender feelings she'd glimpsed. And why had he refused to come inside with his son to play with the puppies in the first place? What kind of person backed away from the chance to play with puppies?

At least Ben hadn't seen him go.

The joy on Ben's face edged those thoughts aside as she told him about the various stages of puppy development. Socialization with people, she explained, was critical to puppies being able to form bonds with their future families, and socializing with other dogs was important so that they would behave well when they met dogs in the future.

The boy absorbed every word. She caught the sparkle of discovery in his eyes and warmed inside.

"I want a dog," he revealed, surprising no one. "A puppy would be great—but I'd like a dog of any kind."

She smiled. "And what does your dad say about that?"

"I didn't ask him yet. He's busy…saving people…and dogs."

There was a wistful pride in his tone that sent a pang of longing through Kate. Ben sensed his father's ambivalence toward this whole dog business, so he wasn't begging or pushing like most eight-year-olds would. He really was a wonderful kid, a remarkable mixture of curiosity, enthusiasm and sensitivity. And those *eyes*. Big golden pools

of wonder rimmed by thick, dark lashes…
just like…

Her next free thought was for the boy's
mother. Was she responsible for the attentive, respectful tone Ben displayed toward
adults? As Kate tried to imagine the woman
who had captured Nick Stanton's heart and
produced such a bright, lovable boy, a knot
formed in her stomach.

Not long after that, she heard Gran's voice
and looked up to find her grandmother smiling down at them. Soon they were watching Gran ply her uncanny magic on the little
scamps.

"She's famous for being able to con-
nect with and teach even the most stubborn
dogs," Kate told Ben in hushed tones. "Puppies adore her. Watch this."

One by one the puppies were lured to
Gran by her special charm. They seemed
to relish the affection she gave so freely as
much as the little training treats she carried
in her pocket.

Ben leaned close to Kate. "They did what
she said. They sat down. How does she do
that?"

Kate gave him a mysterious grin. "We

call her 'the puppy whisperer,' although she seems to have a similar knack with animals of all kinds. You should see her farm. It's practically a zoo out there. And the animals all come running to meet her when she walks outside."

Ben's eyes were as big as saucers as they turned back to Gran.

When playtime was over, the tired puppies gravitated to Nance and climbed over each other to reach her lap. They nestled against her as she sat cross-legged on the floor, petting them. Before long, her lap was full of sleepy pups. Two of them resisted the lure of nap time in Gran's lap to continue exploring and they ended up on Kate's lap, yawning.

As Ben stroked one of the puppies she held, he leaned close to ask, "Are you a puppy whisperer, too?"

She chuckled softly. "I guess so. It seems to run in the family. But Gran has a lot more experience at it that I have."

After a few quiet moments, Ben helped put them in their basket and carry them back to the run where their mother was waiting.

"Where's my dad?" Ben asked, looking

around as they exited the kennel and crossed the old patio to the office again.

"I'm not sure." She frowned as they passed through the kitchen-surgery and the empty reception room. "He stepped outside while we were in the puppy room. Let's go find him."

CHAPTER FIVE

THEY FOUND NICK in the farthest exercise yard with a familiar-looking German shepherd, giving commands and waiting patiently as the dog complied. A teenage volunteer was hanging on the fence near the gate with a leash over his shoulder, watching the interplay.

Kate's jaw dropped as she saw the dog sit, stay, come and retrieve. This was the same shepherd who growled and bared teeth at staff and became a Tasmanian devil when anyone tried to put a leash on him?

Nick seemed unaware of their presence as he worked with the dog, so they waited in silence for a while. The volunteer responded to Nick's request and entered the yard to put something in his hand. The instant Nick turned to the shepherd, the dog's nose was quivering. Seconds later, he was being rewarded with treats and pats on the head, the latter of which caused him to freeze for a moment, still wary after accepting Nick's commands and the treats that meant a job well done.

Nick reached for the leash, and the shepherd allowed him to slip it over his head. There was some resistance when the volunteer tried to lead him back to the kennel, but after a few words from Nick, the shepherd grudgingly followed the volunteer. When Nick turned and spotted Ben and Kate, he headed toward them with a long, military stride that made it seem he could be wearing full dress blues.

"That was him, Goldie's friend, wasn't it?" Ben climbed onto the bottom rail of the fence to greet his dad, his face alight with discovery.

"Yeah, that was him," Nick responded with a smile that made Kate's stomach quiver. Then he stopped by the fence and looked to her. "It seems Goldie's friend has had some major training. Maybe even military. Certainly knows verbal and silent commands."

"And it seems you know how to give those commands," she said, tilting her head, wishing she could see behind that handsome pair of eyes. "Those dogs you knew in Iraq, right? You were a handler?"

"Not really." His smile faded. "I took over a few times when handlers got injured or rotated out. The guys attached to our unit taught us the basics, in case…" He halted and after a moment swallowed hard. She noticed, because she couldn't take her gaze from that muscular neck. Every part of him seemed armored with muscle, impervious— except those eyes, which had darkened and were now avoiding hers.

"You know how to make dogs behave, don't you, Dad?" Ben's grin brought back some of the pleasure to Nick's tight smile.

"Certain dogs." Nick ruffled Ben's hair with a big hand and then drew the boy against his side in a half hug. Kate's stomach dropped. Her knees weren't feeling any too steady, either.

"It may sound strange," he continued to Kate, "but I think he's depressed. It happens to military dogs that lose their handler. They droop physically…lose interest in training… forget how to play."

"I've heard about that, but never treated

it. I think you may be right." Kate looked toward the kennel. "He seemed a lot more energetic just now, not to mention cooperative. Well, now that we know more about him, we can handle him better and start to rehab him. Who knows? Maybe we'll even be able to find him a forever home."

Ben looked up at her and seemed puzzled. "A forever home?"

"That's what we call it when a dog finds people who will love it and make it a part of their family for the rest of its life. A *forever* home."

There was a heartbeat's pause.

"So…some homes aren't forever?" Ben thought about that, and his eyes darkened as the sense of it hit home. "Some people get dogs and kids, then decide they don't want them anymore and just…" He glanced up at his dad, then jumped down from the fence and headed for the sanctuary office.

Kate stared after him, speechless, unable to place what he'd said in any reasonable context. She would never have expected to hear such hurt from such a vibrant and seemingly well-adjusted child. Had she totally misread Ben's relationship with his father? She looked at Nick, but he seemed just as devastated as she was by the emotion packed into Ben's statement.

"What was that about?" she said, shifting directly in front of Nick.

"It's not exactly a secret." Nick's tone flattened and expression hardened as he spoke. "Ben's mother left us right after I returned from my last deployment. He had just turned four, and he took it hard. He doesn't talk about it or about her. But sometimes it comes out…like…now."

"So his mother is…"

"Not in the picture." He produced a tight, humorless smile as he stepped to the side and swung over the fence to stand beside her. "It's just him and me. And my mom. She's a widow, and she moved in with us after Ben's mother left. She's great with him and does everything she can to fill the hole in his life."

"And who fills the hole in your life?"

It was out before Kate could apply a filter—the thought went straight from her brain out her mouth. His eyes widened a couple of degrees, but otherwise he seemed surprisingly undisturbed by the question and the curiosity that prompted it.

"That wound healed pretty quick," he said. "We were apart more than we were together, with deployments and all. It's Ben I worry about. I have to work a lot and don't get to spend the kind of time with him I'd like."

"Understandable." She hooked her thumbs in her pockets. "But then, every parent I've ever talked to says the same thing. Time is the one thing there never seems to be enough of when it comes to kids." She searched his now guarded expression. "If it helps—from an outsider's point of view— Ben seems to worship you. He talks about you a lot and is very proud of how you help people and *dogs*." Back on safer ground now, she smiled. "Fair warning—he wants a dog pretty badly."

"Yeah, I got that. Seeing him with the golden at your office, then with the puppies—it wasn't hard to figure out that a dog request is probably in the works."

"When we were in the puppy room, he said he'd be happy with an older dog. And if I could offer a little advice, that might be a good option for a boy as young as Ben. But all kids want a puppy. The cute factor is overwhelming. I mean—" she remembered his expression in the puppy room too late "—who doesn't love puppies?"

He straightened and focused on her in a way that made her feel like a specimen under glass. Wow. A shiver ran down her spine at the intensity of his stare. *It's personal*, that look said.

She stuttered mentally. *More personal than the disintegration of his relationship with the woman who gave birth to his child?*

A shout of alarm from one of the volunteers yanked her attention to the end of the long gravel driveway, where two dark lumps lay on the pale crushed shell, one still and the other struggling to move. In the distance, hidden by the trees lining the road, an engine revved and tires squealed. Her nerves snapped taut. Someone had dropped off dogs.

She was in motion before she had a chance to think about it. She ran with two other volunteers to see what had been dropped on their doorstep. By the time she arrived, one of the volunteers was on his knees beside a dog that was scarred and bloodied beyond belief. Its head and ears were so swollen it was hard to identify the breed. The other dog, an American Staffordshire terrier—a male "pittie" from the looks of him—struggled to rise, clearly weakened and dazed from loss of blood. There were open, bleeding wounds all over its blocky head and muscular shoulders.

Instinct told her the motionless dog was probably beyond help, so she focused on the Staffordshire thrashing on the stone, trying to make it to his feet. She put both hands on the dog's chest and ribs to try to get a sense of his heartbeat while murmuring reassurances, trying to calm him. It felt like his heart was going to jump out of his chest; he was frantic to escape whatever torment he expected at the hands of humans.

"We need to get him inside so I can work on him," she said to the people gathered around. A familiar pair of arms appeared with a blanket to cover the dog and lift it.

"Ben, go to the car and stay there." Nick's voice was strained as he carried the dog down the long drive.

"But, Dad, the dogs are hurt and I can—"

"Go!" Nick thundered. "Now!"

Kate was aware of the boy heading away from the group, shoulders rounded and feet dragging. She looked up at Nick with a question she didn't get to ask.

"I don't want him seeing this," Nick said roughly. "He's too young. It'll give him nightmares."

Kate nodded and ran ahead to make sure the exam table was clear and to prepare the necessary supplies. When she looked up, Isabelle and three other volunteers were crowding the doorway behind Nick, who settled the dog on the table with a grim expression.

"He's in shock. We have to find out where all that blood is coming from." It was a short-haired dog, but she gave his front leg a pass with the clippers anyway and then thrust the coil of tubing and needle pack at Nick. "Get this going while I check out his wounds." She sensed his hesitation and looked up. His face was taut and his jaw was set, but after a moment he went to work establishing the IV, and her gaze moved on to one of the older volunteers, Harry Mueller, who was just pushing into the room. Harry had been the one trying to help the other dog. "What happened?"

Harry wiped his face on his sleeve and shook his head. "Gone."

"Damn." She froze for a second and then drew a sharp breath. "Well, let's see what we can do about saving this one."

For the next several minutes she worked intently, cleaning away blood and investigating cuts—some jagged rips and others clean slashes. There were fresh scars and lumps that looked like old swelling in several places, including on the dog's head. Part of one ear had been ripped off recently and was only half-healed. The certainty settled in her gut like a stone. "These are fighting injuries."

"Yeah," Nick said, looking around for a place to hang the IV bag, but, finding none, simply held it himself. "From the looks of him, this guy has seen plenty of action. We've heard rumors that they're back in this area. The dogfighting rings."

"But why would they dump their injured off on us?" Isabelle asked from behind Nick. She folded her arms tightly across her chest as she edged around the others to see the damage for herself. "Don't they usually just bury the evidence somewhere out of the way and move on?"

No one said anything for a minute, then Kate looked up at the ceiling to clear her vision, then back down at the wound she was stitching. "Maybe somebody had an attack of conscience."

She quit counting knots after a while; it seemed like she stitched forever, having to layer some in the deeper cuts. Swelling caused some of the lacerations to go together unevenly, leading her to comment that he might not be pretty afterward.

An ache had begun in the small of her back by the time she finished. The group crowded into the doorway had since moved on; only Isabelle and Nick remained.

"That's it," she said, snapping off the gloves, tossing them into the nearby can and arching her back. "That's all we can do. I'll bring over some antibiotics later, and we'll have to watch him closely for the next few days."

"You think he's got a chance?" Isabelle asked.

"A slim one." Kate frowned as she studied her handiwork, then turned to the sink to scrub her hands and arms up to the elbows. Her clothes were a disaster. "Maybe twenty-five percent."

"All that work for twenty-five percent." Nick's voice sounded thick.

She reached for a towel and turned to look at him. "Without that work, his odds would have been zero." She met the storm in his gaze with a calm she had learned at her grandmother's side. "That's what we do… better the odds. We give it all we have and trust in the outcome." She paused and ran a hand gently over the dog's battered, heavily stitched head. Emotion that had been held at bay by professional duty came rushing in.

"You learn early on, working with animals, that you're a conduit for healing, not the source," she said quietly, as much to herself as to him. "We're not responsible for every life we touch. That's a burden too big to bear. After a while the weight of that kind of thinking would paralyze us. It's also a recognition that we're part of the natural processes of life. We help wherever we can, whenever we can, always knowing that the outcome may be out of our hands."

Tears pricked her eyes, and she grabbed her stethoscope to busy herself listening to the dog's heart: slow, but still beating.

Moments later, Gran entered with an anxious expression, towing a young boy behind her.

"Ben and I were wondering what's happening."

Nick wheeled and found Ben moving toward the table where the injured dog lay—swollen, stitched and inert—in a mass of bloody cloths.

"Did he die, too?" Ben asked, his eyes wide.

"What the hell?" Nick ground out before checking himself and bending to take Ben by the shoulders. "I told you to—" He reddened with what looked like chagrin and then glowered up at Nance. "He doesn't need to be seeing this stuff."

Kate watched Ben recoil from his father's anger and rounded the table to intervene. "It's all right, Nick. It's probably not as bad as he might imagine. If you'll let me explain to him—"

"He's seen enough for one day." He turned Ben toward the door and gave his back a gentle push to get him going. "He's just a kid, for God's sake."

Shocked silence descended as Nick rushed Ben out, and the sounds of their departure wafted back through the offices. It took a minute for the tension to dissipate. Kate felt Nance studying her and hoped her grandmother wasn't reading every confusing emotion she was feeling. Nance looked to the door where the two had escaped.

"I've seen a lot of creatures in pain in my time," she said with a concerned look at Kate, "enough to know *that* one is carrying a load of torment inside him."

Kate nodded, her anxiety melting into something softer, something more complicated. It was too late for grandmotherly warnings. She was already involved, heart-over-head, with the trooper and his adorable son.

CHAPTER SIX

KATE STAYED AT the shelter that night, catching a few winks of sleep on the lumpy, donated sofa in Isabelle's closet-size office. In the empty hours before dawn she kept going over the day's events, recalling everything Nick had said and second-guessing every response she had given. She'd be lucky if she ever saw the Stantons again.

Nick clearly had a thing about hurt dogs, undoubtedly tied to his experiences in war zones, and was doing his best to avoid resurrecting bad memories. And Ben had a thing about hurt dogs that produced the exact opposite reaction. He was drawn to them, wanting to help in whatever capacity he could.

By dawn, she was aching from lying on that miserable couch and bleary-eyed from lack of rest. And when she checked on the injured dog, her heart sank. His heartbeat had grown weaker and was giving her a premonition that this case was not going to end well. After all that work…she hadn't lied to Nick, she truly did believe she wasn't responsible for every life she touched. But that didn't mean she didn't get involved with animals or that losing a patient didn't take a toll on her.

Nance arrived early in the morning with breakfast sandwiches and gigantic cups of coffee. Jess came by on her way from an overnight somewhere and agreed to come back later and stay with the dog so Kate could go home and get some rest. Isabelle checked in between sessions with potential adoptive families. And Hines showed up with his new buddy, the visibly smaller but not entirely mobile Moose, to spend a little time with his other charges in the kennels. But overlaying all of that normal activity was a quiet sense of expectation, an air of impending loss. It was almost six hours before the dog's weary heart gave way to the inevitable and stopped beating.

It was all right, Kate told herself. She had done her best—they all had. The pittie had received devoted care at the end. And she went home Sunday night and obeyed Jess's orders to drink a glass of wine, then have a hot shower and a good cry.

Monday morning, on her way to the clinic, she thought of what Nick's and Ben's reactions would be to the news that the dog had died, and irritably shoved those thoughts from her mind. After the way he'd left the shelter on Saturday, Nick would probably never come back to learn what happened to the dog. She'd just better accept it, and ignore this hollow feeling she got at the prospect of never seeing him again.

"Your problem is, you're too serious about men," Jess declared, pushing her to sit on a stool in the surgery. "You've seen this guy all of two times, and already you're losing sleep over him and his kid. I get the uniform lust, I truly do. But Katie, you have to lighten up. Broaden your horizons. Have some *fun*."

For once, Kate was going to listen to her partner's advice. Lighten up. Quit being so serious. She'd seen Nick Stanton all of twice, and only learned he was a father the second time—two days ago. What was she doing letting herself get so emotionally involved?

But both times she had been with him, she had done emergency surgery on a dog with his help, and you couldn't get much more intense than that. Still, she knew that she was taking their interactions too much to heart. Given time, this preoccupation with Nick Stanton would undoubtedly pass.

By the end of the week it seemed to be doing just that: passing. His presence in her thoughts and feelings faded as she threw herself into routine, immunizing, spaying and neutering and treating minor injuries and illnesses. It was actually a relief, she told herself, not to have to worry about someone else's problems.

SATURDAY MORNING, NICK pulled into the parking space nearest the Lakeview Clinic's front door. Ben had had a soccer game and it ran late. He tried to tell his son that the office was probably closed, but Ben was desperate to check on Goldie and Nick was... well, he was a sucker for his kid's wide-eyed plea. He could see the same spiky-haired receptionist at the door, locking up even as they rolled out of the SUV. Ben ran ahead of him to the door and knocked on the glass. The young woman seemed to recognize them.

"Where is Dr. Kate?" Ben asked eagerly as she opened the door. "We came to see Goldie."

"Oh." The receptionist scowled. "She's not here."

Ben's face fell, and he looked over his shoulder to Nick, who was coming up behind him.

"Who's not here?" Nick asked. "The doc or the dog?"

"Both."

"Goldie's gone?" Ben's alarm seemed to surprise her. "What happened to her? Dr. Kate said she was going to be okay."

"She is okay." She smiled reassuringly. "The docs took her out to the shelter a couple of days ago. We needed the room."

Ben turned to him with that determination-melting look of expectation. "We have to go, Dad. I promised her." He was so serious and so determined that the receptionist grinned.

"Who did you promise, the doc or the dog?" she asked.

"Both," Nick said, feeling none too pleased about it.

"Lucky dog," the receptionist said with an appreciative glance at him that made him redden.

As he and Ben turned and headed for the 4x4, the receptionist reset the alarm and finished locking the door, and he could have sworn he heard her add: "Lucky doc."

"GOLDIE, YOU'RE A PEACH." Kate knelt by the crate to examine the way the stitches were holding on the golden's hip and rear leg. "You left your stitches alone and you're finally eating." She gave the dog a pet and tested the fit of the cast on her injured leg. "I know you're bored, being cooped up like this. But we had to keep you in a crate to stop you from trying to get up before you were ready. Well, today's the day. You ready to get up on that leg and walk?"

The golden thumped her tail once, but laid her head back down, looking dejected.

"Come on, baby. You can do this. I know you're weak, but just think how good it will be to pee outside again and sniff the grass where all the other dogs have left messages."

Still no interest in getting up.

Kate backed away a few steps and reached into her pocket for a treat.

"Come on, girl." She held out the snack and glanced at Nance and Isabelle, who watched the dog's listless response from a nearby doorway.

"She's probably stiff from inactivity," Nance said.

"She may not be ready yet," Isabelle offered.

Kate gave them a glower. "Who's the vet here?"

They shrugged and nodded to each other; Kate had a point.

"Come on, Goldie. You have to get up and move around, at least a little." She pulled on the blanket the golden lay on, dragging her with it out of the crate and into the concrete aisle of the kennel.

But nothing, no treat, no request, could induce her to get up on her own. At length, Kate stood over her and grabbed the blanket on either side of her belly, lifting and groaning. "How can you weigh this much? You're skin and bones." She was barely able to get the dog to her feet, and the second Goldie was released, she slumped back onto the floor and looked more miserable than before. Kate sighed and pushed her hair back behind her ears, letting her heart rate return to normal. She scowled at her grandmother, daring her to say a word. Nance, being Nance, had several for her.

"So much for being an animal whisperer."

"WE'RE JUST GOING to check on the retriever, and then we're heading home," Nick told his son, glancing in the rearview mirror to see that his words took root.

"Sure, Dad. And the other sick dog. The pittie. It won't take long." Ben had raised his chin to look out the window.

"No puppies today. No tour of the kennels." Nick thought he'd better reiterate: "We just stop in, see the golden—"

"Goldie."

"Okay *Goldie*. We just stop in to see Goldie and then head straight home. I have to mow the lawn and get the oil changed in Nana's car."

"Okay, okay. I got it."

The instant the car stopped in the parking lot of the shelter, Ben popped his seat belt and flew out door. He ran straight for Harbor's offices and disappeared inside despite Nick's call for him to wait. Muttering things he was glad Ben couldn't hear, Nick closed up the car and headed after him quickly.

He called for Ben in the reception room, glanced into the empty puppy room and then continued on toward the sound of voices in the kitchen-surgery at the rear.

"Where is he?" Ben's voice grew louder with each word. "Dr. Kate fixed him, and he is going to stay here and get better."

Nick found Ben facing a familiar-looking older woman. A second later he recognized the shelter's director, and crossed the room to put his hands on Ben's shoulders. "What's going on?"

"He's not here, Dad. The pittie." Ben looked up at him with frantic eyes. "The hurt dog you helped with. She says he's gone." He wrenched out of Nick's grip and looked under the table and all around the makeshift surgery. "Where did he go? He was hurt really bad."

Nick cringed, sensing exactly what the woman's rueful expression and shaking head tried to convey.

"Ben!" He caught his son by the arm as the boy rushed for the rear door. "Ms. Conti here is the shelter director. She's trying to tell you…she means…the dog didn't make it. He died."

"No, no—you fixed him—you and Dr. Kate. Just like you did Goldie." He grew even more alarmed and looked at Isabelle. "Where's Goldie? She's here, right? That lady *said* she was here!"

Ben yanked free and raced through the rear door.

"Ben—wait!" Nick ran after him, out onto an old back patio. Ben ran toward a long concrete-block building that housed the rescued dogs.

Nick caught up with him near the open door of the building and dragged him to a stop. This was what he had dreaded—this clash of youthful hope and stark reality. Ben was too sensitive and too damned young to be dealing with such life-and-death issues.

"Ben, you have to listen to me. Dogs die." He lifted his son's face and choked on the pained disbelief in his son's eyes. He swallowed hard. It was a second before he could continue. "Sometimes dogs get injured and they die. We try to help them, but—"

"Our best is all we can do" Kate Everly's voice came from the open door, and she appeared a second later. Her presence sent an involuntary wave of relief through Nick, and he felt the tension in Ben's body lessen. She stepped onto the concrete pad outside the door as Ben turned to her with a reddened face and teary eyes.

"What's all this?" she said, watching Ben struggle to contain his feelings. "Oh. You heard about the pittie." She stooped beside Ben and reached for his hands. "It's okay to be sad and cry."

"I'm not crying," Ben said, looking ready to burst.

A tear squeezed through his control and slid down his cheek.

She softened visibly and opened her arms, sinking fully onto her knees as he leaned into her. "All of us were very sad, just like you are now. It's hard to do your best and still have an animal die."

"I'm not crying," he said desperately between gulps of air.

"It's okay. Everybody cries sometimes."

"Not soldiers. My dad doesn't cry."

She looked up and caught Nick trying to blink away the excess moisture in his eyes, and he felt like he'd taken a right-left combination to the gut.

Then she smiled at him.

Sad and sweet.

It was all he could do to hold it together.

"Do you remember what I said about how dogs and people get better?" She set Ben back a few inches and collected his gaze in hers. "Their bodies have special systems for repairing and healing." Ben's head bobbed as he swiped at his face. "Well, the pittie's body was so weak from loss of blood that it couldn't repair itself. All we could do was make him comfortable and help him across the rainbow bridge."

"Rainbow bridge?" Ben took a shuddering breath. "What's that?"

"That's what people say when a beloved pet dies—the animal's spirit crosses the rainbow bridge into heaven. That way, every time they see a rainbow, they can remember their pet and not be sad."

Ben scowled. "Is the rainbow bridge real?"

Kate's sad smile reappeared, and Nick struggled to draw breath against the tightness in his chest. His choked cough made her look up.

"I don't know." She held Nick's gaze for a moment and then looked back at Ben. "But I'd like it to be true."

Ben pushed back from her, bracing for something worse.

"Did Goldie die, too? Did she cross the rainbow bridge?"

"No, no, not Goldie." Kate's relief bloomed like a sunrise as she released him and pushed to her feet. "She's getting better, and we brought her here so she could recuperate. In fact, it's a good thing you showed up today. You might be able to help us with her." She offered him her hand and led him into the noisy kennel. "This way…she's right down here."

Nick followed as soon as he could get his legs to move, shaking off the effects of the exchange he'd just witnessed. He watched them walk down the aisle together, hand in hand, toward a section of crates and felt his eyes sting again. He halted several feet away, rubbed his face and took a deep breath. What the hell was happening to him? He never acted like this—tearing up over—

The golden retriever lay on a blanket in the middle of the aisle with a cast on her leg and a row of stitches he had helped to place on her flank.

"She won't get up," Kate explained as doleful brown eyes stared back at them. "We've tried coaxing and then bribing her with toys and treats, but nothing seems to motivate her to stand." She put a hand on Ben's shoulder. "She seems to like you. I was thinking you might be able to help persuade her."

Nick watched his son's slender shoulders square as responsibility settled on them. He knelt beside Goldie, seeming a little tentative.

"Do you remember me? I came to see you at Dr. Kate's office."

Goldie lifted her head a bit and sniffed, cataloging his scent. After a moment, her head sank back to her paws, and Ben looked at them with disappointment.

"I don't think she remembers me."

"She just needs a little time to get used to you again. She's been through a lot lately."

Kate crossed her arms and leaned a shoulder against the empty upper crate. "Why don't you sit with her for a while, talk to her and pet her. When she's feeling more confident, we can try to get her to stand again."

"What do I say?"

"Just talk. Tell her about your soccer team, your bedroom or your favorite TV program. As long as you're petting her, she'll be happy."

Nick watched Ben pet Goldie and tell her about his soccer team, but what filled his thoughts was Kate.

Her warm, feminine presence—inches away—opened doors in him and produced conflicting impulses. He wanted to explore these feelings further—and to run like hell in the opposite direction. He didn't much like either option. He hadn't felt this uncertain since his first recon in Iraqi hill country.

"You want to help him?" she asked, watching Ben talk to the dog.

"Nah. I'm good." In truth he wasn't sure what he wanted to do at that moment. Except maybe touch her. And he shouldn't. He sank his hands firmly into his jeans pockets.

"In that case, how about a cup of coffee?"

Without waiting for a response, she stooped beside Ben and gave Goldie a pat. "So how about if I steal your dad for a few minutes while you and Goldie spend some time together? Are you okay with that?"

Ben looked up with a glow of purpose on his face. "Sure." And then he turned back to the dog, who thumped her tail in encouragement.

Kate rose and turned to Nick with a glint in her eyes. "Come with me, Trooper, and I'll treat you to the best coffee you've ever had."

While his mind was still deciding, his body took over and headed after her like a needle following a magnet. A very curvy magnet that he figured would cause him a few unsettling flashbacks in the coming week.

CHAPTER SEVEN

SHE LED HIM to the offices, where their coffee machine—nothing as mundane as a "pot"—sat in a corner of the kitchen-surgery. "Our director, Isabelle, graced us with this thing, swearing it was magic, and I think she may be right. Even I can coax a great brew from it, and I'm not exactly a coffee wizard." She grabbed a couple of mugs from the shelf above and pressed some buttons on the machine. She could feel his gaze like a tangible thing, studying every movement she made. Her heart beat faster and she grew self-conscious. Minutes later, she was handing him a mug of fragrant, dark coffee and waving him toward the creamer and sugar.

He added creamer and then leaned back against the counter, one arm across his chest, the other holding the mug as he sampled the coffee. She took a position across from him, leaning against the heavy old farmhouse table that doubled as her exam table, sipping her own coffee and studying the quality of the silence between them.

"Well? What do you think?" she prompted.

"Good stuff. It tastes as good as it smells, which is saying something."

He gave a taut smile before burying his nose in the mug, and once again the silence stretched until she felt compelled to break it.

"He'll be fine," she said, holding her warm mug between hands that suddenly felt chilly. Nick looked up for clarification. His hazel eyes seemed larger, more luminous. "Ben. I know you're worried about him getting involved with these dogs and getting in over his head. But from what I can tell, he's a remarkably grounded kid. As long as he's guided to the right conclusions, he'll be fine."

"And who's going to guide him to these 'right' conclusions?"

"You are."

"What makes you think I know the ones to guide him to?"

"Because you've experienced loss and you got through it."

Skepticism permeated his half smile. "You sure about that?"

She studied the curve of his lips and squelched the urge to lick hers.

"Look," she said, "I don't know you well, I admit. But what I've seen makes me think you're somebody a kid can count on. You do the right thing. You're not afraid to do the work, even if it's thankless or heartbreaking. You're strong and you're not afraid to share that strength. And you love that boy of yours like nobody's business." She took another sip of coffee as she let that sink in. "How am I doing?"

"You should write campaign ads," he said, studying her as frankly as she examined him. Her face began to heat.

"Oh, I'm sure you have your flaws," she said with a self-conscious laugh. "But I have a feeling you're already quite aware of them. Most people are. What they need to be reminded of is their potential…the good and the great in them that can make the world a better place."

"Your middle name wouldn't happen to be Pollyanna, would it?"

"Not by a long shot. Am I embarrassing

you? Too personal?" *Too interested?* she almost said and realized that she was already declaring personal interest as openly as she could. For the first time in her life she felt perfectly fine with that. If he wasn't interested, too, it was best to know it now. Experience had taught her that honesty was the best policy when it came to relationships.

Whoa. Was that what she thought was happening here?

Damn it, Kate—this is only the third time you've set eyes on him—

"Not embarrassed. A little surprised is all. Don't know that I've ever been analyzed so…"

"Correctly?" she offered.

"Neatly."

"Yeah, well, that's me. Neat. And to the point. I'd like to think I have a bit of insight into more than just cats and dogs."

"Well, you're aces about one thing—I am crazy about my kid. I'd move heaven and earth to keep him from getting hurt any more than—" He looked down into his cup, then took a gulp of coffee.

"More than he already has been," she finished the sentence for him. "His mom. I get that. But learning to handle the ups and downs of life with animals might help him learn to deal with the ups and downs of the rest of his life…his *human* problems."

He canted his head, his expression now intent, searching her in a way that made her feel positively x-rayed.

"That what happened with you?" he asked, his voice quiet and all the more intense because of it. "Working with animals helped you put your 'human' problems in perspective?"

She was startled by his conclusion and straightened, setting her mug on the counter. She wouldn't have put it in those terms, but now that he had, there was no use denying it. Having him turn her well-intentioned nosiness back on her was unsettling. But then, she was the one who insisted on getting so personal, and it was *his* son they were talking about. She paused to let her defensiveness retreat and then laid it out simply.

"Ben isn't the only kid to have a parent or two walk out on them."

He absorbed that for moment, searching her, drawing another of his dead-on-center conclusions, then gave a soft, through-the-teeth whistle. "Two? That sucks."

"Big-time." She shrugged, but found herself strangely drawn to explain, which was something she never did. Well, not before the hundredth date, which was about ninety-seven more than she usually had with the same guy. "Fortunately for me, I got dumped on Gran's doorstep, and she knew a thing or two about caring for strays and rejects. She opened her heart to me and filled the hole in mine. After a while I didn't think so much about the might-have-beens, only the what-can-bes. So I know it's possible to survive and even thrive without the traditional 2.0 parents."

He nodded, but it was a moment before he spoke.

"Your grandmother—she's the one Ben called the 'puppy whisperer'?" He gave a slightly crooked smile that made her pulse trip.

"The very one."

"The one with the farm and all the animals?"

"So he talked about her?"

"I got a blow-by-blow. She really has llamas?"

"Yeah, but they're not spitters. She has well-mannered llamas. Except that they're not wild about the ostriches. I think they see them as competition." Relieved that the conversation was taking a lighter turn, she laughed. "And they seem to enjoy making the baby goats 'faint' whenever they run through the yard."

"Goats really faint?" His eyes brightened in a way that could only be called pleasure. She nodded and he chuckled, a low rumble that sent a trill of expectation along her exposed skin. "That would have come in handy a few times in Afghanistan."

"Well, not all goats faint when they're scared. It's a genetic thing, so it might or might not have happened to Afghanistan's goats. Might be interesting to do a little research on—" While reaching for her coffee on the counter, she caught a fleeting glimpse of a something moving across the rear yard and frowned.

"What?" he said, following her line of sight.

"I thought I saw...nothing." She picked up

her mug and was in the middle of a sip when she looked back and glimpsed Ben disappearing inside the small kennel that housed their less cooperative charges. "Oh…"

She was in motion before she could explain, but Nick caught her tension and followed.

"What's happened? What's going on?"

"We left him with Goldie. What's he doing in the small kennel?"

They found him at the far end of the concrete alley, where he was struggling to get the latch up on a run, amid a horrific din of barking.

"Don't!" she called, but it was too late. The door of the run swung open, and a German shepherd—Goldie's German shepherd—came charging out. He just missed knocking Ben over as he whirled to face Kate and Nick.

"Ben, get behind the run's door and stay there!" Nick barked, looking frantically around for something to wrap his arm to absorb the attack he felt must be coming. But the dog slowed for a moment before shooting between them and straight out the open door.

A heartbeat later Ben came running down

the alley after the dog, his eyes wide. "Come on, Dad, we have to get him!"

Nick snatched him back, hauling him up with an arm around his waist while he struggled to get free. "What the hell do you think you're doing, letting that dog out? He could have bitten you!"

"We have to get him!" Ben tried to free himself from his father's grip.

It was hard to hear above the racket the dogs were making, but Kate caught "Goldie" and "him," and grabbed Ben's hands.

"Why did you let the shepherd free? Ben, look at me!" She bent closer. "What has this got to do with Goldie?"

"She needs him." He looked up with tears of frustration gathering, his chest heaving. "He's her friend. He can help her get up."

"So, you came to get him to help her." She looked at Nick, whose arms loosened around Ben, and she saw that he understood what was happening, too. He let Ben slide to his feet. Then she glanced toward the door. "He's loose. And running."

MOMENTS LATER, THEY were all running across the yard after a fast disappearing streak of dark fur. Fortunately, the shepherd had headed for an area thick with fences— the meeting yards. He was diverted by one fence and raced around it only to confront another that caused him to slow further. Sensing pursuit, the shepherd darted through an open gate and raced across a fenced yard that ended too quickly. As he raced around the fence, gathering speed for a jump, Nick's voice made him falter.

"No!" The words and tone had equal impact. "Stand down, soldier!"

A moment later, Nick thudded to stop in the very yard where he had worked with the shepherd a week earlier. What exactly caused the shepherd to hesitate—the familiar location or the familiar voice—was impossible to say, but he slowed and looked at Nick. Some bit of instinct or training asserted itself in his canine mind, and he halted along the fence, standing braced and wary.

Nick stood for a minute, letting his breathing slow, and then began a circuit of the yard, near the fence, talking as he went.

"Just where do you think you'd go, you stubborn mutt? Huh? We had this talk before, remember? The big wide world is not all it's cracked up to be." The words probably didn't matter; it was the sound of his voice, the certainty in it that would convince the shepherd to listen to him. The shepherd fixed on him, seeming less agitated, and as he walked and talked, he felt himself calming, as well.

"There are bigger dogs out there. Meaner dogs. And it's wet and cold and there's not enough food." He watched the dog's reaction from the corner of his eye. "And— here's the kicker—your girlfriend is here. Yeah. Goldie. She's here. And she needs to see your flea-bitten hide." He paced closer, watching for any signs of aggression or flight. "Don't know what she sees in you, but Ben, here, seems to think she's missing you. So you better shape up, soldier. Starting now." He turned to face the dog fully. "Sit."

There was a heart-stopping pause as the dog assessed the man and the command. Then, miracle of miracles, the shepherd lowered his rear to the ground.

"I could really use that lead now," Nick said without easing his stance or taking his gaze from the dog.

Kate entered the yard, walked slowly to Nick and put the leash she had snagged on the way out of the kennel in his outstretched hand. By the time she had retreated to where Ben waited beside the gate, Nick had approached the dog and was murmuring quietly to it. The dog eyed the leash and glanced around for an avenue of escape. Nick talked calmly to the animal, letting him decide to cooperate. It didn't take long. Another order to "sit" brought quick obedience.

When the loop dropped around his neck, the shepherd strained back against the pressure. Nick gave him a little room and called him to "come" and then "heel." Another tense moment passed as the shepherd came to his left side and stood slightly behind his leg.

Nick walked the shepherd through the gate to join them and saw Kate pat Ben's shoulder. They both exhaled with relief. The dog was still skittish, moving at the limit of the leash, but he followed Nick toward the main kennel building. At the door, where Nick paused to let Kate and Ben catch up, the dog's nose came up and quivered.

Kate and Ben went first and found Goldie

still on her blanket, head on paws, her immobilized leg stretched out to the side. At the sight of them, her tail thumped. Then she caught a familiar scent and her head came up sharply, her nose working excitedly.

The shepherd bulleted into the kennel and a moment later he and Goldie were nose to nose and wagging tails. The shepherd sniffed her all over while she examined his legs and underside from her position on the floor. Inspections over, he jumped and turned in circles, making odd whimpering sounds…a canine display of joy if there ever was one.

"Look at her." Kate delighted in the spark returning to Goldie's eyes. "She's thrilled to see him again. And he's acting like a puppy."

"I knew he would help her," Ben said, grinning from ear to ear. He knelt beside Goldie and put his hands under her side and strained to lift her. "Come on, girl. Don't you want to get up now?"

The shepherd stretched his forelegs out along the floor, rump in the air, in invitation. Goldie's front half moved to meet his posture, and her rear struggled to rise on muscles that hadn't been used in too long. Ben struggled to help lift her.

"Wait, Ben. Let her try on her own," Kate said, waving him back. For a moment they watched the golden struggle to rise without putting weight on her broken leg. When she finally reached a stable three-legged stance, she had what looked like a grin on her face. Ben let out a whoop that made Goldie jerk back—using her immobilized leg to steady herself. It took a moment for her to realize she was able to use the cast for support, but soon she was walking with a somewhat awkward hop to meet the shepherd down the aisle.

Their playtime was sweet and memorable but didn't last long. Goldie was still weak, and when she sat down and started to nose her hip and cast, Kate said she might be in some pain from the exertion. She ran to the surgery for a dose of medication.

"How could anyone, seeing those two together, deny that dogs are capable of love," she said to Nick as they stood together watching the shepherd nose and lick Goldie's stitches and then move on to inspect and lick her ears. "He's tending her as if she were a puppy."

"Interesting." He spoke his thoughts aloud. "They have a bond of some kind. Makes me wonder if they came from the same household."

"We may never know. But I can already see that separating the two of them is not a good idea." She frowned. "Which means the chance of them finding forever homes is less than great. People who can adopt two large adult dogs together are pretty rare."

In the end, they decided to move the shepherd permanently to the main kennel and into a run with Goldie. Ben asked if he could write their names on the card the staff kept on the door, and in his neatest hand, he printed *Goldie* and *Soldier.*

"Soldier?" Kate asked as he handed her the card to post.

"That's him," Ben said, pointing to the shepherd. "That's what Dad calls him— Soldier."

Kate looked up at Nick, who blinked in surprise. "So he did." She tried it out. "*Soldier.* Nice name for a shepherd." A grin bloomed on her face. "Good job, Dad."

He felt himself blush but he smiled back. "Anytime."

After seeing to bedding, snacks and water, they left the pair there—curled happily side by side—to rest.

"You should have seen him," Ben told Nance when they saw her in the office later. "He was so excited to see her and they bumped noses and jumped around."

"Well, sometimes we need a friend to help us get well. Good friends make good medicine," Nance said, ruffling his hair. "You thought of getting them together all by yourself?"

Ben glanced at his dad, who gave him a half-hearted look of disapproval. "Yeah, I did. But I won't do it again." There was mischief in his second glance at his dad. "Unless I ask first."

KATE WATCHED HER grandmother charming Ben with her appreciation of his actions and her offhand lessons in life, and stole a glimpse at Nick. He seemed uncertain whether her admiration of Ben's headstrong behavior was such a positive thing. She chuckled, having been on the horns of that same dilemma regarding her grandmother's actions more times than she could count.

"Consider it a good lesson," she said, edging closer and lowering her voice. "One he'll probably remember for some time to come."

He regarded her thoughtfully, then nodded and jammed his hands firmly into his pockets.

CHAPTER EIGHT

"IT'S SATURDAY." JESS checked her watch the next week as she eyed the door to their front office and waiting room.

"So it is," Kate said, glancing up from the computer, where she was entering a treatment plan for the standard poodle she had just seen.

"Closing time," Jess added with a sidelong look at her partner.

"And yet, you're still here." Kate glanced around to find Jess draped over a stool and the counter, looking relaxed. "What? All of your dating apps go down this week?"

"Ooh, aren't we snarky today."

"It's just that you're usually out of here by now," Kate said, glancing back at the clock on her computer screen. "Twelve-oh-seven. Don't you have a hot date or something?"

"Nope. I just finished my last chart note and I'm free as a bird. Thought I'd just hang around awhile and see if any latecomers show up. You know, with hurt dogs or something."

Kate narrowed her eyes. She knew exactly what Jess was doing. "You're wasting your time. The golden is at the shelter. There's no reason for him to show up here today."

"You don't mind if I sit here for a while and see for myself, do you? I've gotta see this guy. LeeAnn says he's hunk-of-the-year material."

"LeeAnn's crazy," Kate said, typing away. "You know that, right?"

"Yeah, but she's a fantastic judge of beefcake. Have you seen the guy she's with lately?" She shook a hand in the universal gesture for *hot*.

Kate chuckled. As it happened she had seen LeeAnn's latest conquest, and he wasn't bad, compared to her usual guys. His shirts had actual *sleeves*.

"Well," she said minutes later as she shut down her computer, "that's it for today." She hung her white coat on a peg by the reception-room door and reached for her keys. "Want to come by the shelter with me?"

"No, thanks." Jess glanced toward the

front door with disappointment and then at her watch. "I've had my fill of needy critters for the week. I'm going to put on my bathing suit, find a lounge chair and take nap before dinner tonight. Going to Tampa. Burns Steak House."

"Ooooh." Kate sighed wistfully at the mention of one of the premier steak houses in the country. "Bring me a doggie bag?"

"Get your own hot date," Jess said with a wicked laugh, breezing past her and out the door, "and your own leftovers!"

THE SHELTER WAS a perfect storm of activity when Kate arrived. She sat trapped in a line of idling cars trying to reach a place to park on an empty lot next to the shelter. Cars trying to exit the parking area were blocked by those arriving, and no one was moving in or out. Gridlock.

"I forgot about this mess." She groaned and leaned her forehead on the steering wheel.

A local radio station had set up to do a remote at Harbor to publicize the work done there, and Isabelle had finagled a couple of restaurants into providing ice cream and drinks for the people who came out to tour the facility and participate in a little fund-raising. The idea had mushroomed and turned into an *event*.

The weather was sunny perfection, and people had turned out in force. There were at least sixty cars jammed into the adjacent field and parked randomly on the county road in front of the shelter. She could see kids with balloons running around; white tents that sheltered refreshments, face painting and information tables; and a throng of people gathered around a small stage next to a van with WSRZ emblazoned on the side. With her windows up and air conditioner blasting, she couldn't hear what the speakers were putting out, so she turned on her radio.

Someone was interviewing Director Isabelle Conti, who sounded breathless with excitement at the success of the first ever "Harbor Day."

Next came an interview with a Harbor board member, who turned out to be none other than Nance Everly. Warm, familiar tones curled around Kate as Gran spoke of caring for the planet and its intricate web of life and "how much richer our lives are when we share them with animals."

As she listened to the voice that had become the foundation of her ethics and her purpose, Kate's irritation melted. "You tell 'em, Gran." She smiled. Her grandmother should have her own show. Daily Lessons on Living. Mandatory listening for all human beings.

Then came some promotion for Harbor's programs, before the DJs spun some golden oldies. Her hopes for the afternoon were evaporating like rain puddles in the Florida sun. She considered going off-road and heading for home when she heard a *whoop-whoop* and looked around. Several cars back, an FHP cruiser with lights flashing was threading its way past cars parked haphazardly on the berm.

Kate sat frozen, watching the cruiser draw closer and emit another *whoop-whoop* to make a car trying to leave the road get back in line. She squinted, trying to make out who was behind the wheel, but the tint of the windows made it impossible to see who was driving. Her heart thudded as the cruiser worked its way to the front of the line, and the trooper bolted out of his car to plant himself at the crux of the traffic jam.

She rolled down the window and stuck her head out like an overheated Labrador, trying to see the trooper who had come to their rescue. He was tall—sweet Lord— with heart-stoppingly broad shoulders. The sight of Nick Stanton, all business in hat and shades, gesturing with those muscular arms, sent a frisson of anticipation through her. He looked just like he had that first night. The fact that she knew Nick's form and movement so definitively should have given her pause. Instead, it gave her a shiver of pleasure.

She jerked her head inside, rolled up the window and flipped down her visor mirror to check her hair and makeup. She hadn't really expected to see him. Why couldn't she have put on a little blush and some mascara this morning? What did it mean that he was here, helping bring order to the chaos Nance and Isabelle had unintentionally created? Was he on duty? Or had he just dropped by to see her? The bleat of a horn from behind interrupted her thoughts.

She threw her Jeep into gear and rolled

forward, craning her neck to catch glimpses of him at work. Just as she expected: every movement was sure and controlled. No one in his right mind would mess with Trooper Stanton. Her stomach seemed to be melting into a pool of goo. He was gorgeous. No, *spectacular.* In the back of her mind she could hear Jess's assessment: "You're in trouble, Everly."

"Get stuffed, Preston," she muttered.

When she reached the head of the line, Nick held up a hand to stop her and approached the Jeep. She rolled down the window.

"Is this part of your patrol route now?" she said, smiling.

"Not exactly." He flashed a handsome smile beneath those intimidating shades. "My mom and Ben heard about this, and he harangued her into coming to see the dogs. I was just getting off duty and said I'd meet them here. Didn't quite expect this."

"Apparently no one did. When you get this mess sorted out, I'll buy you a cold whatever they're serving, okay?"

"Sounds good." He stepped back and

waved her toward a part of the lot that had spaces opening.

After parking, she turned off the engine and paused for a minute to recover. His mother *and* Ben. That was a good thing, right? Meeting the entire family? After swipes with a comb and some gloss she found in the console, she made her way to the center of the festivities. She noticed a number of people in the crowd who had dogs that wore neckerchiefs designating them as Harbor alumnae.

"Dr. Kate!" Ben's voice stopped her in her tracks, and she paused to search the crowd for him. He ran up from the side, face ruddy and beaming. An older woman with short, frosted hair and a lovely softness to her features came up behind him. She would have recognized Ben's grandmother anywhere: same nose, same mouth and those *eyes*.

"You must be Mrs. Stanton." She extended a hand and was pleased by the woman's warm response.

"Call me Sarah. Ben talks about you all the time." She pretended to look around Kate's shoulder. "I half expected a pair of wings."

Kate laughed. "Not even close. How did you hear about this?"

"We listen to WSRZ every morning, and they mentioned it several times. Harbor is all Ben talks about these days—well, that and soccer."

"I want Nana to see Goldie and Soldier," Ben said, bouncing on the balls of his feet, "but they aren't in the kennel. Where are they?"

"Not in the kennel?" She frowned and looked over her shoulder to where Nance stood. "I have no idea. But I know someone who does."

She led them over to Nance and introduced them. Nance's face lit as she shook Sarah Stanton's hand and ruffled Ben's hair.

"Wow. Quite a turnout, huh?" Nance beamed at the crowd milling around them. "Glad you could make it."

"We barely did," Kate said with a piercing look. "The traffic is a nightmare."

"Yeah, well, it's our first time planning something like this. Next year we'll do better," Nance said firmly.

"Fortunately for you, a state trooper saw

the gridlock and volunteered to get things moving." She gave Ben a sidelong grin.

"It's my dad, isn't it?"

"It is," Kate said, feeling an irrational surge of pleasure at the fact. "I saw him as I parked, and he said he was meeting you here." She turned to Nance. "Ben wanted to show Goldie and Soldier to his gran. But he says they're not in the kennel."

"About that..." Nance looked a little chagrined. "We had some drop-offs and needed the space, so I volunteered to take them out to the farm." She focused on Ben. "We didn't want to separate them, so it was the only place we could find on short notice."

Ben looked crestfallen. "But I wanted to see them. Can we come and see them at your farm?"

"Really, Ben, it's not polite to ask that." Sarah Stanton pulled him against her side.

"It's okay," Nance said, bending to meet Ben eye to eye. "I know you've got a special bond with those two, so you're welcome anytime. Kate can tell you how to get to my place, right, Kate?" She straightened, looking like she'd just thought to add, "Or maybe you can show them the way. Bring them out and give them a tour." She caught Sarah's eye. "Those animals are as much hers as they are mine."

Kate watched her grandmother's act and knew exactly where this was headed. It was just her luck to get stuck with a diabolical meddler for a grandmother. She preempted whatever came next by asking, "Ben, have you had ice cream yet?"

"No. They have chocolate and strawberry and peanut butter cup."

"So, you've already scoped it out." She laughed. "What do you say, Sarah? Time for some ice cream?"

Sarah nodded permission, and Kate offered Ben her hand. He took it and bounded along beside her to one of the refreshment tents.

The ice cream was just soft enough and rich enough to make a delicious mess. Chocolate threatened to run down Ben's hand as he hurried to lick the soft edges hanging over the cone and keep it in bounds.

"You're a pro at this, I see." Kate chuckled. "Just try not to get it anywhere that isn't washable. I don't want to annoy your gran."

"Nana wouldn't get mad." Ben grinned at her. "She likes you."

"She doesn't know me. We just met," Kate said, searching the boy's chocolate-smeared face.

"I told her all about you." He licked his ice cream into peaks before biting them off. "And Dad said you're a good vet and a nice lady."

"He said that, did he?"

Ben nodded with a teasing glint in his eyes. "He likes you, too." He took a bite of the cone this time. "And I like you."

"The feeling is mutual, Ben Stanton. You're one adorable kid."

Ben scrunched up one side of his face as if trying to decide if *adorable* was truly a compliment or just something adults felt required to say about kids.

"What? *Adorable* isn't good enough for you?" Kate sniffed with indignation. "Kids these days. I suppose I could call you bright, curious and fun to be around. That sound better?"

"Are you saying I'm smart?" He lowered his ice cream. "'Cause I don't want to be a smarty-farty."

"A smarty *what*?" She choked out a surprised laugh.

"That's what kids call me on the playground sometimes." His voice lowered. "And Wyatt. They call him 'smarty-farty,' too."

"Hmm." She studied him for a moment. "Smart is a good thing. Who doesn't want to learn quickly and understand things and be recognized for it? And farts—well, they're just a natural bodily function, part of being human. Our bodies need to fart in order to expel gases that form in our gut."

He giggled self-consciously. "So farts are *good*?"

"Absolutely." She lifted her chin. "Farts are downright healthy. Benjamin Franklin, one of our country's founding fathers, wrote a book that says we should 'fart proudly.'"

"*Fart proudly*? And here I thought adults were supposed to set a good example for kids." A deep voice from behind sent a jolt of surprise through her. She turned and came face-to-face with Nick. Behind those mirrored shades, she imagined his eyes narrowed in displeasure. Lecturing his kid on the glories of farts, what was she thinking?

"Take it up with old Benjamin, he's the one who wrote it. And I— We just— He was telling me about kids on the playground—"

"The 'smarty-farty' thing," Nick guessed. He took off his sunglasses, hung them on his chest pocket and looked at his son. "The current-day version of 'puke-face' and 'teacher's putz.'" He propped his hands on his service belt, his expression impenetrable, looking for all the world like the four-letter-word police.

Ben seemed to have lost interest in his ice cream, and Kate was suddenly finding it difficult to swallow.

"He just needs to find a couple of zingers to fire back," Nick continued, including Kate in his cool, professional gaze. "Sounds like you can supply him with a few scientific fart facts to help even the score."

Kate jerked her gaze up to find him grinning and she relaxed, then gave his arm a good-natured shove.

"You. I'll do my best to help him come up with something." She smiled up at him and—wonder of wonders—he smiled back. A broad, no-reservations kind of a smile that made her heart skip. This felt so good, it had to be bad. Lord, he looked…

"Thirsty, Trooper Stanton? I believe I promised to buy you a cold one."

Minutes later, they were downing icy lemonade and watching Ben's face being painted like a golden retriever's. Ben's grandmother and Nance joined them, and when Ben's face was complete, they strolled the tent area while Ben did his best dog imitations and Nance pointed out to Sarah various parts of the shelter. After a while they noticed a knot of people gathered around the office porch steps, looking as if they needed help.

Nance hurried over and pushed through the people to find a cardboard box holding four puppies on the doorstep.

"Schnauzers," she said, picking up one small, mewling puppy to examine. "Again."

Kate joined her and looked them over. "Young. Two or three weeks. Their eyes haven't been open long." She searched the immediate area. "Where's the mother?"

Onlookers provided a few details: one had seen a young boy carrying a box, and another had seen a teenager setting a box down by the door. No one had seen a mother dog.

"What did the boy look like?" Nick took over, all business.

Young, came a response. *Maybe ten or twelve*, came another. *Not large. Maybe Hispanic. Thin. Worn jeans and T-shirt. Shaggy hair.*

Kate watched Nick look out over the crowd as descriptions were volunteered. He spotted a matching suspect at the side of a concession tent, peering around the corner at them.

The minute Nick headed in that direction, the kid took off like a rabbit. "Stop! Hey—I just want to talk to you!"

The sight of a uniformed trooper in hot pursuit made people scramble out of his way, and before long, Nick was racing into the field of parked cars after the youth.

As fast as Nick was, the boy was faster, juking around cars and sprinting toward the cover of the tree line, which was thick with palmetto brush. The youth plowed in and was lost in the brambles in seconds. Nick hesitated for one fateful moment, then plunged into the brush after the kid. A loud muffler on a revving engine caught his attention as he fought his way through, and he looked up. An old stake-bed pickup sat on the county road, belching exhaust.

As he followed the trail the kid's passage had left in the palmetto brush—praying the kid had already put any snakes to flight—he caught sight of his suspect nearing that old truck and a bare arm reaching out of the driver's window to gesture impatiently. Nick jolted to a stop as the kid disappeared around the truck. Seconds later it blasted off down the road in a haze of exhaust.

He whipped a glance over his shoulder to gauge the distance to his cruiser, wheeled and ran his "best 40" time to get there before the beater with the kid was completely out of sight. He slid behind the wheel, hit the lights and siren, and peeled out, leaving ruts in the sandy berm. It didn't take long for him to catch sight of the truck again, but they spotted him, too, and hit the accelerator.

Alerts had come into county station about a dogfighting ring out of South Florida moving into the area. He gripped the steering wheel hard as he thought of the dogs that were being starved and mistreated to make them aggressive. But if the kid was part of a dogfighting operation, why was he bringing puppies to a shelter? And schnauzer puppies, at that. They were feisty, barky little dogs, but hardly the kind people paid to see fight.

The truck ran a red light in front of him, and he had to hit the brakes and get his head back into the chase. The truck was in tough shape; the stakes on the bed bowed out and swayed dangerously with each swerve and pothole, and the license plate was rusted enough to be mostly unreadable. Not exactly a prosperous dogfighting promoter.

He gained steadily on the truck and was soon close enough to see that the driver was not much bigger than the boy. But whoever he was, he knew how to handle that truck. Twice the driver skidded into a turn and almost managed to lose him.

In fact, he did lose Nick shortly afterward, with the help of a 150,000-ton locomotive and a railroad crossing. The beater managed to floor it and make it across the tracks just as the barrier arms came down to block the road. Nick slammed on his brakes and flicked off the siren as he tried to glimpse the escaping truck between the passing train cars.

As soon as the train was clear and Nick

could no longer see the truck, he doused the lights, turned and headed back to the shelter.

The field beside Harbor had a few open parking spots when he returned. He paused a moment at the edge of the festivities to catch his breath and realized his arms were stinging.

It had been a while since he had to run down a suspect on foot. He'd gotten some wicked scratches in the palmettos, but it could have been worse. Thank God for khakis and boots.

Ben was waiting with his grandma, Kate and Kate's grandmother.

"Did you catch him, Dad?" Ben ran to meet him, his eyes alight with the excitement of watching his father in hot pursuit.

Nick shook his head, put one arm about Ben's shoulders and held out an empty hand with the other. "Fast little devil, I'll give him that." He took a deep breath and registered the way Kate's gaze was running over him. "Somebody was waiting for him in an old truck out on the road. I caught up with him, but we got separated by a train headed north." He realized Kate's eyes were shining, and he couldn't help smiling at the thought that she'd been watching, too.

And she liked what she saw.

"We were just talking," Nance said. "This is the third batch of schnauzers that have been dropped off recently. We think that means—"

"Puppy mill," Kate said, and looked straight into his gaze.

He sank unexpectedly into those vivid blue eyes. Overheated and still moving fast mentally, all he could think about was touching her—reaching for her skin—stroking her silky hair and tucking it back behind her ear. Her words took a few seconds to register.

"And this batch is without a mother." Her face filled with a becoming color. "Which probably means she died during or after the birth."

"If we could only figure out where to start looking," Nance said, shaking her head thoughtfully—reminding him how many other people were present.

"We have laws and law enforcement, and volunteers who are willing to help us clear those places out," Nance was saying.

"What we don't have is the location of the mill that's breeding these little guys." She picked up one of the pups and handed it to Ben, who nuzzled it with his freshly painted dog nose and then cradled it expertly against his heart. Nick felt his chest tighten at the sight—his son and the little pup, both so young and so innocent—and had to stop himself from taking a step back.

"They're going to have to be fed by hand for a while," Kate said, reaching for one herself. Nick watched her hands go over the whimpering pup and could see her cataloging its condition before she placed it against her chest. He had phantom sensations of being held against her just like that...

His mom's touch startled him. "You got scratched up, Nick." He found her examining the patchwork of scratches he had just earned. "You probably ought to put something on those."

Kate looked at his arms and seemed a little embarrassed that she hadn't noticed. "I have some salve in the surgery that should work." She handed off the puppy to his mom. "You know the way, Trooper Stanton."

CHAPTER NINE

"Hop up." She patted her farmhouse kitchen table, indicating where he should sit, and then turned away to gather cotton, hydrogen peroxide and antibiotic ointment. From the corner of her eye, she watched him grab the edge of the table and boost himself up. Lord have mercy. She could see his muscles flex through his shirt.

"Here we are again, patching up another patient together," Kate said, her mouth going dry as she dragged antiseptic-soaked cotton down the scratches on his hands and forearms. His smooth, tanned flesh was just a few damp fibers away from contact with her fingers.

"We do seem to end up playing doctor a lot."

She looked up to find a dangerous amusement in his eyes.

"No *playing* about it," she said, realizing

that her voice sounded deeper, more intimate. What was she saying? "I *am* a doctor."

"So you are." His short, husky laugh made her fingers tingle. "And a puppy whisperer. A boy whisperer. Are you a trooper whisperer, too?"

"I don't know." She searched his gaze, the intensity there turning his eyes to glowing bronze. She could practically feel her pupils dilating in response. "I've never whispered to one."

"Let's find out," he said, lowering his ear toward her and tapping it. "Whisper to me."

It was an invitation that slid under her skin and along her nerves, raising goose bumps across her shoulders. It was now or never. Could she make a move that might lead someplace…unpredictable?

He was so close, so warm, so— *For once in your careful, overplanned life, take a chance!*

"Trooper Stanton," she whispered, wondering if he felt the vibrations the way she did when he spoke, "you are going to have to apply this ointment twice a day, every day. No forgetting, no complaining. And I want to see you back in a week. Right here.

Think you can remember all that, or should I write it down?"

"Right now," he said, moving nothing but his lips, "all I can remember is how good that feels. *More.* I need more ointment." He paused for a moment, eyes flicking down to her lips, then produced the magic word: "Please."

It almost dropped her to her knees. She put a hand on the table to steady herself. And still he didn't move. Not a muscle. Not even a tic.

More ointment. Definitely.

She glanced down to find herself holding his hand and feeling warmth spreading up her arm from the contact. She squeezed a dollop of the antibiotic onto her finger and rubbed it into the scratches, using it as an excuse to explore the sleek, purposeful architecture of his hands and arms.

"Yes," he said after a moment of watching her.

"Yes, what?" She paused, feeling the strength of his gaze.

"You are a trooper whisperer."

"Dad! Gran Everly says we can come out to her farm." Ben burst into the kitchen, causing Kate to reel back and Nick to straighten abruptly. Beneath his canine face paint, his boy glowed with excitement as he hurried over to them. "To see Goldie and Soldier, Dad. Today. Now!" Then he realized his dad was being treated and came to lean against the table by his father's knees. "Can I help?"

"Why not?" Kate surrendered the tube of ointment with an odd mixture of disappointment and relief. She showed him how to clean the scratches with peroxide and then apply medicine.

"Whoa. I don't need that much." Nick winced.

"He needs the practice." Kate leaned against the counter and crossed her arms. "Keep going, Ben. You're doing great a job."

"Does he get bandages?" Ben asked when he had slathered his father's hands and arms with ointment.

"I doubt they'd stick," she said, gesturing to Nick's gooey skin. "Unless he wants them. How about it, Dad? Want some bandages?"

"I'll manage without," he responded, narrowing his eyes at her.

"Okay, then can we go to Gran Everly's farm? Nana says *she'd* like to go. She's never seen an ostrich up close."

Nick regarded his son and took his time deciding.

"Daaaaad!" Ben jumped up and down. "Puleeeze."

"You going?" he asked Kate.

"Absolutely." She grabbed some paper towels for him and chuckled as he wiped the excess salve from his hands and arms. "I need to check on Goldie and see what other critters Gran has concerns about. I make a house call at the farm about once a week."

NANCE EVERLY'S FARM was Old Florida all the way. A sprawling, white single-story house with wraparound porches and a steep metal roof sat in the middle of 160 acres, two ponds and several whitewashed outbuildings. Untouched woodland bordered the property and merged with another forested area that bore signs declaring it to be a state preserve. Half of the once-tilled land had been reclaimed by scrub growth and young pines, and the rest was pasture dotted with old orange trees. After plentiful summer rains, the grazing was lush and the land-scape was dotted with sundry sheep, goats, and the occasional horse and donkey.

As their caravan of cars crawled up a driveway lined with venerable live oaks, Nick spotted high fencing around certain areas attached to outbuildings, and his eyes widened when he saw what looked like ostriches stalking around one of those well-fenced paddocks. Ben pressed his nose against the cruiser's window, pointing out animals with ever-increasing excitement.

Ducks, geese and chickens strolled around the gravel yard in between the barns, and a noisy peacock sat on top of a porch roof. As Nick parked next to Kate's Jeep, he could hear barking, squawking, cawing and all manner of other animal vocalizations. A couple of horses, a donkey and several goats ran to the fence near the cars to greet them.

Nance, in full earth-mother mode, threw open her arms with a grin. "Welcome to Everly's!" She waved them to the largest barn. "This way!"

"Ostriches, llamas and bears…oh, my!" Nick muttered as he fell in beside Kate for the tour. She looked up and found him smiling.

"No bears." Kate gave a wry grin. "You'll have to make do."

Nance distributed carrots from a bushel basket just inside the barn doors, and they were soon meeting cows, barn cats, a miniature horse a couple of charming potbellied pigs and a number of pushy goats who were happy to settle for goat-chow nuggets when the carrots ran out. A smaller barn—the one with the high fence—housed the ostriches, and Nick enjoyed how much his mother was taken with them. Ben was a little scared at first, but he managed to pet one before they moved on to the llamas.

They behaved just as Kate had said they would: no spitting, no displays of flatulence and no untoward nibbling of the humans. The llamas were downright mannerly, though they might have been influenced by the walking stick Nance carried into their paddock.

The tour ended at the kennel, a small structure with half a dozen roomy runs filled with dogs lucky enough to have been found or adopted by Nance. Goldie and Soldier called this place home for the time being. They would stay in the kennel when Nance couldn't be with them, until they learned the farm's boundaries and got used to the other animals.

"Goldie!" Ben rushed to give her a hug as she came out of the pen, and before long, he was grinning from ear to ear. The dogs wagged tails and sniffed everyone in the party, pausing longest over Kate, who was a smorgasbord of scent and habitually carried dog treats in her pockets. Soldier was soon drawn to Nick and sat down before him, alert and attentive, as if expecting to be given commands. Kate chuckled and said he looked like he was saluting. She went to a nearby bin of toys and grabbed a couple of balls and Kongs, then thrust one at Nick.

"Have mercy on him and throw a ball so he can get some exercise."

That was how they spilled into a well-grazed field out the rear of the kennel—man throwing, dog running and kid chasing everything on four legs. Goldie tried to keep up at first, but then sat down to catch her breath and rest her leg. Ben dropped behind to stay with her, leaving Kate and Nick to ramble across the rolling field toward an outcropping.

"Snakes?" he asked, looking around them.

"Not here—too many animals tromping and grazing this area. Just stay out of the brush."

KATE SAT ON an outcropping, watching Nick shed his inhibitions bit by bit as he played with Soldier. He laughed, ran, dodged, grabbed handfuls of air and uttered a few choice words in appreciation of the dog's evasion skills. Again and again, he threw the ball and a newfound stick or two, clearly relishing the freedom of the chase and way the dog's pleasure in the game matched his.

His full, rich laughter sent a delicious shiver through her. The caution and containment he usually carried about him melted away; this was the man inside that formidable presence. She wanted to wrap her arms around him and hold that man close to her heart. Despite her determination to slow down her runaway feelings…this felt real and good and healthy.

When Nick paused for breath, Soldier carried the stick to the rock where she sat and dropped it on the ground near her feet.

"You really know how to get what you want, don't you?" Kate slid from her perch, grabbed the stick and ran.

"Hey, that's mine!" Nick called, hands on his waist, tone indignant at this egregious flaunting of the "keep-away" rules… at being cut out of the game.

The dog was a bullet, racing her around shrubs and small trees and across hummocks of grassy scrub. Fortunately, she was pretty quick herself and knew the lay of the land. She was able to outfox her pursuer until Nick had joined the chase. He caught her first and reeled her—laughing and protesting—into his arms while Soldier barked and danced around them.

Body to body, defenses down, they were both breathing hard when he relieved her of the stick and threw it over his shoulder for Soldier to chase. He didn't release her right away and they stood for a moment, face-to-face, recovering, until she looked up into his hot-bronze eyes. He lowered his head.

His lips were firm and soft at the same time, and the contact sent tingles through her own lips and out through her cheeks. She couldn't recall ever feeling such a thing before, certainly not with Jared.

This kiss was the most natural thing in the world, soft, searching and a prelude to… whatever was interrupted by an unruly beast of a dog pouncing on them.

Staggering, they broke apart and laughed, and she felt pleasure lingering in every nerve. It had been a long time coming but was entirely worth the wait.

Blushing and uncertain what came next, she retreated to her perch on the rock and was surprised to find that he followed. Settled side by side, they let their breathing return to normal as Nick threw the stick for Soldier and the dog returned it several times.

"You're a natural." She was fascinated by the way he rubbed his hands up and down his muscular thighs, and had to force her gaze away. "With dogs."

"Oh. I kind of hoped you were talking about kissing."

Surprised by his forthright comment, she laughed. "Well, you're pretty darned good at that, too."

"If you ever want to try it again, just say

the word." He glanced at her with a sideways grin that made her heart skip a beat.

"I'll bear that in mind." Seconds later, before she could stop herself, she said, "How about now?"

With a chuckle, he ran a finger down her cheek and used it to turn her face toward his. This time it was like falling down a well. Every fixed point in her universe dropped away and the whole focus of her existence became that deliciously firm contact with his lips. Moments later, his lips softened and moved differently against hers, and she realized he was speaking. She swayed, off balance, until her brain rebooted and she made sense of what he'd said.

"Kid at two o'clock."

Ben came charging into view with Goldie not far behind. "Hey! Where did you guys go?"

Nick maintained awareness of his surroundings even while engaged in something as distracting as kissing—clearly another aspect of his character honed by his time in the military. He slid off the rock, helped her down, and soon they were walking with

Ben through the pasture and around the old orange trees.

The boy talked nonstop about all of the animals he had just seen and how he wanted to help other animals that needed homes. Kate managed to get in a little conservation education, starting with the origins of the farm.

Her great-great-grandfather had moved to Florida as a boy and worked on the Plant railroad to save money to buy some land. He had planted orange trees during the thirties and forties and become a prosperous citrus farmer. In time, his son, Gran's father, expanded the holdings to include a sizable forest near the homestead and raised a family and beef cattle side by side. Each successive generation had studied the ecology of native plants and animals and became devoted to preserving the nature around them. When a state park was proposed nearby, they agreed to donate some of their precious forested land to augment it.

After her husband died in Vietnam and her only daughter joined the military, Nance Everly had moved home to help her aging parents and began to take in animals of all kinds. Then came the day when she took in her daughter's children...Kate and her older brother, Jace. Their father insisted Jace be sent to a military academy for the school year, but Kate was left with Nance full-time.

As Ben and Soldier ran ahead to investigate a miniature donkey grazing nearby, Nick looked around at the idyllic setting.

"What was it like, growing up here?" he asked, studying her as if trying to picture it.

She laughed. "See that tree?" She pointed to an old, widely spread oak in the distance. "I used to climb that daily and sit for hours trying to imitate the birds I heard. But there was a tall cypress in a swampy area at the back that I never managed to conquer. It taught me my limits, again and again."

"I met a few trees and a rock face or two like that, back in my scouting days," he said, gazing at her tree, nodding.

She looked fondly around the remains of the old grove with its aged, twisted surviving trees.

"There were nights when Gran would have to keep watch over a cow or horse giving birth. She let me spend the night in the barn with her. She'd put a couple of blankets down on hay bales for me and I'd lay my head in her lap. Gran always woke me up in time to see the birth. I remember the quiet and the smell of the barn and the way she stroked my hair…"

"No wonder you decided to become a vet," he said with a half smile.

"Those barn nights certainly helped. But it was old Doc Furlong that set me on course. He stopped in pretty frequently to check on Gran's menagerie and I followed him around, pestering him with questions and trying to help. That man had the patience of a saint.

"What really sealed the deal was my first puppy mill raid with Gran. She made me stay back with the trucks and cages at first, to comfort and clean up the little ones that were brought out."

"She let you see that stuff as a kid?" he said, looking unsettled.

"Gran has never been one to soft-pedal life, even to kids. With her, you get the full dose—the bitter with the sweet."

"I'm not sure that would work with some kids," he said, glancing in Ben's direction. She studied his frown, having already seen his opinion on exposing his son to difficult things.

"Well, my brother and I survived, and life with Gran prepared us to handle the knocks life deals out. Her outlook taught me to see the reality of things—even very difficult things—while not being immobilized by it. 'Nothing has to stay the way it is,' she always told us. 'Things can always change for the better.' And 'It's up to us to make things change.'"

"So you decided to change things for animals," he concluded, studying her, giving no hint of what he was thinking.

"I did. I learned she was right—you can make things better. Not perfect. Not everything. But *some things* better."

She thought for a moment that he might pull her into his arms, but he stuffed his hands into his pockets instead. They walked on together, and she couldn't help feeling a little disappointed that the warmth they'd shared earlier was cooling. She looked around to find Goldie lagging behind and went back to check on her.

"She's doing pretty well." Out of habit, she ran her hands over the dog in assessment. "She's certainly walking better than I expected. I swear it's his influence." She nodded toward Soldier, who seemed to sense he was the subject of their attention and ran back to prance around Goldie and make himself available for their general adoration. Kate could tell he was watching Nick.

Nick made a fist and jerked it toward his shoulder. Soldier came alert and sat immediately, watching for another command.

"That's amazing," she said. "That's one of the 'silent commands'? That fist thing?"

"Yeah. Can't always use verbal commands in the field, so military dogs are trained to respond to both." Nick leveled his fist with his shoulder, then straightened his arm out to the side. Soldier stood, ears up, eyes bright with expectation. Nick threw the stick again and Soldier went for it like a shot. "This guy seems to know both."

"Wow." Kate was truly impressed. "I think you guys already have a bond going. Hey, does the FHP use dogs? With a little brushup training, maybe he could be your partner."

She knew it was the wrong thing to have said the minute it was out. Nick stiffened and control replaced the pleasure in his expression.

"The FHP pairs dogs and handlers only with felony officers in the CIU, and they never take a dog without a known provenance. They have to know what they're getting before turning a dog loose in a law enforcement role. Standards for training and certification are strict—they have to be."

He was an expert at answering questions without revealing much. But that in itself was something of an answer.

"And you're not in the— What is the CIU?"

"The Criminal Interdiction Unit." He took a breath and looked away. "I have a young son to raise. I leave handling dogs and chasing drug traffickers to the felony guys."

"I'd think that after Iraq, patrolling highways might seem a little mundane."

"Mundane—" he started to say something heated, but a second thought chilled his response "—is fine. Just damned fine."

There it was again, that retreat from something important. She had to know. She paused and faced him, hoping her genuine concern showed in her face. "Nick," she asked, "what happened in Iraq? It had to do with dogs, didn't it?"

NICK FIDGETED FOR a moment, glancing everywhere but at her. She wasn't going to let it alone, and he was surprised by the thought that that wasn't such a bad thing. Having somebody care enough to confront him and his issues… He looked down and found his gaze trapped in her blue eyes, warm and understanding. His hands came out of his pockets.

Why was it so hard to say what had happened, even years later? He should be able talk about it—at least some of it. And if he could talk about it with anyone, it would be her. She'd been both raised and trained to understand the intricacies of human-animal bonds.

But could he say it without getting lost in those memories and feelings again?

"We had service dogs. The guys got close to them and to their handlers. Me included. They lived with us, ate with us, patrolled with us and helped us stay sane in our downtime." He shifted back onto one leg and took a deep breath. "We saw them get shot and get blown up. Sometimes we had to carry them back to camp in pieces." His throat constricted, making it harder to get the words out. "Other times, we didn't even have anything to carry back."

This wasn't something he had ever really talked about. To anyone. He could feel his face going rigid as the memories threatened to erupt. He rubbed his temples, making himself focus on just the words.

"They saved our lives over there, again and again. Mission after mission, town after town...finding bombs, warning us of attacks, leading us to safe ground...they worked until their paws were cut and bloody and they were so dehydrated they couldn't stand. And they did it all for a kind word and a pat on the head. We traded them— their strong bodies and loyal hearts—for an extension on our own li-ives."

His voice cracked. He swallowed hard and shut his eyes to banish that familiar warning sting. He felt her reaching for his hand, and his knees nearly buckled as she threaded her fingers through his.

"You can't imagine what it's like to hear your men...guys who had to clear out IED-infested buildings, and face insurgents and ambushes, and stare down death every damned day…to hear them late at night…in the dark…crying in their bunks because…a dog they loved died in their arms."

He sniffed and took a deep, shuddering breath. "I can't help wondering if it was a good trade, their lives for ours."

For a moment, he was back in the desert, everything the color of sand—the ever-present smells of exhaust, machine oil and dirt in the air—the unmistakable *brap-brap* of distant gunfire, the thud of boots moving single file down a dusty road, the jingle of tags, the constant thirst…the smiles on dirt-and-sweat crusted faces when the dogs came up…the promise of treats and jocular offers to share bunks on the cold night ahead…then the limp paws…the sharp, coppery scent of blood on dusty fur…the pain wrenching deep in his gut…

Something tugged him back from the brink. He sucked a sharp breath and refocused his eyes. She was holding both of his hands, watching him. The pain in her face matched his own, as if she had somehow glimpsed the memories he fought to put away, and he realized it was her presence that had kept him from getting lost in the past.

"I'm sorry, Nick."

"For what?"

"For what you went through over there. For you having to live with the memory of it. Most of all, for pushing you to tell me and making you relive it. I won't do that again." She squeezed his hands. "But if you want to talk about it ever, I'll listen. And I'll do my best to understand."

He felt her warmth, her invitation reach into his chest like the benediction it was, loosening a constriction on his heart, giving him room to remember again without fearing that he might not be able to *stop* remembering. In that minute, he understood that this woman, this remarkable vet was a once-in-a-lifetime find: as compassionate as she was lovely, as wise as she was desirable. And he sure as hell didn't want to screw it up with his mountain of military-grade baggage.

"It's okay," he responded, concentrating on the sweet pressure of her fingers between his. It seemed somehow more intimate than kissing her, which he wouldn't have minded right now. For the first time in forever, he wanted to feel that kind of connection, that sense of being anchored by someone else. The realization surprised him. "It's just a little too easy to slide back into all that, and I'd rather stay in the here and now."

"Dad?" Ben stood twenty feet away, holding a stick up out of Soldier's reach while staring at them in surprise.

CHAPTER TEN

"Oh—hey, kiddo," Nick said. "What have you been doing?"

"You're holding hands," Ben said, seeming puzzled but also pleased. He apparently knew enough about the world to understand that holding hands meant men and women really liked each other.

"As a matter of fact, we are." Nick slid back into what Kate imagined was the more comfortable dad role, directing his son toward the path to the barns. "We were talking, and Dr. Kate was helping me with something. We ought to head back."

Ben nodded, accepting that as he trudged toward the path indicated by his dad's outstretched arm. "I'm hungry. Can we get dinner soon?"

"Sure. We'll see what your grandmother has in mind."

Kate smiled to herself as they walked

back to the cars. What he said—*helping me with something*—laid her worst fear to rest. He didn't hold that bit of prying against her. Did he really think she helped him?

They were still walking hand in hand when they came within sight of the front porch, where Nance was serving Sarah iced tea and cookies. She slipped her hand from his and reddened when he frowned. She nodded toward the porch and could tell he got it: *not in front of the mothers.*

Nance packed up some cookies to send along with Ben and declined an invitation to join the Stantons for dinner in favor of doing her evening chores. Kate had no such commitments and was pleased to join them at a restaurant that had just opened on the east side.

She had a wonderful time with Nick, Ben and Sarah. Ben let the grown-ups do most of the talking, but when Kate asked Sarah about Nick's childhood, the boy came to life. Ben bombarded his grandmother with questions and seemed to relish the idea of his dad and Nick's brother, his uncle Michael, doing "kid stuff" and having kid troubles. Kate got the impression that they didn't talk much about the past in the Stanton house-hold, but Sarah now warmly recounted her sons' love of sports and Scouts, their partici-pation in youth groups and school plays, and the family's summer vacations. They had lived in Ohio and Georgia before moving to Florida, and there were stories about Nick and Michael at each place. It was enough to keep them entertained until dessert, which was chocolate cake for some and Key lime pie for others.

Kate had to field a few questions about her own history; where she had lived and the frequent moves of her early life with mili-tary parents. She was sorry to see dessert end, and not just because the Key lime pie was to die for. They walked Sarah and Ben to Sarah's car, and then Nick walked her to hers.

She paused, wondering if it was the right time.

"How about if you and Ben come for din-ner some night this week? I have to warn you, I just moved into a house and things are still a little chaotic. You two would be my first dinner guests."

Nick smiled. "Any night but Tuesday. Soccer practice. Or Thursday. Soccer practice."

"Friday night it is. Any allergies I should know about?"

"Not one."

"See you at…six thirty?"

She smiled all the way home. Then she opened her front door and remembered the seven-foot albino Burmese python that had gotten loose in her garage and prayed that it would just stay lost for a while longer.

"IF YOU SHOW up at my house, you're a dead woman," Kate said with narrowed eyes and just enough heat to show she was serious. It was Wednesday and the clinic was hopping—they had a waiting room full of anxious dogs, indignant cats, uneasy birds and an iguana that wouldn't eat.

"Come on." Jess spun on her stool, abandoning the microscope she was using to scan a Rottweiler's feces for parasites. "You've got to at least let me see this guy."

"You'll see him." Kate turned back to counting out antibiotic tabs for a sheltie's bladder infection. "Eventually."

"If you don't kill him with your cooking first," Jess snarked.

"Hey, lay off my cooking. You'd have starved in vet school if not for my spaghetti."

"Yeah, yeah." Jess waved that old claim away. "What are you planning to feed him?"

"Simple fare. Steak and baked potatoes. Corn on the cob. I unearthed the grill from—"

"Don't tell me you're going to try to grill steaks for that guy. And on that rusty antique Weber of yours." She stood and squeezed the bridge of her nose as if the very notion gave her a headache. "One of the cardinal rules of man-feeding is *Never try to grill food for a man.* Men all consider themselves experts on grilling. If you try to do it for them, they either feel emasculated or insulted, and end up nitpicking the food to death. Lord, didn't Nance teach you anything about the male of the species?"

FRIDAY EVENING CAME before Kate was ready for it. With Jess's "wisdom" weighing on her mind, she had decided to forgo the grill in favor of her well-practiced spaghetti, salad and garlic bread, followed by a dessert of pound cake, fresh peaches and ice cream.

She left the clinic a couple of hours early to give herself time to find a tablecloth in her moving boxes, rustle up some cloth napkins and stick the flowers she had bought in a crystal vase left over from her Jared days. Satisfied that the table would pass inspection, she started on the food.

The sauce was bubbling, the bread was ready for heating and the pasta water was simmering by the time the doorbell rang. She opened it to greet two faces that made her heart beat faster. Ben blurted out a "hi" and darted inside to explore. Nick looked abashed as he handed her a bottle of wine and headed after his son, admonishing, "Don't touch, Ben. Remember your manners."

"There's nothing here that he can hurt," she said, smiling as she followed them into the sparsely furnished living room. Her new house was a modest three-bedroom Florida-style stucco with a two-car garage, set on a lot at the end of a cul-de-sac. The main feature of her living room was a huge blank wall that led up to a white-beamed cathedral ceiling. The adjacent wall was entirely covered with floor-to-ceiling bookcases containing books and artfully placed curiosities—the only real decorating she'd managed thus far. The rest of the furniture was an aged sofa that faced the bookshelves, an equally venerable coffee table, and a pair of bean bag chairs between the bookshelves and the coffee table.

"As you can see, I'm still putting things together. This is larger than any place I've lived in the last ten years. I'm still trying to figure out what to do with all this space—" she pointed to boxes in the corner and under the front bay window "—and with all of that."

"If you're anything like most women, you'll have it filled up in no time," Nick said with a chuckle, before realizing what he'd said. "Not that you're like most women. I mean, you are, but you're certainly not... You're more..." He glanced around and found Ben reaching for a big rock on one of the shelves. "Hey, what did I say about—"

"Wow. What is this, Dr. Kate?" Ben held a large, sand-colored rock with what appeared to be symmetric ridges running parallel across the top.

"That is a mammoth's tooth. Fossilized." She joined him in front of the shelf wall and Nick came along. "My dad and I got it when my parents were stationed in Oklahoma. I must have been six or seven. There was a dig not far from the base, and he took me out to see it. Apparently teeth are pretty common in such finds, so one of the professors in charge let us have it."

"This is just one tooth?"

"Yep."

"Imagine what the tooth fairy would have to shell out for one of those," Nick said, getting a laugh from Ben.

"Cool. Mammoths were huge." Ben's eyes sparkled as he placed it back on the shelf. "And this? It's purple and—are those diamonds?"

"No, it's a geode." She smiled and moved him into a sunbeam to help him see how it could sparkle. "These are quartz and fluorite crystals—the purple is also known as amethyst. Water penetrates rocks and finds itself trapped with a lot of minerals to unload. Over hundreds, even thousands of years it deposits the minerals in arrangements that form these crystals."

She had him turn it over to see the plain, rounded bottom. "The rock looked just like this when somebody found it. You'd never know from the outside that there was something so beautiful inside."

He kept turning it over and over in the light, fascinated by the refracted light and deep colors. He looked up moments later with the joy of discovery in his face. "This is so cool. Wait till Wyatt hears about this."

"Okay, I better get back to dinner. You can look all you want—just don't drop anything, okay?"

"Okay," Ben said, carefully laying the geode back on the shelf and scanning the display for another treasure.

"Want to come and open this bottle for me?" she asked, leading Nick into the kitchen and then handing him back the wine he had brought.

"Nice house." He looked around while she searched a drawer for a corkscrew. He sniffed. "Even smells new."

"I have all but one bedroom painted, and

I've done some planting in the backyard, but I still have a ton to do."

Nick watched her move around the kitchen and load pasta into a pot of water as he opened the wine. This was an interesting change from her practice and the shelter, where she was an authority and mostly business. Seeing her here, watching her go about simple hearth-and-home tasks, brought up feelings in him. *Distinctly pleasurable feelings.*

"So, both of your parents were in the military?" he asked as she handed him the opener.

"My father still is, as far as I know." She slipped the garlic bread into the oven and started tearing lettuce into a large glass bowl. "My mother died in an IED explosion in Mosul in '08."

That news hit him like a punch in the gut. As his shock faded, he searched her for visible signs of pain or bitterness, but found only the same gentle determination that never failed to fascinate him. She was a puzzle, Kate Everly. She had faced some damned tough breaks in life and, from all indications, had come through with her soul intact.

"I'm sorry to hear that," he said, meaning it.

"Thank you." Her smile was small and determined as she continued to focus on making the salad. "I hadn't seen her for three years before we got the news. She'd send the occasional card or present. She was more a cautionary tale than a person to me, by then. I was never tempted to follow her example and make the military a career."

"What about your father? Do you ever hear from him?"

"Once or twice when I was in high school. He sent a check when I graduated." She paused to recall, then said, "I think it paid for one of the fruit trays at the open house Gran had for me."

He detected a subtle tightness in her movements.

"Then how about this brother of yours? Ever hear from him?"

"Once a month, like clockwork. We weren't together much, once our parents split up. But we've become fairly close in the last few years." Her smile warmed. "He's a ranger."

"Special forces?" He paused in the middle of pouring the wine.

"No, not military. He's a Smokey-the-Bear kind of ranger. He's at Grand Teton National Park, overseeing human-bear encounters—trying to keep tourists alive." She chuckled. "He's a real animal guy, an expert at tracking and all kinds of woodcraft. He could keep you alive in the mountains with only a paring knife and a safety pin."

"Remind me to get lost only in the Grand Tetons," he said, echoing her chuckle. And he made himself say, "Who else is in your life? Any other...attachments?"

"If you're asking about men—I was engaged for a while." She washed tomatoes and sliced them into the greens. "It didn't work out."

"Mind if I ask what happened?"

She paused and then reached for a cucumber. "He was career military, on the fast track to his first star."

"Okay. Not what I would have expected, given your *feelings* for the military," he said, edging closer, searching her mask of concentration and watching her graceful hands.

"The military is kind of a love-hate thing for me. There are aspects of it I can't help admiring—it's part of my childhood, my history, my heart. And yet, there are things that I despise about it—one of those things being what it does to marriages and families."

"I get that," he said, surprised by the connection between his own family breakup and hers. "Probably more than you know."

She looked up at him, and he could see recognition in her eyes. She was sensing the connection between their stories, too.

"So what happened with your four-star wannabe?" he continued.

"It turned out that we had very different ideas about things."

"Like what?"

She cut the cucumber slowly and deliberately, parsing her words with equal precision. "Like whether a reunion with an old pilot ex-girlfriend just back from deployment should include a hot-and-heavy workout between the sheets. He didn't see the harm in it. I did."

He gave a low whistle. "How long ago was that?"

"Eighteen months—wait, closer to two years now."

"What a dumb shit—pardon the language." How could anyone with half a brain cheat on a woman as gorgeous and smart and giving—as *remarkable* as Kate Everly? "I hope he gets his stars, then," he said with a razor-like edge, before his voice dropped to a mutter she could still hear, "right up his butt."

She stole a surprised look at him and laughed.

"My sentiments exactly. But in truth, it worked out for the best. Jess and I had always talked about opening a practice together, and when the marriage thing fell apart, I was free to do just that."

"It looks like a going concern." He picked up his glass and took a sip. "I'm not much of a wine guy, but this isn't bad."

She tasted the wine he handed her and then gave it back to him.

"Very nice." She dressed and tossed the salad as she talked. "The practice is doing okay—better than expected, in fact. People down here love their animals and don't mind paying a few vet bills."

"Your partner, Jess—does he have a family?"

"Not yet." Her eyes twinkled. "Jess isn't quite *domesticated*."

He followed, carrying the wine, as she took the salad to the dining-room table. When she returned to the kitchen to check the bread, he watched her bend to look in the oven and felt his stomach drop. Such a gorgeous— Ben's voice from the living room saved him an inopportune response.

"Can I look at these books, Dr. Kate?"

"Which books?" she called out as she tested the pasta.

"The ones on the bottom shelf."

Nick went to see what his son was asking about and found him holding a book that seemed to be about animal obstetrics. He frowned and was just about to nix the access when she called from the kitchen.

"Sure, if you're interested. Those are books from my vet school days." She came to the arch leading to the kitchen, wiping her hands on a towel. "Some of the pictures are kind of icky, but you can look if you want to—after dinner. The spaghetti is just about ready, so you need to wash your hands and then pick out what you'd like to drink with dinner." She pointed toward a hallway. "The powder room is right there."

Nick watched her smile at his son and caught the way Ben smiled back as he headed for the powder room. There was already something there—a real understanding. She seemed to know just what the boy liked and how to respond to his adult way of looking at the world. He followed and found Ben washing his hands, *with soap*, and shook his head.

"So, I take it you like spaghetti," she said later, watching Ben shovel the last of a monumental pile of spaghetti into his mouth. Nick lowered his fork and watched Ben swallow before answering. Not talking with his mouth full… Nick couldn't take credit for that.

"I love spaghetti. Gran makes it once a week for us. But she doesn't eat the spaghetti part. She eats the sauce over some stringy, whirly things she makes out of zucchini." He screwed up his face. "She made me taste it once. Yuck. Can I have seconds?"

Nick had to chuckle. "You know, we really do feed the kid. I can't believe how he's chowing down."

"So I guess my spaghetti passes muster." Kate laughed as Ben held his plate and she piled on a second batch of pasta and meat sauce. They both watched as he poured on the Parmesan cheese. She made a point of looking around the corner of the table at his lower half.

"Where are you putting all of that? Salad, spaghetti, bread...are you going to have room for dessert?"

Ben's eyes flew wide. "I always have room for dessert."

"That I can vouch for," Nick said, twirling up another bite of pasta. "And this is really good spaghetti. Family recipe?"

"Not really. Gran wasn't much of a cook, so I had to become one or starve. I just experiment until I find a way that I like a certain food. So, my repertoire of recipes isn't exactly vast." She chuckled. "I'm only partly domesticated."

"Well, after saving lives and tending to sick animals all day long, I can understand not being in love with cooking. I kind of feel the same. Though I do enjoy grilling a good steak now and then. And ribs. There's nothing more satisfying than producing a stack of great ribs." He sighed. "Except maybe eating them."

"Okay, the next meal is on you and your grill," Kate said with wry assessment. "That is, if you're up for it."

He chewed thoughtfully, prolonging the suspense for a moment.

"I can't let a challenge to my grilling skills go unmet." He watched uncertainty enter her expression and felt a twinge of guilt for not saying what he meant. She deserved things straight up, and he needed her to know he was meeting her halfway. "And I don't think Ben and I could find anybody half as pretty or as interesting as you to ask to dinner."

Her cheeks filled with color.

"Good save, Stanton. You were close to forfeiting dessert."

Cleanup didn't take long with Ben ferrying dishes into the kitchen, Nick rinsing and Kate loading the dishwasher. Before long, they were in the living room, Kate parked in front of the bookcases on the sofa across from Ben and Nick, who occupied the beanbag chairs at the foot of the bookcases. Ben had collected a pile of books from the lower shelves and was going through them with eager eyes.

Nick made faces of horror and disgust meant for Kate alone. He was only half-kidding. Graphic anatomical diagrams in living color weren't exactly his idea of great Friday night entertainment. Kate seemed to enjoy his silent commentary; she stifled grins and her shoulders shook with silent laughter.

"This is all very enriching, I'm sure," he said after the third or fourth photo essay on flesh damage caused by fly-borne parasites, "but don't you have a television? Maybe some Disney Junior or Nickelodeon?"

"Daaaad." Ben looked up, appalled by the suggestion. "This is science stuff. It's important." He looked back at a picture of a cow that was being eaten alive by larvae of the botfly. "And it's *cool*."

Nick threw up his hands in the universal gesture of surrender, and then looked at Kate. "You're turning him into a ghoul. Since he met you he's all about blood and guts and now larvae—" He halted at the way her expression was sliding toward full horror. "Okay, not a ghoul exactly. But he's become strangely bloodthirsty for an eight-year-old, don't you think?"

With every word he spoke, her eyes widened more. She stared at him with anxiety that slowly turned to horror—before she launched herself bodily at him.

CHAPTER ELEVEN

"HEEEEYYY—I ONLY MEANT—" He brought his arms up in time to take her weight and found her falling against him. Suddenly his face was pressed against her breasts and his arms were full of waist and bottom. He heard things falling from the shelves and felt her jerk and spasm against him, wrestling with something.

He lifted her up enough to turn his head and glimpsed fat coils of shiny mottled-yellow skin—

"Arggghhh!" The reaction came straight from his gut; he tossed her aside and scrambled out of the way. Not especially gallant, abandoning her to whatever the hell that thing was.

THIS WAS HER nightmare come true. Kate had groaned internally as she watched the young python slither along the top of the bookcase.

It *would* have to make an appearance when Nick was opening up, giving her compliments and getting personal. The damned thing reached the corner of the bookcase in a heartbeat and began to slither downward…and along a shelf…then stretched out into space right above Nick's head where he sat on the beanbag chair. She didn't know whether to warn him or— The damned thing was dropping fast and she had to get it before it landed on his neck. Frantic to keep man and beast separate, she jumped off the couch and lunged for the snake.

Every part of her was suddenly in contact with Nick as she lay against him with her outstretched hands full of young, muscular and probably hungry python. She had just gotten a good hold behind the head when Nick shoved her back and rolled out of the way. She lay on her side, wedged between the beanbag and the bookcases, her arms stretched over her head while a testy snake was doing its best to squeeze her arms to consumable mush. She could hear a worrisome litany of "Shit, shit, shit!" and "Ben, get away from there!"

As she rocked back and forth, building

enough momentum to scramble upright, her primary feeling was annoyance that the thing should come out now to ruin what might have been a special moment. *Damned cold-blooded reptile.* She couldn't bear to look at Nick as she staggered to her feet, holding the snake and working to keep it under control.

"There's a heavy canvas bag in the back of my Jeep," she said, breathing hard. "If you could get it for me…"

He burst out the door with such enthusiasm that she wondered if he meant to come back. But Ben was still there, staring at the snake with shining eyes, and she heard a car hatch open and close out in the driveway.

"Can I touch it?"

She nodded, and Ben rushed over to feel the coils and stroke the snake just as Nick stormed back inside.

"Ben, get away from that thing!" Nick snapped as he rushed the bag over to where Kate was working to manage the boy-snake encounter *and* maintain her advantage over the snake.

"It's all right, Nick, I've got it. I just need to get it in the bag. Pythons aren't venomous, though a bite could give you a nasty infection." She winced at the glower on Nick's face. *Too much information.* He seemed to have paled under his tan, and the way he held the canvas bag at arm's length told her all she needed to know about his opinion of an evening that ended with bagging a seven-foot constrictor that nearly dropped on his head.

"This is actually a patient of mine. His owner went out of town for a couple of months. I planned to take him to the office, where we have a couple of large aquariums, and keep him doped up on food and sleeping until his owner comes home. They can sleep for weeks at a time, you know." She tugged on the coils and slid her arm free to help guide the snake's body into the bag. She saw Nick stiffen and his fists clench on the opening as the snake slid past them. "But he escaped my vehicle and then got lost in the garage. I couldn't find him, but I figured he'd show himself when he got hungry." She winced as she lowered the head into the bag and released it. Fortunately, the snake kept its mouth shut; it would be tough to convince Nick the snake wasn't lethal if he got a look at its fangs.

Nick handed her the bag and stepped back, sticking out an arm to hold Ben back. He scanned the living room, high and low, for additional threats.

"Got any other dangerous predators hanging around?"

"Nope." She tried for a plucky smile as she tied the bag. "Not that Maury here is a dangerous predator, except to recently thawed mice and rabbits. He's a bit of a shock if you're not expecting him, but he's harmless to people, I promise." She lifted the bag and swung it over her shoulder. "I'll be right back."

Out in the garage she located the pierced metal box with a latch that she had intended to put him in a week ago, and secured Maury for the night. Now came the hard part: facing the fallout of this unexpected *Wild Kingdom* encounter. Squaring her shoulders and saying a desperate, short prayer, she strode back into the living room.

"Okay, who's ready for dessert?"

"Me!" Ben called, jumping up from the chair and heading for the kitchen.

Nick was slower to follow.

The calm was surreal as they washed their hands at the kitchen sink, and Kate got out the pound cake, freshly sliced peaches and ice cream. Ben was full of questions about snakes and, though she feared every answer was driving a nail in the coffin of her budding relationship with Nick, she answered and tried to make snake lore sound as ordinary and nonthreatening as possible. Nick didn't say much as he scooped the ice cream and then joined Kate and Ben in the dining room.

"Mmm," Ben moaned, digging into the peaches and ice cream. "Dad's gotta love this. Peach is his favorite. Nana has to make a peach pie nearly every week."

Kate looked at Nick with silent apology, and it took one very long minute for him to respond.

"Okay, the snake thing—I was almost out the door on that one. You barreled into me like a halfback, and when I saw the size of that thing, well, I'm not a big fan of snakes." He took a deep breath, and she could see he was trying hard to be fair. "But you got it in the bag, and I remembered you said something about peaches earlier. I figured as long as nobody got bit or suffocated or crushed, we might as well stay for dessert."

She relaxed and thanked heaven for whatever help it provided.

Ben enjoyed the peaches and ice cream, and Nick seemed to, as well. But Kate felt some of the warmth had drained from the evening. After dessert, she chose a couple of animal books from her collection to loan to Ben, and Nick looked at her backyard and offered a couple of suggestions on landscaping.

It was nearly nine o'clock when Nick said it was getting late and Ben had soccer the next morning. He coached Ben through a "thank you for the spaghetti and peaches and ice cream," and looked unsettled when Ben asked her if she would come to his game the next morning. She waffled noncommittally under Nick's gaze, mentioning Saturday clinic hours and how hard it was to leave on such short notice. "Maybe another time." He gave her a hug before Nick ushered him out to the SUV and installed him in the back seat.

Nick came back to the porch where Kate

stood with crossed arms and an uneasy feeling in the pit of her stomach.

"Thank you for dinner," he said, looking at his feet.

"You're welcome," she said quietly, and screwed up her courage to apologize. "Look, Nick, I'm sorry about the whole snake thing. My life is sometimes crazy, but that doesn't mean *I* am. I just have animals around all the time. Some of them are a little odd and some are unpredictable, but it's my job to care for them."

"Some warning would have been nice."

"What? That I'd lost a young python in my house and had no idea where or when it might show up?" It sounded even worse when she said it aloud. She looked a little sheepish. "It never occurred to me that it might reappear tonight. Okay, maybe it crossed my mind…once. Anyway, Ben seemed to love it."

"Yeah, well, about Ben—" he avoided her eyes "—I don't like him being exposed to dangerous things. It's my job to protect him."

"Protect him? Did you see him tonight?

He was charged up and loving it. He wasn't one bit afraid of a seven-foot python."

"That's what bothers me. He's too young to realize true danger. He just charged in to get his hands on the thing. He needs to learn control, and until he does, I have to exercise it for him."

"He's your son—you have to do what you think is right," she said, wishing she could reach out and draw him back across the distance spreading between them. "But he's a bright, curious, gutsy kid. He has to try new things and learn by doing. It's in his bones. Surely you can see that."

His head came up and his eyes darkened.

"What I can see is that he needs a firm hand. And limits."

He held her gaze for a moment, and she had no clue where to go from there. Try for another platitude on child rearing? Plead for another chance? Or just be honest.

"I care about him, too, Nick. He's an amazing kid," she said, wishing he could somehow see the depth of feeling in her heart. "I would never do anything to hurt him. And I would never let him get hurt by an animal in my care. I want to protect him, too."

He was silent and motionless for a heart-stopping minute, searching her, then he leaned in…to plant a kiss on her *cheek*.

"Good night, Kate."

He was halfway down the sidewalk to his vehicle before she realized what had happened. Her cheek burned where his lips had brushed it, and for a moment she held her breath. That dry, infuriatingly proper little kiss took more feeling than it gave.

No matter what he had said, it didn't feel like good-night…it felt like goodbye.

As she stood there, feeling drained and boneless, her heart sank into an old emptiness she hadn't experienced in a long time. Memories surfaced from the bottom of her consciousness, potent and unwelcome…another time she'd watched someone she loved walk away.

She didn't notice when he stopped on the sidewalk or that he just stood there with his back to her, legs braced, fists clenched and shoulders rounding. She couldn't see the muscle in his jaw flex or cords become visible in his neck.

She couldn't move. Every bit of energy she possessed was required to keep her upright and breathing.

Inside. Now. Do not let him see you dissolving into—

The sound of footsteps brought her gaze up. He was coming back up the walk, moving fast, filling her vision and jolting her heart into a quick, erratic beat.

He didn't hesitate or pause to gauge her reaction. He didn't explain, negotiate or make excuses. He clamped his arms around her waist, covered her lips with his and in a heartbeat was breathing warmth and feeling back into her.

With him against her, around her, caressing her, her shock quickly melted. His long, thorough kiss worked magic in her, and she responded with an embrace that contained all the joy she could summon. Instinct took over, guiding her response, and for a small eternity there was nothing but him and her—lips to lips, body to body—and this eruption of need and longing. And *loving*.

Sometime in that earth-shattering kiss, she realized she was falling in love with Nick Stanton.

By the time the kiss ended, his cheeks were flushed and his breathing was ragged. Cradling her face between his hands, he ran his thumbs over her lips and said, "Kate... my Kate...my beautiful Kate," and she realized—even if he didn't know it yet—that he might be coming to love her, too.

Moisture rimmed her eyes, and her lips felt thick and conspicuous as she looked up into his eyes and read in them the same things she was feeling...desire, certainty and the promise of *more*. Boyish giggles reached them, making him draw back a few inches, but he didn't release her. Instead, he gave her a hot, reckless, very untrooper-like grin. On the side of her body away from Ben's notice, he ran a hand down her hip.

"Soccer, Kate. Tomorrow at ten?"

She nodded.

His grin was as broad as his face as he strode out to his SUV. When he opened the door to climb in, she could hear Ben taunting his dad about "...kissing Dr. Kate!"

She managed to close the front door behind her before sliding down it to land on the floor on her butt.

"Oh, hell, yeah. Tomorrow." She grinned, feeling more than a little intoxicated. "I frickin' *love* soccer."

CHAPTER TWELVE

KATE LEFT WORK the next morning with a story about needing a dental cleaning and only being able to schedule on a Saturday. Jess scowled, clearly suspicious, but in the end agreed to see Kate's last few patients to allow her to leave in time for the "appointment."

She arrived at an athletic complex she had driven by a thousand times and found herself in a maze of fields, bleachers, and rows of folding chairs, coolers and strollers. It took a while to find where Ben was playing—it *would* have to be the field farthest from the parking lot.

Sarah Stanton spotted her as she arrived, waving and gesturing to an empty folding chair beside her. As Kate sat down, a cheer burst from the crowd and Sarah explained that Ben's team had just scored. Moments later Nick was at her side, crouching on one knee as he watched the boys on the field and tutored Kate in all things soccer. When he slipped his hand over hers on the arm of the chair, she melted inside.

During halftime, as the boys were fed oranges and Gatorade, Nick introduced Kate to several other parents, who were surprised to learn she was one of the vets at the new Lakeview Animal Clinic. As they talked, she caught some of the moms eyeing Nick's impressive physique and smiled. She thought he was pretty darned spectacular, too. But when Ben threw his arms around her, she hugged him back and didn't bother to check the moms' reactions. Nick's broad smile at seeing it was all that mattered.

Ben's happiness had evaporated by the time the game was over. They had lost by one goal. On the walk back to the SUV he kicked at gravel with his cleats and growled, "I stunk. I'm a crummy player. We all stunk—except Koshi." Koshi was the kid who scored both of their goals. Nick grabbed Ben's hand to slow him and talked in solemn tones about "playing classy."

"Every player has good games and tough games—times that you play like a champ and times you stumble around on the field like a chump. That's all part of learning and training your growing body. But the important thing is that you do your best. You play hard and then you learn to accept the outcome—win or lose—with good sportsmanship. That's why you line up and shake hands at the end of the game…learning to be a good sport."

It was a hard lesson for an eight-year-old to understand, and the loss seemed to matter more to Ben because Kate had been there to see it.

Knowing he was looking to her for a reaction, she nodded firmly to underscore Nick's words about winning and losing. It sounded like well-worn "guy-speak" to her, but it was probably also a rite of passage for boys Ben's age. Learning to take your lumps on a sports field taught self-control but just as importantly, it taught hope. There would be another try, a next game, a second chance… if not on the sports field, somewhere else in life.

"Determination and hard work," she heard Nick say, "are worth more than talent any day. And you've got plenty of both, kiddo."

She took a satisfied breath as Nick squeezed Ben against his side. Her prediction that he would know the best way to steer his son had been right on target.

At the mention of his favorite Mexican restaurant, Ben's spirits rebounded, and soon they were seated in a booth at Acapulco, talking about soccer and the possibility of basketball in the coming winter season. Ben wasn't keen on signing up; he said he'd rather take bike hikes with his dad, use his telescope to chart more stars at night and try fishing. Plus, he had to help with the dogs.

"Can we go to Gran Everly's farm and see Goldie and Soldier after lunch?" He cocked his head like a curious puppy. "Puleeeze."

"Mrs. Everly may not want visitors this afternoon—she may not even be home," Nick said, frowning.

"No, remember, she said we could come anytime. Right, Dr. Kate?"

Kate stalled for a minute, trying to decide which one to disappoint, Ben or Nick. "That's right. She did say that."

"Are you going?" Nick asked, tossing the decision into her lap.

"I have to stop at the shelter first to check on a couple of animals, then I could swing by the farm."

"Well, I have a ton of things to do at home," Sarah said to Nick. "Can you drop me off before you go?"

"No problem." He turned to Kate. "How about if we meet at the shelter and go out there together?"

"Sounds good to me," she said, remembering their last visit to the farm and the way they had been together. Her body warmed in anticipation of a repeat engagement. "I don't think it will take me long. And you know, I'm kind of looking forward to seeing Goldie and Soldier."

"Can I ride with you, Dr. Kate?" Ben asked, catching her off guard.

"It's fine with me, if—" She looked to Nick, who gave in to his son's eagerness and nodded.

THE PARKING LOT at Harbor had a few more cars than usual for a Saturday afternoon. "Must be a carryover from last week." Kate parked on the grass near the office and Ben hopped out, saying he wanted to see the puppies in the main kennel. "Okay, but check in with me in the surgery in a few minutes. Your dad will be here soon."

Before she reached the front door, it opened.

"There you are." Nance dragged Kate inside. "We got him."

"Got who?" Kate pulled back to slow her down.

"The schnauzer kid. Caught him red-handed this time."

"The boy who dropped off the schnauzer puppies?" It took a moment for that to sink in. She followed her grandmother into the kitchen-surgery where she found Isabelle, Hines Jackson and volunteers Harry Mueller and Linda Hoskins gathered around a small figure seated on a straight-backed wooden chair.

As she got closer, the boy's head came up, his big brown eyes filled with fear, distrust, and worst of all, resignation. That helplessness struck Kate harder than his thatch of unkempt hair or rail-thin body or the worn clothes that looked like two or three generations already had passed through them. His bony shoulders and scrawny legs said he seldom had enough to eat, and his calloused hands spoke of hard labor, both of which made it difficult to tell his age. He could be anywhere from eleven to fourteen.

"Who is he?" She looked from one member of the group to another.

"He don't say," Hines answered, frowning. "Maybe he don't speak English."

"Habla inglese?" she asked in her limited Spanish. He lowered his head and stared at his hands as they ran nervously up and down his thighs.

To the group she said, "How did you find him?"

"Hines and Harry caught him sneaking around the back of the kennel, trying to get into the puppy runs," Nance supplied.

"Why would he do that?" Kate said, studying the boy. "If he brought them here, why would he try to steal them back?"

"We don't know. He refuses to tell us what he's doing here or where he got the puppies he brought us," Isabelle put in.

"He tried to run at first, but we caught him," Harry added with a grin. "Hines is a heckuva lot quicker than he looks."

Kate crossed her arms, thinking of a way

to get the boy to open up to them. "He looks like he needs a good meal. Maybe if we got him some food and gave him a chance to get used to us, he'd open up."

Harry and Linda went for some food, Isabelle got him a soda from the fridge and Hines pushed his chair up to the table in the surgery. Kate dragged another chair from Isabelle's office and sat down with him, smiling sympathetically, giving the tension in him a chance to unwind.

He wouldn't touch the soda at first; he just stared at it. But after a few moments, he licked his dry lips. He was thirsty and probably desperate for a jolt of energy. Kate nudged it closer to him on the tabletop.

"It's all right. It's yours. Nobody is going to hurt you here. But I think you already know that. It's why you brought us the puppies, right?" She nudged the soda can still closer. "We don't want to hurt you or make you stay here. We just want to know where the puppies came from."

Minutes later, he surrendered the last of his resistance to her soft approach and reached for the soda. He drank eagerly, as if he were starved for liquid and energy. At

Kate's suggestion, Isabelle brought a second can, and then she and Hines left Kate and Nance alone with the boy.

"What is your name, son?" Nance said quietly. "I'm Nance Everly and this is Kate Everly. She's the veterinarian who takes care of the animals here."

The boy looked at Kate with surprise, and Kate knew that he understood what her gran had said.

"You do speak English, don't you? You know what we're saying." She moved a little nearer to him. "What is your name? You're not in trouble here, I promise." She touched her heart to show she meant it. "We just need to find the place those puppies come from. I bet there are more puppies there who need help." Her smile took on a tinge of sadness. "Am I right?"

The boy set the soda back on the table and pushed it away.

One minute, then two passed as Kate searched for another approach. Footsteps sounded and she turned to the door just as Ben burst into the room, red-faced and little out of breath. "The puppies are sleeping— all in piles—so I didn't—"

His gaze fixed on the boy and then moved to Kate and Nance.

"Who's he?"

"We don't know," Kate said, extending her arm in an invitation Ben accepted. He came to her side, and she wrapped that arm around his shoulders. "Maybe you could ask him."

Ben studied the boy and took a deep breath.

"I'm Ben. What's your name?" It was said with openness and simple curiosity that worked on the boy's defenses. His eyes flitted between Ben and Kate, observing the bond between them, and finally surrendered.

"Miguel," he said softly. "I am Miguel."

"Good to meet you, Miguel," Kate said, breaking into a smile. "Ben, here, is a good friend of mine." Ben said hello and waved awkwardly, looking a little uncertain. "Do you live around here?"

"Not so near."

"With your family?"

The boy shrank back against the chair, and she sensed he was afraid to reveal his circumstances.

"Okay, you don't have to say. But you brought puppies to us...more than once. That was you, wasn't it?" When he nodded, she continued, "Why did you do that, Miguel?"

He looked at Ben, who was watching eagerly for the answer.

"I hurt for little ones. No mama. No food." The boy reached for the can he had given up earlier and gulped the soda until it was drained.

"How did you know about the puppies?"

He thought about it as he rubbed his stomach under his shirt.

"My uncle. He work for a old woman. He make me work, too." His big eyes lost something as he remembered. "Old woman, she don't feed dogs good. Once, she sell little dogs." He waved a hand past his shoulder indicating a time gone by. *"No más."*

Kate and Nance exchanged glances.

"How old are you, Miguel?" Kate asked, and he lowered his eyes.

He shrugged. "Mama, she die and my uncle...um...took me."

"So you live with your uncle and work sometimes for this woman who has the puppies," Kate summarized, and he nodded. "Who else knows that you're here? Who drove the truck last week when you brought the puppies?"

"Alejandro. My cousin. He drive us to work. He say it not good, what she do. My uncle work on houses today, so Alejandro help me get puppies to bring."

That explained how he'd escaped the day Nick chased them. "Are there more puppies and dogs there?" He nodded again. "Where is this place? Is it near here?"

Once again he hesitated, and at that moment Harry arrived with a burger, fries and a huge chocolate milk shake. Miguel's eyes bulged as the meal was placed before him, and when he realized it was meant for him, he looked to Ben, who grinned. Miguel attacked it like he was starving.

Nance left to tell Isabelle and the others what was happening.

"Miguel, you don't like what they're doing, do you?" Kate asked as he finished his food. He shook his head and swallowed hard. "We don't, either. It's wrong, and we'd like to stop it. Would you help us? Will you tell us where this place is?"

It took a while for him to reply. He wrung his hands, clearly afraid of the consequences should he be caught helping them. Kate thought he was probably in trouble already, since he'd been caught and his cousin probably knew it. He seemed to be coming to a decision as he looked at Ben's friendly face and watched Kate's gentle treatment of him.

"I cannot tell where, but—" he chewed his lip "—I show you."

CHAPTER THIRTEEN

HINES KNEW THE rural roads of the county better than anyone else, but Kate argued that her Jeep would take back roads better, and he grudgingly agreed to let her drive. Isabelle started to make phone calls, while Harry and Linda headed for a storage shed to check on equipment for securing and transporting the animals they would find.

"You have to wait here for your dad," Kate told Ben, who immediately began to argue for a chance to go with her. "No, you have to stay here with Gran. Your dad will be here any minute, and I don't think you'll be going to the farm. You'll have to see Goldie and Soldier another time."

She gave him a hug, remanded him to Nance's care and went into the office to tell Isabelle that she and Hines were going to take Miguel to find the breeder's location. Isabelle was already on the phone with a friendly judge, getting the legal process moving. She motioned for Kate to wait a moment and produced a county map from a desk drawer. Kate declined with a grin.

"I've got Hines."

"Still, things change and it's easy to get lost on those back roads," she said, pushing the map into Kate's hand. "Good luck."

After a quick trip to the bathroom and a stop in the kitchen for bottles of water, she headed out to her Jeep and found Hines in the front seat and Miguel in the back with Nance. Kate glared at her grandmother.

"Where's Ben?"

"With Harry and Linda—out by the shed."

Kate's glower downgraded to a dark look.

"What?" Nance said with her chin up. "I'm not going to stay here to babysit and miss all the fun."

"All right," Kate said grudgingly. "Buckle up."

When Miguel wasn't scanning the roads for landmarks, he was pointing at familiar farms where he and his uncle had worked. He seemed genuinely eager to help them find the puppy mill. Hines delivered a history lesson on nearly every bit of land they passed—who had owned the acreage and what they had grown, who married whom to join properties and who lost which parcels in a poker game. After forty minutes and what seemed like as many miles, Kate heard a familiar voice from the cargo area: "Can I come out now?"

She put on the brakes and when they were stopped on the shoulder of the ill-paved county road, she turned in her seat. Confronting her were two faces, one brazenly unrepentant and the other glowing with heat and excitement.

"What the heck is he *doing* here?" she demanded of Nance. "You said he was with Harry and Linda."

"He *was*. For a while. But he wanted to come, and I figured it couldn't hurt."

"I begged her to let me come," Ben said, worried by her irritation. "I want to help, too."

"You went on puppy mill raids with me when you were not much older than him," Nance said, crossing her arms and refusing to be cowed.

Kate thought of Nick's reaction to that

very fact and steamed at the fix her grand-mother's meddling had put her in. "How am I going to explain this to Nick? He doesn't want Ben anywhere near such a thing. He said so in no uncertain terms."

That registered with Nance, who looked less confident but still made no apology.

"He get over it, Katie," Hines—always a source of good sense—declared, patting her arm. "We not in danger. We jus' lookin'."

All of which was true, she realized, and prayed Nick would see it that way, too. She took a deep breath, gave Ben a hard look and picked up her phone to call Nick. She had no reception. "Dead." Her heart sank.

"Climb over and get into a seat belt right now," she ordered Ben. "You and I have to talk about your headstrong behavior, young man."

She watched until he was installed safely between Nance and Miguel, then turned and put the Jeep in gear. As they moved on, Hines tried to distract them with more historical commentary and Kate wrestled with misgivings. She should turn the vehicle around and take Ben straight back to the shelter, but that was half a county away by now, and she couldn't bring herself to let this lead go. They couldn't come this far and not find the place where animals were suffering.

Everyone grew quiet as the roads deteriorated into narrow, dusty farm roads. The navigation screen showed nothing but green with occasional lines that indicated road crossings, and even Hines had to stop and orient himself from time to time. But Miguel seemed confident they were in the right area and watched eagerly for things he recognized.

"There!" He pointed to trees crowding the road ahead of them. "Old woman—she live there." A rustle of anticipation stirred in the Jeep.

Kate lowered her window and rolled slowly forward until she located an opening in the growth that turned out to be a track for vehicles. An aged mailbox was mostly covered by weeds, but she was able to make out faded letters on the side: Crowder. Miguel pointed and said the house was farther down the road.

Kate had her phone on the dashboard, prepared to take pictures as they moved along the edge of the property. They spotted what was once a cleared area but was being re-taken by vegetation. A house came into view through the scrubby growth, a sagging patchwork of construction badly in need of paint. Other structures were visible behind it—a ramshackle barn surrounded by sheds with rusting tin roofs. Old farm equipment sat here and there, and pens were visible around some of the structures. As she slowed the Jeep further, she heard barking.

She snapped photos as far as her phone's camera would focus, and Nance suggested she try adding the farm as a destination on her navigation system. She did just that, then rolled quietly by the property to stop a few hundred yards beyond the clearing.

"I didn't see anything obvious," she said. "We need to get a closer look. I'll have to go back on foot—use the trees and brush as cover."

"No, no." Miguel shook his head, alarmed. "Old woman has gun. Shoot at people who come." He motioned circles around the side of his head. "She...*loco.*"

"She's crazy?" Ben asked, watching Miguel eagerly.

"Sí." Miguel nodded. *"Crazy* old woman."

"Ain't a good time to go nosin' around, Katie," Hines said gravely, casting a meaningful look back at Ben. "Folk in these parts—they don't take kindly to strangers."

"Then I guess we'll have to come back another time," Kate said, reading his cautionary look and weighing the possible consequences. "We have to have more than this to get a warrant. We need pictures."

Miguel popped his seat belt and slid forward. "I get pictures. She not shoot me. I make pictures for you."

It was brave of him to volunteer for such a mission, but she couldn't be responsible for sending him into a dangerous situation.

"He's got a point," Nance said, studying Miguel's determined face. "The old woman knows him and probably would just think he was there to work. He's probably the only one who could get in and get the proof we need to start things rolling."

"She's right, Katie," Hines chimed in. "Miguel here, he could get in an' out quick. He's a smart kid. He'll be okay."

It was a tough decision. She searched Miguel, knowing Ben was watching. She chewed her lip. "Do you know how to use a phone camera?"

Miguel wasn't familiar with her phone, but he caught on quickly and took photos of each of them in the Jeep and of the trees outside for practice. After nodding through numerous warnings, he slipped out of the vehicle and quickly disappeared through the woods in the direction of the Crowder farmstead.

The wait was excruciating. Even Hines grew jittery as thirty minutes, then forty-five passed. Kate had to turn off the engine to conserve gas and they rolled down the windows, grateful it was too early in the day for mosquitos. Ben climbed into the rear cargo compartment to keep watch for Miguel. The heat, confinement and waiting began to fray his young nerves, and he asked repeatedly what could be taking so long and if they thought Miguel was all right. No one had an answer for him.

Just when Kate was ready to leave the vehicle and go in search of him, Miguel appeared through the trees and they all heaved a sigh of relief. Ben wanted to vault out of the Jeep to meet him, but Nance restrained him.

"What happened?" Kate asked as Miguel slipped back into the vehicle. "Did she see you? Did you take any pictures?"

"Give the boy a chance to get his breath," Hines chided.

Miguel laid his head back against the seat but produced Kate's phone and held it out to her. She quickly woke up the screen and went to her pictures. With Nance and Hines looking over her shoulders, she found shots of sad-eyed animals in small cages made of chicken wire, and dirt pens filled with feces...dogs so matted and overgrown they were scarcely recognizable. She closed her eyes and swallowed hard.

"Here. Take this." She handed the phone to Nance, told everyone to buckle up and started the Jeep.

The trip back to the shelter took less time than the trip out. Kate was determined to drive Miguel home, but he was just as insistent that they drop him off at a small gas station and convenience store in a rural part of Manatee County. He said his cousin stopped there often, and the clerk would let him use a phone. She stepped out of the Jeep with him and managed to tuck some cash into his

shirt pocket—for emergencies, she said—
and included one of her business cards from
the Jeep's console.

"You're such a brave young man, Miguel."
Her throat tightened. "I wish we had a way
to repay you." She watched his big, dark
eyes moisten, and couldn't resist the urge
to draw him into a hug. Something tugged
in her chest as she felt his thin arms circle
her, and realized he was trembling. After a
moment, she released him.

"That card has my number. Promise me
you'll call if you need help."

Miguel looked from her face to Ben's,
Nance's and Hines's. A wistful expression
came over him. "I call you." He ran across
the parking lot and into the convenience
store.

Hines's deep voice sounded reverent as he
gave words to what they all were thinking.
"God bless that boy's brave heart."

CHAPTER FOURTEEN

NICK PACED BACK and forth on the porch outside Harbor's offices, fists clenching and jaw taut with anger he was struggling to master. Isabelle Conti was less than convincing as she assured him that Ben was with Kate. From years in the military and the FHP, he could tell when someone was holding back information.

She'd said they had gotten a lead on the puppy mill and had taken a drive into the country to try to find it. What she hadn't said was the nature of that lead, whether it could be trusted and what possessed Kate Everly to take his son along on such a risky venture.

"She knew I was swinging by the shelter to take them to the farm," he said to Isabelle. "Why didn't she wait to talk to me before taking Ben out to the back of beyond with her?"

"It seemed like something we had to act on fast." Isabelle avoided his gaze. "I don't think she intended to—to be gone long."

"Just what was this *intel* that had to be acted on right away?"

Isabelle looked ready to bolt, and he softened his approach.

"Please, Isabelle, I have to know. Ben is with her, and she knows how I feel about exposing him to such things."

Isabelle sighed and waved him inside, motioning him into the kitchen. She made him a coffee as she talked.

"We caught the kid you chased that day—the one who dropped off the puppies. Kate got him to tell us who he is and where the puppies came from. He was scared half to death. He took a risk telling us that much, Nick. He said his uncle works for the old woman who runs the place, so he may be in trouble if the uncle finds out he helped turn her in.

"When he agreed to show them where the puppies came from, Kate told Ben to stay here with us and wait for you. But I got busy making phone calls and lining up support to clear out the place." She reddened. "I thought he was with Harry and Linda, out in the kennels. When I went to look for him, they said they had seen him heading around the side of the offices. That was where Kate had parked."

It slowly dawned on him. "You mean you don't know for sure that he's with Kate?"

"I tried calling, but cell service is spotty out in those rural areas. I couldn't get her."

"How long ago was that?"

"An hour or so."

He pulled a chair out onto the porch and sat staring at the road, holding his half-empty coffee cup.

He thought he and Kate had an understanding regarding Ben's welfare: that he intended to keep Ben safe and to discipline his headstrong tendencies. She must know he'd be beside himself with worry—not sure where they were or when they'd return—unable to contact her.

As the wait stretched on, he recalled Kate's words on her porch the other night. She cared about Ben, and she said she wanted to protect him, too. But she couldn't feel the responsibility for his son that he did.

And what did it say about her that she'd put locating a puppy mill above his son's safety? Could he trust her judgment? The woman had pythons running loose in her house, for God's sake!

And Ben—what did it say about his son that he insisted on going along on a mission to find a place where dogs were being starved and mistreated? That he had a good and caring heart, and that he acted more on feelings than common sense. He was so grown-up in some ways, and so very much a kid in others.

Those thoughts gradually tempered his anger at what originally looked like Kate's careless betrayal. He made himself recall her fondness for Ben and her matter-of-fact treatment of his curiosity and impetuous behavior. She treated his intelligence and drive to learn with what could only be called respect. He was not just a kid to her, he was a person, and she wanted to foster his unique curiosity and love of learning. But she could no more predict when he would switch back into kid mode than he could. That made dealing with him a real challenge.

Strangely, just having some time to think about it brought things into better focus for him. Ben didn't need somebody to shepherd his schoolwork or keep him busy with activities. He was already motivated to care about others and to learn and grow and discover. What Ben needed was an older, more experienced guide to help him fill in the gaps in his development, to steer him past the pitfalls of youth and inexperience. Sarah had tried to tell him something like that, but he hadn't quite understood what she was saying.

Could he do that, be that for his son?

It was almost an hour later that Kate's Jeep pulled into Harbor's parking lot, and he could see by the tension in her face that she was dreading his reaction. He wasn't certain what was happening between them or how he felt about this incident anymore, and he wasn't ready to process it with her right now. He did know he needed to have a serious talk with his son.

When they spilled out of the Jeep, he was surprised to see Hines Jackson and Nance with Kate and Ben. He hadn't realized they were along for the ride. Had Isabelle mentioned that?

"I'M SORRY, NICK," Kate said as she walked straight over to him, and he stepped off the porch to meet her. His face was set and unreadable. "I tried to call, but I had no service out there."

"So Isabelle said. You might have found time to call *before* you took off for God knows where."

He transferred his gaze to Ben. "And you, young man, have some explaining to do. You know better than to go anywhere without asking. You clear all invitations with Nana or me."

Ben reddened and looked at Kate. She raised her eyebrows at him in a "see what happens" expression.

"It wasn't exactly by invitation," she said, wondering if Ben was going to be punished for his recklessness and feeling on some level he should be. But then, who would punish her gran for encouraging it? "He climbed in the back of my Jeep, and I didn't know he was in there until we were already far away. We decided not to waste the chance to collect evidence for a warrant, and Miguel went into the barns and pens to take pictures."

"Miguel?" he asked, looking between her and Hines, who had come up behind her.

"Boy that brought the puppies," Hines said.

"Hines and Harry Mueller caught him near the kennels this afternoon," she said, wishing he would meet her gaze. "We got him to show us where the puppies came from, and he volunteered to go in to take pictures." She pulled out her phone and handed it to Isabelle, who had just come out of the offices. She immediately began to flip through the photos.

"Gutsy kid," Hines said. "Said he'd go in because the ol' lady knew 'im and wouldn't shoot 'im."

"Shoot him?" Nick turned a glare on her. "What the hell?"

"Apparently the old woman has a shotgun and is not fond of strangers," Kate explained.

"And if you'd take a look at the photos, you'd see why going out there was so important," Nance said, planting herself beside Kate with her arms crossed. "The place is a pigsty. And worse. Those dogs need rescuing."

"Oh, my God," Isabelle said, looking up from the phone, her tanned face paling. "This isn't just a puppy mill, it's a...charnel house. Who would treat any creature this way, much less small, defenseless dogs?" She tried to hand Nick the phone, but he took a step back and looked at Kate.

"I'll call you." He grabbed Ben by the wrist and headed for his vehicle.

It was all she could do to keep from running after him. Or yelling "See what you've done!" at her pigheaded grandmother. She stood with clenched fists, her heart sinking as she watched his SUV accelerate out of sight.

No one would meet her gaze. Even Nance knew this episode had caused a rift between her and Nick.

"We need to talk," she said to her grandmother. "Now."

Isabelle excused herself to download the evidence to her computer, and Hines mentioned that he had a couple of stops to make before going home to Moose. Moments later Kate and Nance were alone in the kitchen, staring at each other across the kitchensurgery table.

"Nick has every right to be upset," Kate said, bracing her hands on the tabletop. "He doesn't want Ben seeing things that will give him nightmares, and I—I think he has the right to make those decisions. I respect his desire to protect his son."

"Just because he has no great love for animals, doesn't mean—"

"It's not that he doesn't love animals. In fact, it's the opposite. He had experiences with dogs in the military—pretty harsh experiences, from the sound of it. He's a single parent, and he doesn't want Ben exposed to things he's too young to understand. I don't think that's too much to ask."

"You were exposed to things and you turned out okay," Nance said testily. "Kids shouldn't be sheltered from reality. You went on a mill raid when you weren't any older than him."

"Just because I survived it, doesn't mean—"

"Survived it? I couldn't have kept you away with chains and padlocks. You were rarin' to go—you were furious about those dogs."

Kate paused a moment, trying to put her

thoughts together. "I was a different kid. Ben's been through a lot in his short years."

"Like what? Like losing a mother *and* a father? Like being separated from your brother and being sent to live with a grandmother you hardly knew? Like crying yourself to sleep at night for weeks?"

Kate leaned back and crossed her arms over her chest, feeling memories rising, things she had long since forgotten and would rather it stayed that way. She took a deep breath, fighting the pull of the past, and realized Gran thought Kate was criticizing the way she had been raised.

"Gran, I don't regret one minute or one experience I've had with you. I love you with all my heart—you helped make me who I am." She could see hurt lurking behind the defensiveness in Nance's face. "All I'm saying is that Nick has a right to raise Ben as he sees fit. And if I'm— If *we're* going to be a part of his life, we have to respect that."

"Even if he's dead wrong?" Nance asked.

"Who's to say he's wrong? You?" She paused a second to rein in her irritation. "You may not realize it, but there were people who thought the way you raised me was pretty extreme. Some of my friends' parents had trouble letting them come to our house for overnights. Remember how Zoe was always too busy and Rachel always wanted me to come to her house instead? Their parents thought taking in all those animals was a little weird and that the shelter stuff was too intense for their kids."

"Pansies," Nance muttered.

"No!" Kate realized she'd have to get tough to get through to Gran. "They were just parents who had different ideas about what was good for kids and what wasn't." Her voice rose. "Your way isn't the only way to be in the world. Other people have a right to their own values and ideas."

Nance studied her, sensing there was more to this than letting a kid sneak along for a bit of reconnoitering.

"This is about Jared, isn't it? You're still angry that I wouldn't accept him—that I said he wasn't right for you."

Kate's shoulders sagged under the weight of her frustration.

"No, it's not about Jared. What you said was true, and I knew it. If I married him,

I'd never have been able to practice as I had always wanted to. I was willing to do that—to make my career secondary and find part-time vet work wherever he was stationed—until I realized he wasn't the man I thought he was. I could never have trusted him the way I needed to. That's why I broke it off with him. That was why I came back here and opened a practice with Jess. I wanted a life based on love and honesty and genuine caring."

"And you think Nick Stanton can give you that?"

The skepticism in Gran's voice was hard to take.

"I think he can," she said, stepping out onto a ledge she had been avoiding in her own mind, "given time."

Nance closed her eyes for a long moment. "What makes you think he wants the same things? Kate, he's got issues. What if he can't get through them to meet you half-way?"

"Now that does surprise me," Kate said irritably. "Haven't you always said, 'There is no problem, however big, that love can't solve'?"

Nance opened her mouth and then closed it and looked down.

After a moment, Kate slid around the table to put her arm around her gran's shoulders.

"You're always telling me I need to get a life. Well, I intend to. And I think Nick Stanton may be the one I want to share it with. We just need a little time." She bent down to meet Nance's lowered gaze and found moisture in her grandmother's eyes. "And we'll need your love and support."

NICK WASN'T SURE where to start, so he came right out with it as they drove home. "What possessed you to climb into Kate's vehicle after she told you to stay there and wait for me?" He adjusted the rearview mirror to see Ben in the back seat.

"I…I wanted to go and help. That other boy, Miguel, he got to go." He looked up to see his dad's eyes in the mirror.

Was it a simple matter of wanting to be included? The pull of belonging could be a lot stronger than orders you didn't like or understand.

"He knew the way, and I wanted to help, too."

"And what did you think you could do to help?"

"I don't know. But I thought Dr. Kate might need me." He sounded younger by the minute. "I wanted to help her like you did."

He knew Ben adored Kate Everly and her scientific knowledge and earthy wisdom and devotion to healing. He couldn't blame the kid; *he* adored her, too. So a part of this was Ben wanting to earn Kate's approval, even admiration, by being helpful.

It hit him: Ben's adult-like interests and intelligence were accepted and encouraged by the adults around him, and that led him to think that he could do things adults could do. He didn't yet understand the difference age and experience made in the freedom to make his own decisions. Add to that his innate curiosity and lack of experience with the world.

"She said Miguel was brave to go take the pictures of the dogs and puppies." Ben interrupted his thoughts with yet another question. "Do you think he was brave, Dad?"

This was headed off track. Shouldn't he be sentencing Ben to a grounding or something?

"How old is this Miguel?" he asked instead.

"I don't know. Hines said he was maybe thirteen. But he's not much bigger than me, so he could be twelve—or even ten."

"Well, for a twelve- or thirteen-year-old boy to volunteer to sneak into a place he knows is dangerous—where someone has a gun—I'd say that's pretty brave."

"But he didn't have to fight anybody or anything like that."

"Do you think he was scared?" Nick asked, wondering if he should stop the car and have this discussion face-to-face.

"Maybe." Ben frowned. "Probably. So maybe he wasn't so brave."

Jealousy, then, Nick thought. *Ben* wanted to be the brave one.

"What do you think bravery is, Ben?"

"Standing your ground when somebody tries to hit you." Nick saw his son watching him in the mirror. "Like soldiers. They're not afraid when they go to fight—they know what to do. Right?"

"So you think soldiers aren't afraid? That being afraid is not brave?"

"I—I guess."

"Well, I have to disagree. Most soldiers I have known were afraid at one time or another—sometimes they were afraid a lot. They were in foreign countries with people who spoke different languages, had very different customs and didn't trust them. They didn't know who was a 'friendly' and who was an enemy, and they could be shot or attacked at almost any time. Do you think they had reason to be afraid?"

"I guess." Ben frowned and chewed his lip. "But aren't soldiers trained to not be afraid? Because how can they fight and protect people and stuff if they're afraid?"

"That's the point, Ben. They may be afraid or sad or angry or lonely—but they do their jobs anyway and face down guns and rockets and ambushes. Brave is about what you do, not what you feel. It's okay to be afraid sometimes. Fear can keep you from doing dumb things and getting yourself hurt or in trouble."

He turned into their subdivision and slowed the SUV to a crawl so they could finish this talk. This was the hard part...

"So what do you think would have happened if *you* had gone to take those pictures instead of Miguel?"

"Me?" Ben seemed surprised. "Well, I would have been quiet in the woods and ducked from tree to tree, like on TV. And I'd go to the first place and open the door and take pictures." He held his hand out in front of him and made clicking noises while depressing an imaginary button. "And then the second barn and then whatever other places they keep dogs and puppies."

Nick was struck forcefully by the naïveté in Ben's thinking. "Like on TV." He could imagine himself doing all of that, but didn't know yet the difference between thinking something and being able to do it.

"What if that old lady spotted you and came out with her shotgun? What if the dogs saw you and started barking? What if you fell and got hurt or broke the camera? What if the doors were locked and you couldn't get inside the barn? What if there were big dogs running lose to attack intruders?"

Ben sat with his hands clasped between his knees, his eyes flitting back and forth over the images Nick had just seeded in his fertile mind. His shoulders rounded, and Nick felt a pang of guilt. He didn't like having to poke holes in Ben's illusions of adulthood. Was he being too hard on the boy?

After a while Ben looked up, having made a decision.

"I guess it was best that Miguel went to take the pictures." He had gotten the message, and Nick felt a weight lift from his chest. It might be only one of many such steps toward maturity, but at least he had hope now that he could help Ben negotiate them.

"You guess right. Miguel knew the layout and the possible hazards. A successful mission requires that you think of all the angles and have as much information as possible." He nodded in genuine appreciation of Ben's honesty. "You'll make a good mission commander someday."

As he pulled into their driveway, he glimpsed Ben staring thoughtfully out the window. They walked up the sidewalk together, and he couldn't keep from ruffling Ben's hair.

"But don't think you're getting off easy, kiddo. You disobeyed a direct order, and that means you've got KP duty for the next two weeks."

CHAPTER FIFTEEN

KATE TRIED NOT to watch the clock, but by 8:30 p.m. she was mentally bracing for disappointment or worse. When the phone rang at nine o'clock, she made herself take time answering.

"I wasn't sure you'd call," she said in spite of herself. "I thought you probably were furious with me."

"I was," he responded, "for about ten minutes. Fortunately, you took another hour and a half to get back. I had time to think."

"Uh-oh." She tried for a lighter tone. "What about?"

"About Ben and me, and you and Ben, and you and me."

"That's a lot of thinking." She made herself breathe. "Want to tell me how it went?"

He told her all of it: Ben acting so adult but also acting like a kid, wanting her approval, and wanting to be like his dad. Every statement sounded like true insight and, taken together, like a solid foundation for a father who understood and had dealt compassionately with his son.

"So, being a kid is complicated, huh?" she said, hoping the smile in her voice survived being bounced from cell tower to cell tower.

"I guess. I don't remember it being this tough when I was a kid."

"It probably was, but you didn't see it. Ask your mom." When he rumbled with what sounded like a laugh, she continued. "Does that mean he's not on restriction until he's eighteen?"

"I forgot you know military lingo." She could hear a smile in his voice and imagined a glint in his eye. "KP for two weeks. Garbage runs, compost runs and he has to scrub down the cans and recycle bins."

"That's not so bad."

"He's suffering, believe me. We've postponed all talk of getting a dog for a while."

"Ouch." They both paused, though it didn't seem strained. "Now, what about the you-and-me part of the thinking?"

"That I'd rather say in person. You up for some company?"

"I am." She tried not to sound too eager. "But you have to give me a few minutes to get all the snakes and tarantulas back in their cages."

He either coughed or laughed; she couldn't tell which. "I'll be there in fifteen—make that twenty-five. I have to shower."

She stood looking at the phone after they'd hung up. Shower? Did guys shower right before they ditched someone? *Not likely.*

He arrived promptly after twenty-five minutes, elapsed time. She opened the door and felt a tingle of excitement at the sight of him in jeans and a polo shirt that made his hazel eyes look almost green. Hints of soap and shaving lotion teased her nose as he stepped inside. The minute the door closed she stepped back and clasped her hands to keep them from trembling. She offered him something to drink but he declined, so she led him over to the sofa, where he perched on the edge.

"So, what did you want to talk about?" She struggled for composure.

"Us. You and me. I've done some thinking. And no, I didn't strain anything." He cracked a brief smile, looking like he was preparing for something momentous.

"I like you, Kate." He ran his hands up and down his thighs. "A lot. And I want you to know it. You're up front about things. No games. At least none I can detect."

"Smart guy. I like to keep things simple. The curves life throws at us makes the geometry complicated enough. Why add to it?"

He relaxed noticeably and slid back on the sofa.

"You know, I was pretty good at geometry. It was one of my favorite subjects. If they'd had it in college, I'd have been a four-pointer."

She laughed and felt some of the tension drain away.

"That's another thing I like about you—your laugh."

"Oooh, you've made a list. And some of it's personal."

"It's all personal—about as personal as it gets. I find myself thinking about you on the road, after a traffic stop, in the station house, in the damned shower…"

Her eyes widened at that, and whatever

was wrapped around her stomach suddenly released it.

"Now we're getting somewhere." She edged closer so that their knees touched. "Fair warning, I have my own list."

"You do?" His whole countenance brightened.

"Your eyes. Did you know they change color with everything you wear? And I'm starting to be able to read what's happening in them."

"That's a good thing?" He looked down at her fidgeting hands.

"Maybe not in law enforcement, when you're grilling a suspect, but when you're beside someone you're involved with—"

Every muscle in his body had just gone on alert. She read the importance of that reaction in every line and sinew of his frame.

"Is that what we are? Involved?" he asked.

She fought a potent urge to grab him and kiss him witless. The man was so controlled, so measured, so damned rational…it was making her crazy.

"Let's see what the evidence shows," she said, making a point of her patience as she counted it up on her fingers. "You think about me a lot, I think about you a lot. You like kissing me, I like kissing you back. You like being with me, I like having you around. You find me attractive—I hope— and I think you're downright yummy. I could have you for dessert. The way your shoulders move in that uniform shirt practically drops me to my knees." He looked a little stunned—either that or amazed.

Her face blanked. "Did I just say that out loud?"

It was hard to tell which when he didn't say anything for what seemed forever. When he did speak, his voice had dropped an octave.

"I'm gonna wear that shirt every day for the rest of my life."

It took her a minute to translate that.

"So you don't mind being the subject of my fevered daydreams?"

"Uh, that would be *no*." His grin was adorably lopsided, and in that moment, she glimpsed the boy he had been. His expression was the embodiment of wonder, the joy of unexpected discovery.

It amazed her. He acted as if he were surprised that she might want him. Did he honestly not know how utterly male and devastatingly sexy he was?

When he reached for her hands, there was such hope in his face that she felt her heart skip. It was only then that she realized how important what was happening between them was to him.

"I'm head over heels for you, Nick Stanton. You don't have to say anything back— you just have to know that I'm here and I care very much for you."

He looked down at her hands, cradled in his, and stroked her skin with his thumbs.

"I've never met anybody like you, Kate. You amaze me. You're good and kind-hearted, you're smart and educated and funny. I've smiled and laughed more since I met you than I have in years." He paused, glanced at her and then back at their joined hands. She shifted one of her hands to stroke his. He watched for a moment.

"I've had a lot to deal with in these last few years. Cashing out. Iraq and Afghanistan. Combat. Trying to be a dad after Ben's mother left. I still have some stuff to figure out and other stuff to put behind me. I'm no prize, but I'm making progress."

"So I've seen. Even with dogs. Enough that you might reconsider getting Ben a dog?" She knew she was pushing, but couldn't help teasing him. "Or a puppy?" Something dark flitted through his expression and she realized she had said the wrong thing. Dang it!

"The puppy thing. I'm sorry, Nick. I don't understand, but I want to." She had to shoot straight about this, too. Because of her work, her life, this was going to come up again and again. "Help me understand so we don't have to tiptoe around this."

"I really don't want to talk about it—not when…"

NICK LOOKED INTO her warm, open expression and realized it might be the best time, the only time for him to talk about it. If they were going to continue seeing each other and getting more involved, it would come out sooner or later. And if she thought it was dumb or as crazy as it sometimes sounded to him—a badass ground pounder's PTSD focused on dogs and *puppies*—he should know it now. He held her hands tightly and braced himself.

"It was Iraq. Our camp was just outside the old city walls, and we were running daily patrols through unsecured areas of the city. Relations with the locals were tense, and we were told to keep a low profile— no loud music, no drinking and no fraternizing. We were going stir-crazy until we found a dog and her newborn puppies hiding in a stack of old wooden supply crates at the edge of camp.

"My guys adopted the brood—saw to it they had food and water and a safe place to sleep. Then one day the mother dog disappeared. Dogs don't have the same place over there as they do in our culture, so who knows what happened to her. Before that, she would sometimes leave the puppies for a while, but this time she didn't come back, and we figured she'd gotten run over or even shot while running the streets.

"After that, my guys fostered the pups… shared rations with them, leash-trained them and took them on patrols riding in their gear pockets. The pups became a bit of normal in a foreign and hostile environment. They were something personal to care for and protect. Looking back, they came to mean too much to us. It was like we blocked out the hatred, threats and violence around us when they were with us."

"That makes total sense," she said with a sympathy that brought a lump to his throat. "Dogs are so connected to us humans. They can touch us in ways even other humans can't."

"Yeah, well, I probably should have stopped it before it went so far. But the little things were so cute, and morale improved. They became our mascots, our buddies... watching them chase and growl at tennis balls, and sleep sprawled on their backs or curled into balls was our entertainment. They ate with us, slept with us, went on patrols with us, and in the end, helped us salvage our humanity."

His gut tightened as he descended into still more potent and disturbing memories. These were things he had never told another living soul—not even the army shrink who debriefed him at the end and diagnosed him with what he called a mild form of PTSD.

"What were their names?" she asked. That simple inquiry helped anchor him more in the present.

"Baby, Mad Max, Einstein, Bono, Slick and Lady Gaga." He rubbed his eyes as he recounted the names, wishing he could rub what came next from his memory. "Things got tense in the city as the insurgents got reinforced, and one day when we rolled out of our barracks at dawn, we found Max hanging from the rope of the flagpole in the middle of camp—tied up there for us to see. He had been choked to death...but not before he had been...abused."

He was gripping her hands hard, but she met that pressure with her own hold on his. She was in this with him, that contact said.

"I'm here," she said softly. "Stay with me."

He took a deep breath and nodded.

"One of the worst parts was— It had to be somebody we knew, somebody who brought us information or came to our camp to get help from our medics for their children and old people. Somebody knew how much those pups meant to us and sent us a message in a way that would really hurt. It was then we realized we couldn't trust anybody, not even those we were trying to help.

It was a pretty damned hard thing for my guys to accept."

He wondered if she could feel his hands starting to tremble. She must have, because she squeezed them tightly and resettled herself closer.

"I've never seen men so sick and despondent." His mouth dried and his voice grew husky. "The guy who fostered that pup went a little nuts—grabbed his gun and started for the nearest city street. It took four of us to take him down. We talked the captain into putting him on sick report for a few days to get him out of the area and give him time to come to his senses. After that we kept the remaining pups close. They were never out of our sight, and we watched everyone who came into camp.

"Then word came down that we were pulling out, and the captain emphasized that there would be no room on the trucks for 'livestock.' We continued to hope until we were told in no uncertain terms that our dogs would not be going with us. The guys were furious at first, and then frantic. But we had no idea where we were going or what conditions we would find.

"The day we left, I had to make the choice—between my orders and my guys, between the dogs we'd come to love...and my duty. It broke my heart. I had to physically shove several of the guys onto the truck.

"The dogs were trying to jump up onto the truck to be with us. When the convoy started to move, the dogs grew frantic and came running after us. It was chaos. Some of the men tried to jump off the truck, others tried to hold the guys on. They were shouting at each other and cursing—then we heard a shot and one of the dogs fell. Then another. And another. The bastards were waiting on rooftops and in alleys, watching us go and taking the chance to hurt us one last time. We could hear the dogs yelp as they got hit and see them struggle to get up before they took more bullets."

Tears welled in his eyes, and Kate released his hands to put both arms around him.

"My men pulled out guns and tried to spot the shooters." He halted between sentences...reliving every moment...every revelation costing a payment in pain. "In the end, Baby was the only one left running— she just wouldn't give up. And Jimmy Nicks, who had fostered Baby, picked up his rifle and sighted Baby's heart…and put a bullet in her." Tears slid down his face and he looked away, barely able to hold back a sob. "He loved her too much to let her suffer or be shot to a bloody pulp."

"Oh, Nick." She pulled his face around to hers, and she had tears running down her cheeks, too. "My God, Nick. I'm sorry. So very sorry."

He wrapped his arms around her, pulled her onto his lap and buried his face in her shoulder. The weight that had lain on his heart for five years seemed lighter as he held her against him. The pain wasn't gone—it might never be—but it was not as sharp or as crippling as before.

He held Kate close as the emotion began to drain away. People usually saw him as big and strong and even impervious. But Kate looked deeper, saw the pain he suffered from things he had experienced half a world away. He hadn't been blown up or lost a limb or an eye, but he carried internal damage…like a lot of vets from a lot of wars.

She stroked his hair and kissed the side of his face.

"'Give sorrow words,' the Bard said," she murmured into his ear. "Each time you talk about it, you peel back another layer of hurt and loss and your burden gets a little lighter. Anytime you want to talk, Nick, I'll be here to listen. I know how being military separates you from ordinary life and can make you feel like an outsider in your own home, among your own people."

They sank back on the cushions holding each other, sometimes talking, sometimes just savoring the closeness and deepening connection between them. He spoke about cashing out and about his decision to join the FHP. She told him about her life with her parents before their breakup, and about living in other countries…events and experiences that meant she could understand how he felt.

It was late when they went to the kitchen to get something to drink. He put his arms around her waist as she poured soda into glasses of ice.

"You are an amazing woman, Kate Everly," he murmured into her hair. She melted back against him, loving the feel of him against her and around her and sensing that he felt the same pleasure.

"Hasn't anybody ever told you that 'amazing' is in the eye of the beholder?" She laughed quietly and turned in his arms. "I think you're pretty amazing yourself."

"After all I said?"

"After that and a whole lot more." She ran her hands up his chest to circle his neck.

"I promise you, I'll try my best to be good to you and good for you. I want you in my life." He took a deep breath. "And I don't want to screw it up. I want to take it slow and easy. I want you to trust me and feel like it's right...every step of the way."

"I get it," she said, placing her hands on the sides of his face.

He looked up.

"That's what I want, too, Nick. I want what is between us to grow and become something—no, not just good, I want it to be *spectacular*. And it will be." She tilted her head, her lips parting to meet his. "Because it already is."

CHAPTER SIXTEEN

THE STATION WAS busy Friday evening when Nick arrived for a late shift, feeling like he was seeing everything fresh. The previous night with Kate had cleared some of the haze of guilt and uncertainty he'd been living in for the past five years. He had a direction now, and a connection that could form a life-giving bond with a woman he both wanted and respected. There was an ease in his gait because he felt more comfortable in his own skin.

Fellow troopers Perez and Harlow looked up when he strolled into the briefing room. They were doing their coffee thing and studying the dailies, so he grabbed a cup of brew and slid into a seat beside them. The rest of the shift filed in behind him.

"What's new?" Nick asked.

"Dogfighting. North and east, around the

Hardee County line. Combs found a couple of dogs on the side of County 42," Perez said.

"Carcasses, really," Harlow added. "Slashed up pretty bad. Just tossed out—dumped by the road like a heap of trash."

"Bastards," Nick growled. Why was it always *dogs*? "I'd love to get those jerks in my sights."

"You might get your chance, Stanton." Watch Commander Garrity strode into the room with a clipboard to begin the briefing. "Hardee County's sheriff called. He's shorthanded and asking us to back him up on this dogfighting business, so stay loose and alert. And if you are called in, remember, they're taking the lead.

"Meanwhile, we've got hot cars coming down I-75 and a couple of BOLOs from Tampa for escaped prisoners—one may have stolen a car—thought to be headed south…check your sheets." He handed out paperwork with mug shots for the BOLOs and a list of high-end cars that were missing. "So, basically, business as usual."

As they headed to their cruisers, Perez elbowed Nick and grinned. "Hey, if we find those dogs, maybe you can call your hot veterinarian friend in to help." But if he was hoping for an embarrassed reaction, he'd been mistaken.

"Yeah." Nick gave him a wicked grin. "I just might do that."

MOUNTING A PUPPY MILL raid was a little like planning a military invasion, Kate thought as she watched the troops assemble in Saturday's predawn hours to check equipment and discuss strategy. They had chosen to go in early, when they believed they could expect less resistance. Voices were tight with tension as the staff and volunteers greeted each other and colored armbands were passed out to assign people to duties. They had no idea how many animals they might have to deal with, but from the pictures they estimated more than sixty.

The previous day, a local judge who was friendly to the Manatee County Humane Society—his wife was on the board—had viewed their evidence and issued a warrant. Then he'd called a friend in Hardee County, next door, and gotten a judge there to do the same, since the farm looked like it straddled county lines. The Humane Society staff had called the Hardee County Sheriff's Office to ask for deputies to serve the warrant, and Isabelle and Nance had spent the rest of the day making calls to volunteers. They also arranged kennel space with other organizations, plus fostering for animals that might be in good enough condition.

Kate and Jess had been at the shelter since before five. They'd agreed to evaluate and triage the seized animals. They'd had Lee-Ann reschedule appointments, packed up plenty of supplies and loaded the back of Kate's Jeep with equipment.

Kate had tried to call Nick to tell him what was happening, but she knew he was on patrol and probably not available. She left a cheery voice message that was short on details. Jess heard her make the call and fixed her with an indignant look.

"Reporting in to each other already?" she said, crossing her arms over her white coat. "I can't believe you've let things get this far without letting me thoroughly *vet* this guy. I mean, he could be...a..."

"Great guy?" Kate gave her a sly smile. "He is. And he's a state trooper, so he's already been vetted. By the state of Florida."

She looked over to see the first cars pulling out onto the darkened road. "Time to go."

They climbed into the Jeep, and Jess found a rock station on the radio with hard driving music that seemed in keeping with the occasion. Kate pulled out behind one of the vans, and soon they were speeding through the surrendering darkness, heading north and east. The line of vehicles stopped twice, the first time to check directions and the second to pick up their Hardee County Sheriff escort.

A lone patrol car sat at a crossroad with his light flashing, waiting for them. A deputy got out, and, with a flashlight, showed Isabelle, Nance and Liza Pacheco, the Humane Society president, the warrants they needed to serve. Jess glanced at Kate, and in the dim light from the dashboard, Jess looked a little green.

"It's really happening," she said, her voice constricted.

"Yep."

"You anxious?" Jess was clearly feeling a few nerves herself.

"A bit." Kate had to be honest. "But once the action starts, it all becomes real and nothing matters but the work." Her smile felt tight. "You'll be fine." She gave Jess's hand a squeeze. "Just think of the dogs."

"Yeah. The dogs." Jess leaned her head back on the headrest and took a heavy breath.

Dawn provided enough light to recognize the farmstead beneath its ragged canopy of trees. The deputy threaded his car through the overgrown driveway and inched his way toward the house, his progress made visible by his headlights. Nance, in the lead truck, drove past the property, where she then made a Y-turn and drove back to park on the side of the road nearest the house. About half of the other vehicles followed her lead, parking behind each other, and the other half—Kate included—parked on the side of the road across from them. A few of the volunteers left their cars so they could stand where they had a better view of the proceedings.

Kate slipped forward, making her way through the scrub vegetation to stoop on the slope below the cabin. Jess joined her and together they watched the deputy approach the house on foot. His body was bent as if to make it a smaller target, and even from a distance he seemed to be quaking in his boots.

"That's all we get? Barney Fife over there?" Jess exchanged dubious looks with Kate. "What if the old lady decides she doesn't want to hand over her dogs?"

Kate shrugged. Then one corner of her mouth drew up in a half smile. "We could always sic Gran on her."

The deputy circled to the front of the house and worked his way through the yard to the sagging porch. The sound of his knock carried a long way in the still morning air. They waited and watched.

Then the door was flung open and out came the double barrel of a shotgun, which sent the deputy scrambling back off the porch in an undignified retreat. An old woman appeared behind the gun, filling the doorway with a mixture of absurdity and danger. She wore a ratty bathrobe and no shoes, her white hair stuck up all over, and her mouth was sunken—missing teeth.

"Get outta here!" she yelled, brandishing the shotgun and looking for all the world as if she meant to use it. "Off my porch… stinkin'…Nazi!"

They heard the deputy say something about "Hardee County" and "Mrs. Crowder" and hold out the warrant. The gun waved wildly and went off with a boom.

Cries of surprise and horror came from the volunteers and most of them—even those still in cars—ducked for cover. The deputy rushed to his cruiser, backed it frantically around to point his engine for the driveway and gunned it back to the road. The cruiser screeched to a stop across the road, blocking it, and the deputy lurched out while gripping his radio and blurting out, "Backup. I need backup! Shots fired at the Crowder farm in northwest Hardee!"

NICK GOT THE call he dreaded just as he was heading back to the station for reports. It had been a fairly routine shift, where just his presence in the flow of traffic was enough to turn most motorists into model citizens. Now he was stuck with the Hardee County backup action he had hoped to avoid. The universe seemed hell-bent on driving home a point with this dog thing, but he didn't have a damned clue what it was. He had just entered the coordinates into his GPS navigation system when a second message came across the radio, one that jacked up the seriousness of the situation: "Shots fired."

He flipped on his light bar and hit the gas.

He spent half the fifteen-minute ride airborne, and the other half being slammed against his seat as his cruiser bottomed out on the storm-rutted back roads. He tried to prepare himself for what he'd find: suspects pinned down and trying to cover an escape by shooting at outnumbered deputies…dogs caged in filthy vans…run-down RVs and makeshift tents…garbage strewed around…

He came across the last rise and hit with a thump that jarred his vision of the wooded area he was entering. Something was across the road ahead, and he glanced at his GPS to find he was almost at his destination. The "something" was a white car with a green "sheriff" strip and a light bar. As he closed in, he spotted other cars beyond the Hardee County cruiser. He scowled. Dispatch had said nothing about civilians being present. In the center of the road between the rows of cars stood a uniformed deputy and a knot of people who seemed to be intent on getting some message across.

They spotted his cruiser and lights, and pointed. A second later, the deputy was running toward him. Nick looked around for other county cars and found none. Where the hell were the rest of the Hardee County deputies? They were taking on a dogfighting ring with a single deputy and a bunch of civilians?

"Thank God you're here." The deputy— "Krum" by his nameplate—halted by the car as Nick stepped out and put on his hat. "The old woman's crazy as a bat, and that bunch—" he pointed at the group huddled in the road some distance away "—isn't much better. They're ready to storm the old lady's house and she's already fired once—at *me*." He nervously tugged on his service belt. "Damn near got me."

"Where are the rest of your guys?" Nick asked, searching the motley collection of vehicles in confusion, until the sense of it struck. "What old woman?" He did a double take to focus on a Jeep he recognized.

Oh, hell, no!

He half heard the deputy's explanation of

his attempt to serve a warrant; he was busy picking out an all-too-familiar pickup truck and a couple of figures in the group now watching him. This wasn't a dogfighting takedown, this was a puppy mill raid. His stomach felt like it deflated and slid south in his gut.

KATE KNEW THE minute he stepped out of the cruiser that Nick was not going to be happy about this. Of all the troopers to send to help out on a puppy mill raid, why did they have to send him? She was in motion before she had a clue what she was going to say. His face darkened as he left the sputtering Deputy Barney—that really was his name, Barney Krum—and headed straight for her.

"I'm sorry it's you, Nick," she said as they met. She wanted to reach for his hands but wasn't certain if that would be wise, considering he was here in a professional capacity, and she could guess he would rather be anywhere else in the world right now. "We had no idea the old woman was so combative—"

"Or so well armed," Nance said as she came up behind Kate with several others at her back. "Glad it's you, Nick. We can sure use your steady hand here. This is Chet and Jamie Dunlap." She gestured to a middle-aged couple wearing jeans and farm boots. "They live back down the road, saw the flashing lights as we passed and came over to see what was happening. Tell him what you told us, Chet."

Dunlap, a barrel-chested citrus farmer with thirty-years of sun damage on his face, nodded and gave Nick an earful.

"The old woman's been gettin' worse for years. But she used to be a crack shot back in the day, and she does love them guns of hers. She's got a mess of dogs in there. Used to breed good pups, but now, who knows? You can hear dogs barkin' day and night… clear down to our place when the wind is right."

"She lives there by herself? Anyone else around?" Nick asked, flicking looks at Kate and Nance.

"No," Jamie said, staring up at Nick. "She's been alone for some time. Except for that nephew of hers. Jerry something— I don't know if he's a Crowder. He comes around once a month when she gets her social security money. He was supposed to help out around the place, but he hasn't turned a hand in years. The place is fallin' apart. God knows what state those poor dogs are in."

"Has she ever shot at anyone before?" Nick asked, frowning at the picture they painted.

"Don't think so," Chet said. "But there's a first time for everything."

Kate watched Nick's jaw harden and his hands ball into fists as he assessed the situation. She wished with all her heart he hadn't been the one dispatched here. The conditions they'd encounter and the tragedy they'd uncover could prove worse for him than anyone else in the rescue crew. He felt things more deeply where dogs were concerned. From the signs, it was going to be a heartbreaking afternoon all around.

As if someone flipped a switch in him, he was suddenly in motion, heading for the driveway. "Stay here," he told Kate when she tried to follow, "and keep these people back. Krum, you call for some EMTs and tell them to make it fast. You'll need to go and meet them and lead them in here. Make sure they know it's a psych situation—no sirens—and tell them we may need to *Baker Act* someone."

He was in control as he strode up the weedy drive; Kate could see it in the set of his shoulders. Something in her chest swelled painfully as she watched him do what he seemed born to do: look danger in the eye without blinking.

If anyone could talk to her, he could.

CHAPTER SEVENTEEN

NICK STRODE INTO the weedy mess that had once been a front yard and paused to remove his hat, service belt and the sunglasses that were hanging from his pocket. He laid them on the ground and then removed his service piece from its holster and tucked it into his waistband against his back. Taking a steadying breath, he headed for the front door, which opened the minute he came in the old woman's sights.

The warped and peeling door slammed back against an interior wall and a disheveled old woman appeared in the opening. A shotgun hung loosely in her hands, and her red-rimmed eyes were wide and full of fear.

"Get off my land!" she shouted, lifting the gun and pointing it in Nick's vicinity. "B'fore I blast yer head off!"

Nick stopped ten feet from the porch and

opened his hands out at his sides so she could see he wasn't hiding anything.

"Miz Crowder? Miz Clara Crowder?"

The sound of her name, spoken so forcefully, flustered her for a moment. She lifted her feet, one after the other, and her mouth worked oddly, as if she had trouble speaking. "I'm—I'm Clara. I'm Clara…Crowder. Who're you?"

"I want to help you, Miz Crowder," he said, watching her furrowed face and age-yellowed eyes as she struggled to make sense of what was happening. "I'm Nick Stanton. Your neighbors are concerned about you and wanted me to come and check to see that you're all right."

"I got no—neighbuhhh—" She seemed to run out of energy for the word, paused, then raised the gun and her voice. "Go. You get off…get away. It's my land. My place." She swept the gun barrels to the side. "I'll blast yer head…clean off!"

The shouting must have taken most of her energy; the gun drooped again in her hands. Nick considered rushing her, but mere seconds later she was back in combat mode, and he was glad he had hesitated.

He could see her drawing on her thin re-
serves as she forced herself to defend her
property.

"I'll go, Miz Crowder," he said, raising his
hands in a gesture of surrender. "But before
I do—you hear that?"

Again the gun came up.

"Hear what?" She was trying to yell, but
it now came out strained and hoarse.

"The dogs, Miz Crowder. Can't you hear
your dogs barking?"

"Stupid things—bark all the time. Nothin'
wrong with that."

"I think there is, Miz Crowder. I think
some of them are in trouble and they need
help. They need care." He paused to see how
she was taking that and was encouraged by
the way the gun lowered an inch.

"That's what these people came to do—"
he waved toward the cars visible through the
brush and the people standing behind them
"—to help you with your dogs."

"My dogs!" she shouted, though it came
out with less force than before. "They're my
dogs."

"I don't want your dogs, Miz Crowder."
His voice softened as he tried to lull her,

every word carrying the weight of truth. "I just want to help you. I can see you need help. And I know you're exhausted, I can see it. How long has it been since you had a good hot meal with a piece of pie and a cup of coffee? You must get so tired, taking care of everything by yourself. Your nephew— Jerry, is it? He's supposed to help you, but he doesn't, does he? He just comes and gets money and goes away again."

"Jer-ry? Where's Jerry?" She looked confused, and the gun barrel lowered. "He was here... Jer-ry was. With that boy."

"You need care, Miz Crowder." He began to inch closer, speaking in the same even, reassuring cadence. "You need someone to take care of you and see that you get food and a bath and clean clothes." He was near the porch now, and the old woman was no longer paying attention to his approach. She was just staring off into space, letting the gun droop in her gnarled, arthritic hands. It was amazing that she could hold the thing, much less pull the trigger.

"Let me help you, Miz Clara." He reverted to the local custom of calling ladies by a first name honorific. "Let me help take care of things for you." He was on the porch now, but instead of reaching for the gun, he moved steadily toward the open door. "How about if I get you a chair to sit on?" When she just stood there, shoulders rounded in confusion, he stepped into the house and was hit powerfully with odors of urine, feces and human decay. Holding his breath, fighting the urge to retch, he grabbed the first chair he saw and carried it out onto the porch.

"You're so tired, Miz Clara. You need to sit down." He took her by the elbow, and she allowed herself to be guided to the chair. In the process, he slipped the gun from her hand and held it up for the others to see as he took a breath of relief and fresh air. A cheer went up from the direction of the road.

KATE WAS FIRST to reach them—she ran the rest of the way through the brush and onto the porch, her eyes wet and heart full. She had crept from the road toward the house and heard nearly every word they'd exchanged. The courage and compassion he showed filled her with an eruption of love she couldn't contain. He looked at her across the old woman's nodding head, and she said, "You're amazing, Nick Stanton."

His face softened only slightly, but in his eyes she read the warm, heartfelt response she needed.

THE AMBULANCE ARRIVED QUICKLY, but without the sirens that could have frightened old Mrs. Crowder. Kate and Nance had found a blanket for her and gotten her some warm cocoa that one of the volunteers had packed. She seemed to have retreated into her memories and was barely responsive when the EMTs asked her routine questions. They gave her a quick evaluation and then a light sedative, then put her on a gurney and phoned in an approach to the nearest hospital.

The sun was well up when the ambulance left. Nance and Isabelle gave the signal for the volunteers to suit up in their protective gear, then gathered them for a few last instructions before going in. Meanwhile, Deputy Krum and Nick checked the premises to be sure no one else was around before letting the rescue begin. The place seemed deserted—except for the rows and stacks of cages and pens containing dogs in every heartbreaking condition possible.

Nick was stone-faced when he came back down the road to the group, who were now dressed in disposable white coveralls. He nodded to Nance, who called, "All right, people. Let's go in and get 'em."

A small forward group went in with clipboards and cameras to document the number and condition of the animals. Behind them went a group carrying travel crates of various sizes, blankets and towels, and bottles of water. Nick watched their determined expressions, knowing from what he had glimpsed earlier that some would be in tears before the morning was out.

And when a young voice called, "Dad!" he whirled just in time to meet Ben's tackling hug full-on. He hadn't recovered from that shock when he got an even greater one. His mom came up beside Ben with her arms open and her eyes moist.

"What the hell are you—"

She threw her arms around him and hugged with all her might…which blunted his prickly response. He set her back with a scowl. "You brought him here? What the hell were you thinking?"

"Don't give me that look," she answered

with a fierce expression. "Nance called to tell us about the rescue and ask if we'd like to donate or to foster one of the animals. Ben begged to come—he wants to help and so do I—so we volunteered. And before you get all indignant or outraged, he and I are staying down here with the vans. They need people to calm the animals and hold them while they get used to being out of the cages. That's our job—the holding and reassuring. Ben will be by my side the whole time, and we won't be going anywhere near the rough stuff."

Nick could see by the spark in her eyes that she was determined to do this. He looked down at Ben, who sensed his dad had just been trumped the way only a grandmother could.

"You were great, Dad." He grinned. "The way you talked that old lady into giving up her gun…you're the bravest trooper in the FHP." His face grew impish. "And you just said the H word *twice*."

Nick expelled a breath of frustration. Determination and adoration were a tough combination to overcome. He looked up to catch Kate and another white-coated woman struggling with a couple of folding tables and boxes of supplies. He surrendered with a nod to his mom, who hugged him tightly. "Your son is right, you know. You are the best."

"The best what?" he asked, his mind and heart both elsewhere.

He saw his mom smile when she saw who had captured his gaze.

"The best *everything*." She pointed to Kate and gave him a push. "Ask her."

He ran after Kate and quickly caught up with her.

"Let me." He pried a table from her hands and carried it up the drive to the examination station they were setting up in the gravel yard equidistant from the house, barn and pens. When he looked up, he found the other woman, a tall, lanky brunette, staring at him.

"You're the trooper. The one who brought that pair of dogs in," she said.

"I guess I should get used to that designation."

Kate watched their encounter and smiled at Nick's confusion.

"Nick, meet my partner, Jessica Preston."

She gestured between them. "Jess, meet Nick Stanton...rescuer of dogs, apprehender of highway evil-doers and more importantly, a very special someone."

Jess stuck out her hand to him. "We meet at last," she said with a twinkle in her eye.

At that moment, their first patient appeared, a small, towel-wrapped creature cradled in Linda Hoskins's arms. The volunteer's eyes were wide, and she looked a little pale.

"I know you're not ready yet, but—" her voice cracked "—I just had to get this little thing out of there."

It was going to be a tough day for a lot of them, Nick thought as he saw Kate wince when she took the bundle from Linda. He realized it would take a toll on her, too. Despite her philosophy of acceptance and her soothing, rational pronouncements, she was deeply affected by this cruelty to animals she had dedicated her life to helping.

He seized plastic drapes from the box and spread them over the two tables, then took the scale from Jess to stack on one end. "You just take care of them." He fished nitrile gloves out of the boxes for her and Jess, and then nodded toward the puppy. "I'll see to the rest."

The first heart-blow of the day came moments later when Kate peeled the toweling from the animal and discovered it wasn't a puppy at all. It was tiny dog that was mostly skin and bones and teats. "She's given birth recently." She looked to Linda. "Was she with puppies?"

Linda shook her head and began to stroke the trembling dog. Kate looked around, swallowed her reaction, then went immediately to work...weighing the dog, attaching a plastic collar for identification and noting on her paper record, "Seven pounds. Severely malnourished and undersized. Whelped recently, but no sign of puppies."

Kate had Jess position and hold the frail little dog as she examined teeth and ears and palpated the abdomen. The dog's small head looked like a miniature adult's except for the big dark eyes, which were too large and too lifeless to be normal. The little female lay back in Jess's hands, trembling, but resigned to whatever fate they decreed for her.

"So, this is what it's like," Jess murmured to Kate, who nodded somberly. Before five minutes were up, Jess had a patient of her own to evaluate. Then another. And another.

The story became all too familiar: the dogs were females—mostly miniature schnauzers and what looked like poodles or poodle crosses—all of which were underweight, filthy and full of worms. Most showed evidence of having given birth and were missing fur where they had lain on the chicken wire of cages for much of their lives. Their feet showed evidence of old cuts that had gone untreated. The few males were a little better off from not having had to share their meager nourishment with unborn puppies.

"I was kind of feeling sorry for the old girl when they carried her off," Jess said angrily, tears rimming her eyes as she straightened from listening to a little heart that would never beat again. "But after seeing this, I'd flip the switch on her final cocktail myself."

NICK WATCHED THAT first dog with silent horror…the frail little body and crumpled rear quarters that hadn't had room to move and develop proper musculature. It was as small as a puppy but with more mature features.

The listless, pain-filled eyes were what finally made him bolt from the tables. He found himself on the driveway moments later and paused to get his bearings before heading to Kate's Jeep to fetch more supplies. There was now a line at the exam tables, and the waiting volunteers were using bottled water to clean the animals so they could be examined.

Nick deposited the supplies, tried not to look at the animals too closely and strode off in search of Deputy Krum. He found the kid leaning on a post by a stretch of downed fence at the rear of the property. From the smell, he figured Barney's breakfast lay on the ground nearby.

"It's terrible," the deputy said. "I never imagined... Right under our noses..."

"Any idea how many dogs we're talking about?" Nick turned his face into the humid breeze to avoid the smell of sickness.

"I heard them say more than sixty," Barney said, wincing at the taste in his mouth. He spit into the bushes. "Didn't stick around after that to hear more."

"Well, we need to look around, maybe take a few pictures." He glanced back over his shoulder at the barn and sheds, and braced himself. "We ought to find out the extent of the operation. The shape the old woman was in… I can't believe she could keep track of this many animals, much less feed or try to sell them. And who would buy them—so filthy and unhealthy?" He gave Barney a thump on the shoulder. "I want to see if there's any sign of that nephew of hers."

Barney grabbed his camera from a nearby stump, and they walked the perimeter. The puppy operation didn't seem to cover a large acreage. All around it, native trees and palmettos grew in tangled masses of shrunken, moss-laden branches. They swatted at mosquitos disturbed by their movement along what appeared to be a path running by the line of rotting fence posts and rusty wire.

At one of the corners of the property, they spotted what seemed to be another path heading back through the trees and undergrowth, beyond the fence line. Trampled vegetation, mostly. "Hard to say if it's related. Take a shot of it and let's finish the perimeter first," Nick advised.

Barney took a photo for future reference,

and they continued fighting their way along the path. There was something oppressive in the air—a heavy, damp scent of decay that probably came from some swampy areas they passed, repugnant enough to make them want to hurry this reconnaissance along.

At the far corner, they were stopped by the sight of animal bones in a clear space on the far side of the fence. The bones seemed fairly new but had been picked clean. Nick strained through the fence to retrieve a skull while Barney worked to keep his stomach in place.

"You smell that?" Barney caught a scent on the air, grimaced and jerked his chin back.

"A dog," Nick said, head down, absorbed in examining the skull. "But a bigger dog. Not like any of the little guys they're rescuing. Look how broad the head was." He recalled what Perez and Harlow had said about finding carcasses dumped beside a road. "There could be a connection between this place and the dogfighting ring."

"Anybody who would keep dogs like that," Barney choked out, going a little green, "wouldn't blink at making them fight." He swayed slightly and grabbed his stomach.

After Barney was sick again, Nick steered him down the path, away from the bones and whatever had unsettled his stomach again. While the deputy rested, propped against a tree, Nick took the camera to get photos of the remains. He caught some of the same scent that had sickened Barney. God, it was terrible—revolting—then the air lifted and it faded. When he returned, he had to sit a few minutes to let his own stomach settle.

"It's not just you, buddy. There's something bad out there," he said, staring off into the mass of vegetation.

He'd heard terrible stories from veteran troopers who had been in the patrol for years. Were the fight operators just taking advantage of the old woman's dementia to use her land? Or did somebody associated with this puppy mill participate in the fighting operation?

"Wish I had some VapoRub," he muttered, covering his nose. "I have a feeling I'll be smelling this place for weeks."

"I've got some in my cruiser," Barney said

with a wan smile. "Out on these backwoods roads, you never know when you'll come across a nasty smell and I—I kind of have a touchy stomach."

They finished their perimeter search near the house, applied VapoRub, then took flashlights and pry bars with them to investigate some of the padlocked doors on the ramshackle sheds. Inside, they found chains, crates for transporting dogs, crude spiked collars of various sizes, and dog-sized harnesses and cruel-looking muzzles. It was hard to believe the old lady might have had a use for such things in a puppy breeding operation.

"We need to get some evidence guys out here," Nick said as they stood looking at the house, remembering the smell and dreading entering. "Looks to me like this whole place is a crime scene." Barney nodded, and they headed for their cruisers.

Nick tried not to stare at the dogs in the pens as he passed. But even a cursory glance showed all were malnourished, and some were covered with scratches and unhealed sores. They barked and snapped at each other as they crowded the sides of the pen whenever a human came close. Humans approaching meant food, and they had to compete for whatever meager fare was provided. He halted after he passed by one pen, closed his eyes and tamped down harrowing memories and fierce emotions that threatened to disable him.

KATE WAS SWAMPED. Triaging such a large group of animals was like that. Able to be rehabilitated or permanently disabled? Contagious or noncommunicable? Savable or too damaged to allow to suffer more? She had seen it all before and worked diligently through the heartrending rubrics created to help make medical decisions possible under extreme circumstances. Then she came to some listless puppies that were barely breathing and probably hadn't been fed in a while. No mother was tending them; she probably had ended up in the ash- and bone-laden steel drum that served as a crematorium on the property.

"Come on, baby, breathe. Breathe for me," she murmured as she bent over, her stethoscope on the puppy's side as she rubbed its flaccid belly, trying to coax a breathing response. "Come on. You can do it…you can do it. You just open your lungs and pull…breathe…and we'll find you a home and a family…just breathe…please God…*just breathe*—"

Someone grabbed her shoulders and pulled her up and away from the puppy. She struggled until the sound of her name penetrated the haze in her senses. "Kate! It's gone—it's finished. Take a step back." Her eyes focused on Jess's anxious face, and she gradually relaxed her grip on the failure that had knocked her sideways.

She looked back at the sad little body that never had a chance to live or grow…much less to know a full belly or the touch of a loving hand.

"Take a break, Katie," Jess said gently, grasping her shoulders. "You're getting too close. You have to step back and regain some perspective or you'll be useless here." She pushed some of Kate's hair back out of her eyes. "Go, get something to drink. That's an order."

"Okay, okay. You're right." She put up her hands in surrender and turned to walk away—only to run into a brick wall that smelled astringent and enfolded her like a cloud. She looked up to find herself in Nick's arms. He was staring at her with concern and not a little exasperation.

"You've been hard at it for hours, Kate," he said, holding her fully against him. "You need a break, and I know just the place."

He led her down the driveway to the vans that were open and, for the moment, mostly empty. Sarah and Ben greeted her warmly and showed off their charges: furry little dogs with big, luminous eyes. The sight of those sweet faces and Ben's and Sarah's pleasure in giving them comfort was a balm for her bruised heart. She sat down in the open door of a van while Nick got her some hot chocolate and a doughnut to revive her energy. When she finished her snack, he pulled her to her feet and walked her down the road to help clear her head.

"Thank you, Nick." There was still a tinge of sadness in her smile.

"Somebody has to take care of the doc so she can take care of the patients."

"What is that smell?" She sniffed his shirt and scrutinized the swipe of gel under his nose.

"We found some bones, and Deputy Krum broke out the VapoRub." He grinned. "He's not a bad guy, just a little green. He's been helping me search the place."

"Bones? Dead dogs?" She stopped.

"Don't go ballistic on me," he said, taking her hands in his. "We found some bones…a dog that…didn't make it." He winced. "Me and my big mouth. I shouldn't have mentioned it."

"Me? What about you?" She searched him for signs of duress. "Was it really just bones?" She scowled. "Are you okay?"

"Sure. I'm a guy. I can compartmentalize."

She stared at him, surprised.

"What? My mom still watches *Oprah* reruns."

She almost laughed.

"Yeah, you compartmentalize beautifully—until you can't anymore. Look, I don't want you to have to deal with more terrible memories."

"That makes two of us. So how about we make a memory of a different kind?"

He reeled her into his arms and gave her a kiss that smeared stinky salve all over her upper lip. It was such a good kiss that she didn't even realize what had happened until she pulled back and—"Ewwww!"

He chuckled, and she swiped her upper lip with the back of her hand.

Then he really laughed, and she did, too.

It was a purging kind of laughter they both needed to clear the tension that coiled around their nerves and heightened their emotions. When it passed, she slipped an arm around his waist, and he rested an arm around her shoulders to walk back to the rescue vans. There were more volunteers holding animals now, taking a break from the intense work of clearing the sheds and pens, and everyone grinned at Kate and the big state trooper as they returned to the group.

When Kate went back to work, Jess was ready to take a break herself. Before she left, she stretched and looked around to be certain Nick wasn't in earshot.

"Holy crap, Everly, *that* is your trooper? You might have said he's a dead ringer for Chris Hemsworth with a bad haircut."

"I like that haircut. It goes with the uniform." Kate treated herself to a wicked grin. "So, he meets with your approval?"

"Approval? Hell, you'd better scoop him up and marry him, or I'm gonna have to make a run at him myself!"

It was the last lighthearted moment Kate was to have that day.

The next time she saw Nick, he was standing across from one of the filthy pens of barking dogs, his gaze dark and focused on something that clearly disturbed him. She handed off the little female miniature schnauzer she had just cleared for transport, rolled her shoulders and announced she needed a five-minute break.

It was a measure of how absorbed he was that he jumped when she slid her hand into his. "Are you okay?"

"How could anybody be okay with something like this staring you in the face?" He squeezed her hand. "The dogs in that pen weren't bred here. Shepherds, retrievers and mixes—how did they get here? And there are those guys." He pointed to several emaciated dogs pacing the fence. They had short hair, square heads, heavy jaws and plenty of aggression. "Fighting dogs."

Kate thought a moment, uncertain why that would make a difference. "Does it matter? They're neglected animals that need our help."

His face was set with concentration, and whatever conclusions he was drawing were locked inside.

No matter how he tried to convince her otherwise, elements of his past were awakened by evidence of the cruelty of this place. He was clearly trying to hold it at bay, but she could feel its intensity rising in him. What if she couldn't be there to help him through it this time? She glanced back at the exam station where volunteers now sat on the ground waiting with their charges in their laps, cleaning them with water and antiseptic wipes, rocking them and sometimes even singing softly to them. They needed her. She had to go back.

Torn, she pulled him around to face her. "Promise me that you won't go into the barn without me." He frowned, and she squeezed his arms as if to force his concession. "*Promise me*, Nick."

He nodded, and she rose on tiptoes to give him a soft kiss.

NICK WATCHED HER go back to work and felt the tie between them—anchored in his heart—stretch across the distance. She wanted to protect him, just like he wanted to protect Ben and Sarah and her. He never wanted Kate to have to experience the kind of horrors he'd seen. But then she had already seen the effects of human cruelty at its most evil and destructive. She was dealing with it right now, working with her whole heart and mind to repair some of that damage. And she still had time and worry left over for him.

He closed his eyes and saw in his mind glimpses of remembered horrors she couldn't protect him from. All around him were reminders—dogs that were dying even as they were being saved; animals in pain that might never know a healthy day or a loving home.

Desperate to escape those thoughts, he started to walk, heading for the perimeter again. He reached the rear of the outbuildings, where he had found Deputy Krum earlier. He put his hand on a weathered fence post and stared at the ground for a time, trying to clear his thoughts. Something about the grass and weeds near his feet drew his attention. The vegetation had been flattened near the downed fence wires. In fact, there were bare spots in the grass and weeds— long, thin patches—*tire tracks*. Damn, why hadn't he seen it earlier?

He followed those tracks until they disappeared beneath vegetation again, but the path of flattened grass was still plain to see. Half a mile later, the tracks emptied into an old orange grove with ranks of gnarled, half-bare trees still standing. Most of the tracks among the trees were overgrown, but some looked fresher, deeper. Suddenly all of the evidence came together. Dog bones, crates, chains, spiked collars, machetes…fighting dogs…stolen dogs used as fighting bait.

He'd been right. He closed his eyes and stood listening, drinking in the sun and the heat and the sense that he was meant to find that back entrance—that he'd found clues to the case the universe had been rubbing his nose in.

Dogs. That was why it had to be dogs… because dogs got his attention like nothing else would, got his emotions involved the way nothing else could. They got him reconnected…to a woman and to himself and to goodness, caring and *love* the way nothing else had. He opened his eyes on a world of brighter, truer colors and felt his chest expand as he inhaled the grove's orange blossom–sweetened air. It was a moment of pristine clarity that fit pieces of his shattered inner self back together.

He headed back for his cruiser to call in a report. For the first time in months—years—he felt a sense of rightness inside. He and all of this dog stuff were meant to come together.

He passed the broken fence, the sheds and the half-empty pens before he noticed the relative quiet. Most of the rescue crew had withdrawn to the vehicles to rest, take stock and regroup.

Nance rushed out of the main barn with a bundle in her arms. "Nick! In there!" she called, jerking her head toward the barn. "This one's giving birth right now and the first pup isn't coming right. I heard the sounds of puppies trapped in the back. They need help—right away!"

Nick froze, then looked around for Harry Mueller or Linda Hoskins—somebody, anybody he could press into doing what he'd promised Kate he wouldn't do. This wasn't his job. He was here to provide legal support for the operation and to discover evidence relating to the dogfighting operation. He was here to help put away criminals whose contempt for life corrupted the most loyal and loving creatures on earth.

He was here to help save...dogs...

Nance hurried to lay her precious burden down on the table before Kate and turned to yell, "In there—hurry!"

Puppies. With a growl of surrender, he turned toward that barn and whatever calamity Nance Everly trusted him to solve. Because that was what he did. He saved people. And dogs. And puppies. He found himself repeating his old lament with a twist. Why did it have to be *puppies*?

He stepped into the barn and found chaos all around—rows of poorly made wire cages had been stacked on one another. The floors of the cages were bare wire so that whatever feces or urine came from above fell on the poor animals below. The cages were empty now, many pulled down and smashed after the dogs were removed. But the remaining stench and filth were testimony to the conditions the inmates of this hellhole had endured.

Light bulbs hanging from single wires provided some illumination, but as he neared the back, shadows took over and it was hard to see if the lower cages were still occupied. The silence gave him hope they weren't.

He came to a break in the cages and turned on his flashlight. He'd discovered an equipment area; rusting farm tools and machine parts lay in piles and hung from the walls. He listened, trying to locate the puppies, and heard a faint mewling sound coming from the far side of the room. He searched the area with his light, found nothing, then stepped over and around cast-off tools to listen again.

A chill went through him as he heard the plaintive sounds of a puppy calling in the dark. The sound mingled with memory… yelps of pain and fear he had carried in his head for five years…cries that he could never comfort, caused by pain he could never relieve.

That was not today. He jerked his thoughts

back to the present and forced himself to breathe.

These cries he could do something about.

Steeling himself, he headed to the rear and saw light coming through the wall that separated the barn from a lean-to structure propped against it outside. He knelt in the corner and put his eye to the widest crack between the boards.

A small, round body, dark with white feet, lay on a floor of dirt and moldy straw. It raised its head and gave him a glimpse of a little black nose. This was a young one, alone and scared, and its eyes weren't opened yet. Where was the mother? He stuck his hand through the opening and touched the puppy's soft coat. But his hand had barely fit through; he could never get the puppy out that way. He needed to widen the opening.

There were tools all around, but not a single saw. He grabbed a pickax and used it as a lever to pry away some of the age-hardened wood, pulling it away in splinters. The sound and vibration caused renewed mewling from several little throats. More than one pup. He made a hole large enough to get the closest one out, feeling the little thing quiver in his hand as he laid it against his chest to warm it.

Paradoxically, he received as much warmth as he gave. The feel of the cool, damp nose and the silky feet softened something inside him. And there were more inside. He located some straw, made a nest and laid the puppy in it. Alone and cold again, it mewled for its littermates and mother.

"Hang in there. I'm going for them, too."

He looked through the hole he'd made and spotted two others. He pulled them out, one by one. Each squirmed in his hands and burrowed straight for his heart as he placed them on his chest and carried them to the nest he'd made. Together again, they comforted each other with shared warmth.

A fourth puppy lay motionless in the dirt, and he couldn't tell if it was still breathing. He nearly threw his shoulder out as he strained to reach the puppy. He had to make a bigger hole.

Grabbing the pickax, he took bigger swings at the boards and cracked them higher up. But the wood there was even harder and resisted.

"Damn it—I want in there!" He jammed

the pick beneath one edge of a board and pushed fiercely, willing it to give and allow him access to that little life. The wood cracked but remained solidly nailed. He put his feet against the boards and used his back and legs. One board finally broke, sending him shooting against a roll of cage wire that scraped his spine. It hurt like a son of a— *gun*.

Shaking off the pain, he went back to the opening he'd made. The puppy hadn't moved. But he looked up and his heart almost stopped. Beyond the puppy, trapped in a coil of wire, bleeding from her neck, was the mother dog. Small and thin, exhausted from the birth of her pups, she lay with her head and forelegs trapped and barbs from the wire slicing into her skin with every movement she made.

"Oh, God." At that moment it truly was a prayer. His heart sank as she saw him and moved her head enough to meet his gaze. He sucked a shaky breath and reached for the puppy. The little body was still warm, but seemed limp compared to the others and was barely breathing. He had to get it out to Kate and Jess. But the mother—if he took her puppies out now, she might die before he got back to save her.

It was a cruel choice—so similar to one he'd made that day in Iraq that it could only be his penance for that fateful decision. Do the right thing for your men…or the dogs… but know as you do so that someone will die. That was a soldier's unearned hell: good always tainted by bad, peace bought by horrific violence, saving some lives at the cost of others.

The mother dog raised her head to look at him despite the way the wire bit deeper into her flesh. Pain glittered in her dark eyes. But he understood what he saw in them. *Save my babies*, she said with those big, sad eyes. A mother's plea.

At that moment, suspended in time and battling remembered grief, the protective wall that had formed around his heart cracked.

"No." He scrambled back with the puppy and shoved to his feet, unwilling to make that fateful choice.

Kate's words came to him: "We can't do everything, but we can do something. We can always do something." He looked at the little body in his hands and realized this wasn't penance, it was a second chance.

"There has to be a way."

He whipped off his shirt, wrapped the puppy in it and set it in the nest with its littermates. Then he grabbed the pickax and swung it at those boards with all his might. Again and again he pounded that stubborn wood, pouring his anger and frustration into each swing of the pick. When that stubborn wood finally gave, he was almost shocked. Panting, he pulled pieces of shattered wood out of the way.

"I don't know how you got in here—" sweat ran down his face as he stepped through and crouched beside her "—but I'm going to get you out."

The mother dog looked up at him as he studied her entanglement, and when he spoke softly to her and stroked her head for reassurance, she licked his hand. At that moment, he'd have given his right arm to see the little thing freed.

He untangled her legs first, threading them through the wires, careful to avoid putting more pressure on her neck. One by one, the loops of steel released their grip on her, until only two remained. These coils were tighter, smaller, and he finally understood that without wire cutters, there was only one way to get her out. He carefully inserted his fingers inside the sharp wire, gripping it on each side, and pulled hard. It gave, but only a little and the wire bit viciously into his fingers. He lifted her out into the open and tried again, this time pulling with all his might and lifting—hoping she would slip out. He could hardly believe his eyes when it worked and she dropped to the floor.

"Don't die on me now." He picked her up gently and cradled her in one arm. As he climbed back through the hole, the barn door opened and Nance rushed in, calling his name.

"Back here!" He picked up the puppies, tucking them against his chest and around their mother. With his free hand, he gave Nance the quiet puppy, wrapped in his shirt. "Get this one to Kate, quick. I'm not sure it's breathing."

He heard Nance murmur encouragements to the puppy as she ran.

He could feel the mother's heart beating against his arm, and the other puppies squirmed and rooted against him as he carried them out into the late-afternoon sunlight. It was hot and humid and bright, and he felt strangely at peace as he crossed the gravel yard bearing an armful of life.

"I THINK HE'S GOING to make it." Kate pulled the stethoscope from her ears and looked up, strain giving way to hope in her face. "He just needed a little help breathing." She stared at Nick, and he knew she was trying to make sense of his bare chest, the bleeding dog and armful of puppies he carried, and the tracks of sweat—or tears—on his dusty face.

He laid the puppies on the table one by one, and then gently settled the mother dog beside them.

"She's lost some blood, but I think she'll be okay if we can get some fluid in her and stitch her up." He smiled at her in a way that weakened her knees. "If you've got a needle pack, I can get you a line started."

Kate rushed around the table and threw her arms around him. He kissed her forehead while she wiped the dusty tracks from his cheeks.

"I had to get them out of there," he murmured into her ear. "But I swear, I'll never break a promise to you again." When she looked up, he saw tears spring to her eyes.

Jess traded looks of surprise with Nance, then propped her chin on her hand and watched with a wistful expression.

"I've got to get me one of those."

CHAPTER EIGHTEEN

THE HEADLINE READ Ninety Dogs Saved in Puppy Mill Raid in the local paper the next day. The Harbor staff was happy to let the Humane Society take the credit and provide facts and photos to the media. All Nance, Kate, Jess and Harbor's volunteers wanted to do was find care and shelter for the rescued animals and then go home to their families to sleep.

Rest, however, was more an ideal than a reality for Kate and Jess. Many of the animals needed significant medical care, and others had issues adjusting to food and close human contact. Each had to be bathed, screened for ID chips, evaluated and scheduled for medical care or rehabilitation. Surprisingly, they found chips in several of the larger dogs and learned they had disappeared weeks ago—possibly stolen. It was heartening to think they could reunite some dogs with loving families.

Nick, on the other hand, spent the next day with deputies from two counties and a couple of fellow troopers going over the Crowder place for evidence of more than the puppy mill operation. They located a previously undiscovered tack room in the barn that contained viciously spiked harnesses, muzzles, hot shot prods and cruder, homemade electrical devices used to administer punishment—tools of the dogfighting trade, no doubt about it. The thought of such things being used on dogs turned Nick's stomach. It got worse when the sheriff's deputies investigated the trail Nick and Barney had spotted and discovered a dumping ground of dog remains—the source of that sickening stench.

Nick was happy to hand over the investigation to the local guys and get back to his station. Routine patrols on highways sounded like sweet duty compared to dealing with such disturbing discoveries. But his overwhelming urge as he headed back into Lakeview was to see Kate and feel the calm that their growing connection brought.

As Nick walked into the clinic, Kate looked up from treating battered paws and skin problems discovered when volunteers shaved matted dog hair.

"You look tired," she said, letting him lead her outside, into the shade of the laurel oaks around Harbor's old farmhouse. She studied him as he pulled her into his arms. "What's happened?"

"It's what we thought. A lot of stuff going on out there. None of it good."

"What did you find?" she said, half-afraid to hear what other horrors the place held.

"I don't want to talk about it. I just want to hold you." He sank his nose into her hair. "God, you smell good."

"After two days of sweating?" She nestled more fully against him, feeling fatigue settling in and grateful for the support of his muscular body. "It must have been bad if you think I smell good right now."

"You always smell good," he murmured.

She pulled back enough to see his face. "I haven't had a chance to tell you how much it meant to me to see you with...those puppies yesterday."

"Yeah, well…they needed help and I… couldn't just walk away."

"Even if it was painful for you?"

He went still, and she could see him working to make sense of his thoughts and feelings. He was the amazing embodiment of all of the complexities of human nature; hope and fear, strength and weakness, self-doubt and confidence, confusion and clarity. And in that moment, she quit falling in love… because she had just landed—fully, irrevocably—in love with Nick Stanton.

"I just figured… I owed some dogs for helping get me home in one piece. I can't return the favor directly, but I could help others. Maybe even the score a bit."

"Dogs don't keep score." Tears rimmed her eyes and her voice was thick and low. "You know that, right? They just love you, accept you for what you are and invite you to love them back. And that trust and unconditional love can work miracles on a battered heart."

"I guess it can," he said, gazing into her eyes, stroking her cheek. He took a deep breath, seeming a little surprised at what was happening between them.

"It takes time, Nick." Kate released him and took hold of his hands instead, threading her fingers through his. "And patience and caring. You have all of that and more from the people who love you. Including me."

She held her breath for what seemed a small eternity. Did he realize what she'd just said to him?

Then he bent his head to kiss her, and the relief and pleasure of it poured through her with thick, reassuring warmth. She relaxed instantly. This was a behavior she could read with 100 percent accuracy.

Moments later, a soft buzzing sound made him pull back enough to reach for the phone in his pocket. "Sorry—call from home.

"Hi, there…°Sure. Always." He listened. "Aww, that sounds great. Give us half an hour. Make that forty-five minutes." He gave a husky laugh that made her shiver. "Yeah, well, she's a girl and she may want to do something first…like freshen up. Girls are like that."

Girls. She smiled. He had to be talking to Ben.

"Time for some R & R, Doc," Nick said

as he clicked the call off. "We could both use it."

Kate glanced back at the shelter. The animals all had been triaged, and the paws and ears and baths were being finished by volunteers. She looked up at Nick. There was nothing she wanted more than to be alone with him...someplace soft, quiet and private. But the minute he mentioned grilling burgers and his mom's prizewinning potato salad and chocolate cake, she ruefully decided that private time could probably wait.

She checked in with Isabelle and the volunteers, and then headed home to shower and change clothes. She knew it was the right decision the minute she walked into the Stanton backyard and was greeted and hugged as if she were long-lost family.

"You just sit and relax, Kate. You've had quite a week." Sarah put raspberry lemonade in her hand and directed her to a lounge chair. Then Sarah paused and glanced at her son. "We all have."

Kate sank gratefully into the lounger, taking in the large, well-landscaped yard. She caught Nick's eye and smiled.

"Your yard is huge. And beautiful. These

trees—it would be perfect for a dog." It was out before she realized what she'd done.

Nick caught the way Ben's ears perked up and shook his head with a wry expression as he laid burgers on the grill.

"One of these days, maybe."

Relieved, if a bit disappointed, she let it drop. Ben came to sit on the foot of the lounger and bombarded her with questions about the dogs that he and his grandmother had helped.

"Hey, now," Nick said, coming to sink into a chair beside hers, "give Kate a break. I promised her some R & R from all the animal stuff." Ben looked disappointed until he added, "Why don't you show her your telescope and star log while the burgers are cooking?"

For the next fifteen minutes, Kate was kept busy with Ben's accounts of star watching and the details of various telescopes he hoped to have someday. Before she knew it, Nick was settling a plate containing a burger and mouthwatering sides on her lap. "Stay where you are," he insisted. A moment later he handed her a napkin and silverware.

"You didn't have to do that." She poured gratitude into a tired smile.

"Yeah, I did. Can't have you fainting from starvation." He brought his plate to the chair beside hers and set his beer bottle on the patio by his feet. As she watched, she realized he was wearing shorts and had pretty darned memorable legs. Unfortunately, she was so tired she could do little more than appreciate them from afar.

"Hey, Dad," Ben said as he munched his burger and chips. "There's lots of dogs at the shelter who need a home now." He had ketchup smeared across his cheek. "Why don't we get one?"

Kate held her breath, watching Nick think as he chewed and swallowed. After a long minute, he drew a deep breath.

"What do you think, Mom?" He turned to Sarah, who seemed surprised. "Maybe we could get one of those little dogs—a Chihuahua. They don't eat much. That would be economical. Or maybe we should get one of those hairless guys. I can't stand the thought of dog hair in my breakfast cereal."

Ben's initial squeal of interest turned into a groan of horror. "Noooo! We need a real dog—a big one we can play with—one that can guard the house when Nana is here by herself."

Nick put on a puzzled look. "Not a puppy, then? I thought you liked puppies."

"I love puppies, but we need a grown-up dog—one that already knows to pee outside." A cough from his grandmother made him turn to her. "It's okay to say *pee*, Nana. Dr. Kate says it's a normal body function, like farts. So, it's no big deal."

Kate shrugged like she had no idea what he was talking about.

"Well, I don't know." Nick seemed befuddled by the notion of a grown-up dog. "Where would we find such an animal? It would have to be one we liked and that liked us. And it would have to have manners and follow orders. I couldn't put up with a dog that didn't follow orders."

"Daaaad!" Ben caught on to his dad's teasing. "You know where there's a dog like that. *Two* dogs like that. Goldie and Soldier. Please? Can't we get one of them?"

"I don't know," Kate said gravely, trying not to overdo it. "It would be a shame to part them."

"Then we could get both of them. Our yard is big enough. And we've got trees and places for them to dig and a goldfish pond for them to play in. Goldie could sleep with me and Soldier could sleep with Dad—"

"Whoa." Nick waved his fork in objection. "Who says I want to sleep with a dog?" He glanced at Kate with a mischievous glint in his eye. "I may have other plans."

"Well, then, he could sleep with Nana." Ben looked hopefully to his grandmother. Her shudder of horror made Kate and Nick burst out laughing.

"If Soldier comes, he can bed down in the kitchen at night," Sarah declared with authority. "That will make it easier for him to keep an eye on things."

"Well, I'll have to sleep on it." Kate watched Nick melt visibly as he looked at Ben's hopeful face. "Goldie and Soldier seem to be candidates, but two dogs—that would be a big change. How about just inviting them over for a visit first?"

Ben abandoned his plate to throw his arms about his dad's shoulders, and Nick gave him a bearlike hug that produced a sweet ache in Kate's chest. When she looked up, Sarah was smiling and dabbing her eyes with a napkin.

After dinner and a helping of rich chocolate cake, she was ordered to sit back on the lounger and relax. Sarah insisted on carrying dishes and condiments back into the house herself and set Ben to collecting garbage and helping with the dishes. She watched the sky turn a hundred shades of gilt-edged gorgeous as Nick cleaned the grill. Then he offered to show her around the yard.

Every tree had a name, and every shrub and flower had a purpose; keeping insects away, absorbing water from downspouts, feeding honeybees, providing berries for birds. And there was a flourishing herb garden near the house to supply Sarah's desire for fresh seasonings.

"This is beautiful, Nick," she said, slipping her hand in his as they strolled. "How do you know so much about plants and landscaping?"

"When I came back from my first tour, I spent a lot of time planting things." He paused beside an overachiever of a bougainvillea and ran his hand over its brilliant fuchsia blooms. "When you've been in a place that's dry and brown and arid—a place where nothing but strife and hatred grow—you begin to appreciate green. And peace." He shrugged. "I guess I wanted to make a place where life could grow and good things could happen. It didn't quite turn out that way. Every time I came back from deployment the yard would be a mess." He gave a bitter laugh. "Ben's mother didn't exactly share my vision."

"So, you lived here together?"

He nodded. "For a little while. Then she went back to work and asked my mom to come and stay with Ben while she went on business trips. When I got home from my fourth deployment, she had her bags packed—cleaned out every trace of her presence from the house—said goodbye and walked out. I think she wanted to think that Ben and I never happened. Haven't heard from her since."

She was silent for a minute, having a hard time imagining any reason a woman would just walk away from Nick and a wonderful child like Ben.

"It must have made it that much harder

for you to adjust to being home," she finally said, squeezing his hand.

He nodded, raised his head and looked around at the trees and the purpling sky. "But I had Ben. And I'd walk through hell to see him safe and cared for. Those first weeks after she left were pretty bad. He cried himself to sleep and kept asking when she'd be home. That was when I called my mom, took a discharge and joined the FHP."

"A lot to deal with."

"Yeah, but we got through it. My mom was a rock. She spent hours and hours with Ben and helped me make peace with his mother leaving. As much as she could. I can't swear that if that woman knocked on our door today, I wouldn't want to punch her right in the nose." He gave a rueful laugh.

He was probably entitled to that feeling, but she sensed there wasn't much heat behind it. Kate grinned and looked around the beautiful yard.

"You have made a good life here, Nick."

"Yeah. But it could be better." He squeezed her hand. "A lot better."

She raised her face to him with innocent provocation.

"Oh, right. You don't have a dog yet."

He pulled her into his arms. "I'd be tempted to get one, if it came attached to you."

They watched a movie later, with Ben snuggled on the sofa between them, and Nick shepherded him to bed as soon as the credits rolled. Sarah hugged Kate goodnight and headed for bed, too.

When Nick returned a few minutes later, Kate was curled around a pillow, her eyes closed.

She felt his weight settle on the sofa and didn't resist as he pulled her over and into his arms. She opened her eyes sleepily and he kissed her nose.

"Go back to sleep, Kate."

"I ought to…go home," she said, fumbling to sit up.

He chuckled. "You're dead on your feet. If you set foot in that car, I'll have to ticket you for unsafe operation." His strong arms wrapped around her, supporting her in all the right places. "Just relax, sweetheart. I'll get you home before sunrise."

She relaxed into him, savoring the feel of his broad chest and big arms around her.

She hadn't felt this secure, this wanted in… well, she couldn't remember ever feeling this right. So, she did go back to sleep. With a smile.

Nick watched that smile, feeling it wrapping around his heart. And for a few minutes, it was hard to see through the tears brimming in his eyes.

KATE CALLED GRAN the next morning on her way to work. She mentioned that Nick was thinking about taking Soldier and Goldie, that he'd agreed to have them come for a "visit." Nance was surprised, but after a moment gave a quiet chuckle.

"Something happened to him at the rescue. Had to be those puppies. Before then, he wouldn't get near one. Afterward, he couldn't get enough of them. I saw the way he held on to them…and you. Shows he's finally got some sense. With you around, that boy's gonna be all right."

Kate wished she could reach through the phone somehow to hug her stubborn, wise and bighearted grandmother.

"Like my gran always says, good friends make good medicine."

Nance had Soldier and Goldie ready to go the next afternoon when Nick, Kate and Ben arrived at the farm to pick them up. She sent along water bowls and a couple of their favorite toys. Ben wondered aloud if the dogs would be afraid in a new place, then turned to them and hugged each, telling them he'd show them the ropes and they'd love the yard and that he and his "nana" had baked some special dog biscuit treats with peanut butter.

Nance chuckled, elbowing Kate and muttering, "Good luck getting them into the car to bring them back to me."

Kate rode up front with Nick while Ben buckled himself into the middle of the rear seat with a dog on either side of him. As they headed back to town, he told Goldie and Soldier all about the place they were going, including the great backyard, the strict rules—"no snitching or begging" and "no digging around Dad's plants." Nick held Kate's hand and could feel her chuckling silently at the combination of mature tone and kid-like detail in Ben's lecture.

They were halfway home when Nick spotted an old stake-bed truck just ahead of him and had to slow for the truck to make a turn into a convenience store and gas station. Something about the vehicle and its crumpled license plate seemed familiar. He came alert.

Kate looked around the parking lot, remembering the place. She looked to Nick, intending to tell him that this was the place the boy, Miguel, insisted they drop him off. But Nick was already pulling off the road and into the parking lot.

"I know that truck," he said, pulling around to the side of the convenience store. "That's the one that picked up the kid who brought the puppies to Harbor. I'd bet my badge on it."

"Miguel," she prompted as they watched an older youth in jeans, a T-shirt and work boots leave the truck and enter the store. "That must be Miguel's cousin." She was out of the car before he had a chance to object. He opened his door and called her name, but she was already at the entrance and then inside the store.

Miguel's cousin—Alejandro, she remembered—was at the counter. Edging closer, she heard him say something to the clerk in Spanish that included Miguel's name and saw the clerk shake his head. Alejandro looked unhappy, thanked the clerk and bolted back out the door to his truck. She followed but was intercepted by Nick.

"What the devil do you think you're—"

"It's what I was afraid of." She leaned around him to see the old truck pull back out onto the highway. She grabbed Nick's arm and urgently turned him back toward the SUV. "That's Miguel's cousin, Alejandro." As they climbed in and buckled up, she explained, "He was asking the clerk about Miguel. I think he's looking for him. And he's heading for—"

"Clara Crowder's," Nick said, frowning as he put the SUV in gear.

"Did something happen to Miguel?" Ben asked.

"Good question," Kate said with a sharp glance at Nick. A second later they were pulling out onto the road, heading away from Alejandro's truck. "What are you doing? We need to follow him and find out what happened to Miguel."

"I have to drop you and Ben off first," Nick said, his jaw set.

"You're not dropping me off."

"Yes, I am." He gave her a glare, and she glared right back.

"You'll lose him if you do. What if he isn't going to Crowder's? What if he's going to another place Miguel has worked? Just, go, Nick. All we want to do is ask him about Miguel."

"That's all *you* want to do. I want to question him about things the sheriff has been finding out at the Crowder place."

"Then turn around and catch up with him. What harm can it do? From what Miguel said, Alejandro helped him bring the puppies to Harbor. He's a good kid, Nick."

Nick pulled into an office building parking lot, stopped the car for a minute and looked over his shoulder at Ben and the dogs. He gave Kate a grudging nod and put the SUV in gear.

"If he's really a good kid, then he won't mind telling us what he knows." He pulled out onto the highway and put his foot down.

Alejandro's truck soon came into view, and Nick slowed, keeping just close enough to see where he was going. With every mile, Kate grew more anxious. She dreaded going back to the place where she had encountered so many heartbreaking situations. But what if Miguel's uncle had learned he was responsible for the puppy raid? Could Miguel be in trouble?

Even though she wanted to catch up with Alejandro, she wasn't happy that Ben was along and that they had two dogs in the back seat that were not exactly known quantities in touchy situations. *Somebody* would have to stay with Ben and the dogs while *somebody* talked to Alejandro. And she had a fair idea who Nick would nominate for the job of staying behind.

Nick slowed as they reached little-used roads and let Alejandro increase his lead. It was a risk, but he said he didn't want to spook the boy and have him drive off before they had a chance to talk to him. Kate leaned forward, watching the distant plume of dust that showed Alejandro was going exactly where they expected. Fifteen minutes that seemed like fifty passed before they approached the Crowder farm and spotted the truck turning into the overgrown drive. Nick waited a couple of minutes before pulling in and stopping to block any possible exit.

"Stay here," he told Kate and Ben as he

put on the emergency brake and left the engine running. "I'll call for you when it's safe for you to come up and talk to the boy."

"I should be the one to go," she objected. "He won't bolt at the sight of a woman the way he will at the sight of a big guy."

"No. And that's all there is to it. Stay put, Ben, and don't touch anything." He stepped out of the vehicle and she got out as well, her mouth tight with determination. "Kate!" he growled. "Get back in the car."

"I'm going." She copied his loud whisper. "Get over it." She headed up the drive and he muttered a few choice words before striding after her.

The truck was parked in the gravel yard, and Alejandro was nowhere in sight. They halted at the rear of the vehicle, listening, and heard Alejandro calling for Miguel. He *was* searching for his cousin, and it sounded like he was in the old woman's house. They crept toward the back door, which stood open, and focused on the sound of the youth's voice.

Alejandro reappeared in the doorway and surprised Nick. In a heartbeat the youth reversed direction and ran through the house for the front door. Kate ran around the house to catch him and found him headed for his truck. She changed direction and got there just ahead of him, planting herself in front of it with her arms spread.

"Stop, Alejandro! We just want to talk to you!" The youth stared at her, confused by her use of his name. "You're looking for Miguel, yes? We are, too. We think he's in trouble of some kind."

"I don' know any Miguel." He spotted Nick charging toward them from the rear of the house, panicked and tried to bolt around her for the driver's-side door. Kate grabbed his shirt and held him. Nick arrived in time to catch him from behind and lift him off the ground.

"Take it easy! We're not here to hurt you," Nick barked close to his ear. "We know you're Miguel's cousin and that you helped him bring dogs to the Harbor shelter. We just want to know what's happened to him and to ask you a few questions about this place."

Alejandro seemed to realize he had no chance of escape and quit struggling. Nick set him on his feet, but still held him.

"Miguel is missing?" Kate asked, watching for confirmation. A brief nod was all she got. "How long since you've seen him?" When he didn't answer, she moved closer and lifted his chin to make him look at her. He jerked it away, but she persisted.

"You're afraid for him." Her voice softened when he looked down, seeming angry and anxious. "We're worried, too, Alejandro." She paused to let that sink in. "What made you think he might be here?"

"You are doctor?" he asked.

"Yes. Did Miguel tell you how he helped us find this place? Did your uncle find out, too?" The youth said nothing at first.

"Please, tell us what you know. Miguel may be in trouble."

Alejandro jerked, trying unsuccessfully to free himself, then slowly sagged in Nick's grip and nodded.

"Uncle hear Miguel tell me an' he hit Miguel—again and again. I try to stop him— he hit me, tell me he make me a dog, use a hot stick." Nick released him.

Kate took the youth's arm gently and turned it over. Pairs of blackened burn marks ran up the tender inside flesh, evidence of his uncle's abuse. "My God. Did he use that hot stick on Miguel, too?"

Alejandro shrugged. "I did not see. I was…sick."

Nick turned the boy to look at him. "We'll help you search." His voice was hard with barely controlled anger. "If he's here, we'll find him. And we'll see your uncle doesn't hurt him or you ever again."

Kate nodded and gently touched Alejandro's shoulder. He still seemed skittish, but when she asked where he had already looked, he pointed to one of the sheds.

"Then we'll try the barn next," she said, putting an arm around him and leading him toward the hellhole she had sworn never to lay eyes on again.

THE MINUTE HIS dad and Dr. Kate got out of the SUV, Ben realized, Soldier and Goldie started to act funny. Soldier's nose went around the edges of the window, and Goldie sniffed the air for a while, then lay down and tucked her nose under her paws.

"What's the matter, girl?" Ben petted her and was surprised to find her shaking. "Are you scared? Don't be scared. I'll take care of you."

While he was tending to Goldie, Soldier jumped over the console into the front passenger seat.

"Hey, you can't be up there. The car's running. Dad will get mad, and if he does he might not let me keep you." He pointed emphatically at the seat beside him. "Get back here. Right now."

But Soldier whined and stuck his nose to the window, watching the brush outside as if expecting something bad to burst out of it. Before long, he pawed at the dash and then at the door and window, whining louder and barking. He wanted out in the worst way. Ben asked if he needed to go pee, but Soldier didn't seem to hear.

"What is it? What's the matter?" Ben was starting to worry himself. "Come on, don't get me in trouble."

He was relieved when he spotted Kate coming down the drive a few minutes later. She saw what Soldier was doing and hurried to the car. The minute she opened the door, Soldier bounded out, knocking her over.

"Soldier! Come back!"

SHE SCRAMBLED UP and ran after him, but the dog was soon out of sight. The brush was dense and probably full of snakes, and she didn't want to leave Ben alone again. Worried for the dog but unable to do anything to help him, she turned back to the SUV.

"I don't know what happened," Ben told her, looking scared for the first time since Kate had known him. "He sniffed the windows and climbed in the front seat and started whining and trying to get out. I asked if he wanted out to pee, but he wouldn't listen."

She looked over the seat at Goldie, who lifted her head just enough to sniff Kate, then tucked herself into a ball again.

"She's shaking like she's scared," Ben said. "Why is she so scared?"

Kate stroked his cheek. "It's okay, Ben. We'll find Soldier. I think maybe it's this place they don't like. There are a lot of bad smells here, things that would make dogs scared. Believe me, I'm with them. I don't like this place, either. As soon as we find Miguel and Soldier, we're out of here."

She slid out of the car and went around to the driver's side. The engine was running to keep the air-conditioning on, so she simply threw it in gear and drove up the path, through branches that overhung the driveway and beat the sides of the car and battered her nerves, as well.

NICK WAS RELIEVED when Kate went back to check on Ben and the dogs. He had come to agree that Alejandro was a good kid who was genuinely worried about his cousin. He knew all about the barns and sheds; his uncle had made him help the old woman sometimes. As they looked in covered holes and behind doors Nick hadn't known existed, Alejandro talked about how much he hated it there—seeing the dogs starved and hurt and knowing there was nothing he could do about it. Then his uncle started letting him drive the truck, and he and Miguel figured out a way to save at least a few of the dogs and puppies.

Together they checked every place Alejandro knew, until the old woman's house was the only place left. Was it possible that the boys' uncle had even used the old lady's house?

They entered through the back door, braving the stench and filth, covering their noses with their shirts. Every room presented a more disgusting scene than the last: decaying food in old cartons, beer and liquor bottles broken against walls and old cigarettes that were stubbed out on furniture. When they reached the back bedroom, Nick was ready to go, but there was one last door—a closet. When he opened it, his heart almost stopped.

A young boy, barely bigger than Ben, lay crumpled on the filthy floor, his nose pressed to the crack under the door. Alejandro cried out and fell to his knees beside the boy, shaking him and calling his name while Nick checked for breath. He was alive, but clearly in rough shape. Nick picked Miguel up, and as he cradled the boy in his arms, he saw the uncle's rampage visible in the cuts, swelling and bruising on his face.

"We have to get him to a hospital," Nick said, striding through the trash heap of a house. "Meanwhile Kate can look at him, she's—"

He stopped dead on the back porch. A man stood in the yard, medium tall, beer gut, pasty skin and flat, dead eyes. Everything about him said *low-life* and *mean*.

"What the hell are you doing in my house?" the man snarled, revealing yellowed and decaying teeth.

"I take it you are Jerry, Clara Crowder's nephew," Nick said.

"You're trespassing, asshole. I could shoot you where you stand, and no one would convict me. I'd be standin' my ground."

"If you had a gun," Nick said, flint-hard with anger. "And the guts to use it."

"Put the kid down and get out of here. He's none of your business."

"I've made him my business. I'm a Florida state trooper—this is my jurisdiction and this boy is injured. I'm taking him to a hospital."

Jerry transferred his anger to Alejandro. "You—you caused all of this, you and your little rat of a cousin. You'll pay for this!"

Nick stepped down off the porch, heading around doughboy Jerry. "Not if I have anything to do with it."

The honk of a horn distracted him; he glanced up and found his SUV sitting at the top of the drive with Kate behind the wheel.

Jerry spun to look, too, and when he turned back it was with a fist flying.

Nick had no time to dodge and took it square in the face. Pain exploded in his head as Jerry took advantage of his momentary blinding whiteness and moved in with a piece of wood he'd held behind him. Nick sensed another blow coming and bent, covering Miguel with his body. He took a whack across the head but ducked enough to make it glance.

"Alejandro," he gritted out, shoving Miguel into his cousin's arms and pointing to the SUV. "Get him to Kate."

Another broad blow hit his back as he staggered but kept his feet. "Too bad, Jerry," he ground out. "That one just made me mad."

He straightened, blocked another blow with his arm and countered with an explosive punch to Jerry's surprised face. The man staggered back, holding his jaw, then crashing onto all fours. Nick went in for the finish, but before he could drag Jerry upright, something the size of a Mack truck hit him from behind and dropped him to his knees. As he fell, he rolled and saw a short, thick Hispanic man standing over him, holding a long metal pipe with an elbow fitting on one end that made it hit like a sledgehammer.

"You all right, Jerry?" An ugly smirk came over the face of the man who could only be Miguel's uncle.

"Hell, no! He broke my face! Kill him!"

"Kill him yourself. I got more important things to do," the uncle said as he headed after Alejandro. "Come here, you little... Gonna finish you—do it right this time—beat you till there's not enough left to toss in the pit!"

Nick, still reeling from the blows but desperate to keep the brute from the kids, grabbed his ankle as he passed. The uncle stumbled, then turned back with a snarl and raised the pipe. One blow, two, three rained down with frenzied curses—the explosions of pain made it hard to tell where they were coming from next. Pain shot through his arms and the ribs on his right side as he tried to protect his head and roll out of the way.

A growl and a scuffling preceded a screech of surprise that turned into a yelp of pain. The sound of snarling penetrated Nick's pain and he focused—a big dog, a shepherd, was attacking the boys' uncle. It took a second for him to recognize Soldier. He levered himself up, holding his head, and called the dog, who continued to snarl and bite and shake, dodging blows and refusing to release the uncle, until the right word finally came to Nick. "Release!"

Soldier broke off the attack, and the uncle scrambled away as Nick struggled to make it to his knees. Soldier hurried to him to sniff and lick. All Nick could do was wrap his arms around the headstrong shepherd and sink his face into the dog's fur. Every part of him hurt—head pounding, arms and ribs burning, knuckles screaming with pain. But the dog—the dog had come. He cleared his vision enough to look around. Jerry had tried to crawl away but hadn't made it far before collapsing in a heap.

And the uncle—where had he gone?

KATE MET ALEJANDRO at the back hatch and helped him lay Miguel inside and climb in himself.

"Nick—where is Nick?" she demanded.

"My uncle Raul—he came— Man said bring Miguel quick."

She slammed the hatch and called for Nick. She made it to the front of the vehicle when she saw the boys' uncle, Raul, running straight for her...bleeding from his leg and hand, and wielding a length of pipe. His first swing smashed a headlight and his second splintered the driver's window. She scuttled back, then ran, trying to put the vehicle between them. He chased her around the SUV, while inside Ben yelled and Goldie barked frantically.

She wheeled and ran for the house, but he threw the pipe and connected with her shoulder. It knocked her to the side and she stumbled, going down hard on one knee. Only then did she realize Ben was out of the car and running for her.

"Dr. Kate!"

"Ben! No! Go back!"

Terror gripped her as Raul changed course and charged him instead. Ben fought with both fists, but the boys' uncle was a seasoned fighter and managed to pick Ben up with one arm and head for the barn.

NICK HAD MADE IT to his feet and to the rusty fence that enclosed the yard. The sight of Kate stumbling, trying to escape the pipe-wielding assailant galvanized him. Then he spotted Ben and Raul. Oh, God—the guy had his son!

"Dad! Help, Dad—"

Nick had nothing—no gun, no weapon—No! He did have *one*. He looked at Soldier, who sat erect, reading Nick's tension and just maybe his mind. The dog quivered with expectation.

"Attack!" he snapped, unsure if it was the right command for the dog, and giving the hand signal, too. For a split second his heart stopped. But Soldier leaped into action. The shepherd raced past Kate, focused on Ben and the figure carrying him away. The dog gathered himself, leaped and took down both abductor and victim.

SOLDIER WAS ON TOP of Miguel's uncle, snarling and biting with a viciousness that made Kate halt and skitter back until she saw Ben on the ground. She ducked closer to get the boy clear of the attack and grabbed him. Nick arrived, panting and holding his side.

He scooped up Ben in his arms and carried him back a few paces as Soldier continued to attack the man on the ground. Ben threw his arms around his dad, bursting into tears, and a second later, included Kate in that embrace.

Part of Kate—the rational, clinical part of her—was already examining Ben for damage and relieved to find all the important parts intact. "He's okay—just a bump or two. He's okay," she repeated, running her hands over the boy who was coming to mean the world to her. She realized that their shepherd still had Raul pinned and screaming. "Nick, let me take Ben—you have to get Soldier off him."

She headed for the car with Ben, panting and shaking. God help her, for a minute she actually hoped Soldier would eat the man alive.

SECONDS LATER, NICK was over Soldier, calling him off, shouting orders. His voice must have penetrated the rage that gripped the dog, because he eased enough for Nick to pull him back, and then he barked furiously to spend the last of his angry energy.

Raul groaned and thrashed briefly, then went still. Nick risked releasing Soldier to check him and found the man unconscious and bleeding, but not in imminent danger.

Kate rushed back alone, and Nick pulled her into his arms as he took a painful breath. "I feel a hell of a lot better than either of those guys. You need to get Miguel to a hospital."

"Not without you," she said, searching his face. "You've got a heck of a lump coming, and maybe a black eye. We've got to get you checked out, too. You could have a concussion."

"I've got to secure these guys," he said, wincing as he felt his head.

"We'll tie them up and call the local sheriff on the way to the hospital." She pushed him toward the SUV. "I'll drive.

Alejandro, it turned out, knew where there was some rope and how to tie a mean knot. They dropped him off at Chet and Jamie Dunlap's farm down the road, then asked Chet to wait for the deputies at the Crowder place.

Kate drove while Nick spoke to an officer in the Hardee County Sheriff's Office and reported what had happened and where they were headed with the injured boy. They hit Lakeview and went straight to the local hospital, where the emergency staff listened to Kate's report and rushed Miguel into radiology. Nick needed to be seen as well, and while they were at it, Ben had a few scrapes that needed tending.

Kate called Sarah to tell her what had happened and ask her to come and pick up Ben and the dogs. She arrived in record time, full of anxiety until she saw her son and grandson were all right. She hugged them thoroughly, agreeing to take Ben and the dogs home. Nick walked them out to the SUV to transfer the dogs.

Goldie climbed obediently into Sarah's car with Ben, but Soldier hung back and stared at Nick. There were still flecks of blood on his fur, and Nick met those big brown eyes and felt his stomach drop. The dog trusted him, obeyed him, streaked into danger for him. He knew Ben's nose was pressed against the car window, watching his dad with the dog.

Something was coming full-circle, shifting and settling in his heart and life. Soldier. He had a chance to return that trust, that commitment this time. Another part of his heart settled into place as he knelt beside that courageous dog and took his furry head between his hands.

"You did a great job today, fella. You saved me and Ben and Kate—you're a real hero." He pulled Soldier closer and pressed his face into the dog's ruff. "My hero."

In that moment, the decision was made.

"You're not just going for a visit, you know, you're going to stay." He straightened. "You got that, Soldier? You're a Stanton from this day on." Something in his smile and in the whoops of joy from Ben inside the car registered in the dog's mind. He grinned a tongue-lolling grin and jumped all over Nick, who ruffled his fur and hugged him.

"Okay. Go, climb in."

When Soldier was hugged eagerly and tucked in the back seat beside Ben, Nick leaned down on the car door to give one last order. "Ice cream for Ben and dog cookies for the hero, there," he said to his mom. "As many as he wants."

"Yes, sir," Sarah said, giving him a crisp salute and a beaming smile.

BACK INSIDE THE emergency room, the mood was still somber. While they waited for results, Nick and Kate sat together holding hands, watching a nurse clean Miguel's bruised face and treat his cuts. The sight of him lying there, so small and defenseless, weighed heavily on Kate. She felt responsible for what had happened to him, and every minute his health hung in the balance only added to her guilt.

"He is just a boy," she said to Nick over and over. "How could someone do that to a child? Beat him like that and leave him in a closet?"

"How could anyone do such things to kids or dogs?" Nick said, leaning forward and propping his hands and head on the side rail of Miguel's bed. Clearly, he was still recovering, and Kate rubbed his back and asked if he was all right. He nodded. "I'll be okay." He paused, then looked at her with sadness in his eyes. "In this job, I see the best of people and the worst. Sometimes it seems like there isn't much in between."

"The best and the worst," she said quietly, drawn to him all the more because she felt the same. "Even though I know there are millions of loving pet owners out there, it's the mean and stupid ones who seem to stick in my head. Why is that?"

CHAPTER NINETEEN

THE ER STAFF cleared Nick, diagnosing a mild concussion and a couple of cracked ribs that would earn him some sick leave. They prescribed rest and, at his request, only over-the-counter pain meds.

With one worry out of the way, they focused fully on Miguel and were relieved to see Alejandro arrive at the hospital, courtesy of Deputy Barney Krum, who had picked him up from the Dunlap farm.

The deputy brought word that they transported the two men, under arrest, to a Hardee County hospital and that Jerry Crowder was tripping over himself to inform on a dogfighting ring in exchange for lesser charges on the assault. With his information, they were poised to make more arrests and rescue more dogs.

Alejandro was checked out medically, and then came to sit with them by Miguel's bedside, holding his cousin's hand and speaking softly to him in Spanish.

A major concussion was Miguel's diagnosis. His brain had started to swell, and his prognosis was guarded for the moment. If the swelling didn't worsen, he might wake in a day or two, the doctors said. If it worsened, he might slip into a coma.

When they transferred him upstairs to ICU, Nick and Kate came out into the waiting room to find Nance, Isabelle, Jess and Hines keeping watch for him, too. She filled them in on all that had happened and how Soldier had attacked the boys' uncle, Raul, to save them. That was when Nick announced that Soldier and Goldie were not only at his house for a visit, but were now at their new home. Nance hugged him, and Hines shook his hand, congratulating him on acquiring a fine pair of family members.

Kate was happy to hear Nick's decision; it lifted her spirits briefly. But soon enough everyone left and she, Nick and Alejandro trekked upstairs to ICU to check on Miguel.

They took turns sitting with Miguel in his room and talking to him, telling him about the rescued dogs and how he had helped save dozens and dozens of them. They told him that he and Alejandro weren't going back to their uncle ever again. Alejandro looked doubtfully at her, but she gave him a definitive nod and he shrugged, unwilling to put much faith in her declaration.

Kate went home that night feeling older than her years and emotionally battered. Nick offered to stay with her, but she kissed him and sent him home to Ben and his new family members. She took a long, warm shower, climbed into her soft bed and tried not to see Miguel's injured face every time she closed her eyes.

After a fitful night, she called Jess to ask her to take Kate's patients for the day, only to learn it was Sunday, and she didn't have patients scheduled at all. During the trauma, she had lost all track of time.

"Katie, are you all right?" Jess said. "You need me to come over?"

"I'm okay. Just feeling responsible for all the world's ills and troubles."

"Oh, is that all? I was afraid it might be something serious," Jess said with a wry, sympathetic laugh. Overwhelming responsibility was something they had both dealt with at times—one of the pitfalls of the profession. "You need a good bottle of wine and a couple of hours alone with that big trooper of yours."

"For once," Kate said with a sigh, "I totally agree with you."

When she got to the hospital that morning, she found that Miguel's color had improved. Poor Alejandro had spent the night in a chair by Miguel's bedside and seemed to be wasting away with worry, so she sent him down to the hospital's café with twenty dollars to get some food while she sat with Miguel. Nance showed up, and Kate sent her to check on Alejandro and make sure he ate well. If anybody could do that, it was her gran.

Kate talked to the unconscious Miguel, apologizing for putting him in such danger and promising to help him find a good home when he awakened. Knowing he loved animals, she told him about her patients, relating funny stories that he couldn't laugh at and interesting facts he would never remember. The occasional beep of IV monitors and the ever-present hiss of the oxygen filled every silence, reminding her of her duty to heal and protect those who couldn't protect themselves. She felt helpless and angry.

Time, she reminded herself again and again, was the best healer. But it sounded lame and even patronizing now that she was on the waiting end. Every hour that passed sent her spirits a bit lower.

Nick arrived midday and offered to take the watch for a while. She refused, instead sitting with Nick, talking and reading to Miguel. The afternoon sped by, and it was growing dark when Nance returned to the hospital to insist Alejandro come home with her for a hot meal and a night in a proper bed. He would have objected, but Kate gave him a half hug, during which she whispered, "Don't argue, just go with her. You need to take care of yourself so you can be here for Miguel. We'll call right away if there is any change."

Alejandro nodded and followed Nance with rounded shoulders and fatigue-weighted steps.

NICK WATCHED AS Kate literally worried herself sick and didn't know how to help her.

"I tried to do the right thing," she said

at last when they stepped outside to let the nurses work on Miguel. "Tried to help save dogs…and look what happened." Her voice was dry and strained. "A sweet, good-hearted young boy is paying a terrible price for what I did.

"I knew his uncle was involved, but I coaxed him to tell us about the puppy mill and to show us where it was. I knew it could get him in trouble, but I wanted that location so badly." She leaned against him. "I shouldn't have pushed."

Nick put his arms around her, feeling suddenly like he was hardwired into her emotions, sharing them in a way he had never experienced with anyone else, not even Ben.

She was dealing with some of the same feelings he had felt during and after Iraq. The realization dawned: it wasn't just a soldier's dilemma. Good people put themselves in harm's way to do something good…sacrificing so that others may live in freedom and peace. People here at home fought battles of conscience against long odds and strove to make the world a better, safer place. Their fight, their sacrifice, could be just as traumatic for good and loving hearts as what happened in a war zone.

She turned in his arms and buried her face in his shirt, her shoulders quaking as she fought to contain her grief.

"Come on, Kate." He led her down the hall to a deserted waiting room and settled on a sofa beside her. A sizable ball of tissues later, her tears had stopped, and he lifted her chin to look into her eyes.

"I must be a mess," she said, trying to look away, but he tugged her gaze back to him.

"You're the most beautiful thing I've ever seen," he said with complete sincerity.

She melted visibly and stroked his cheek.

"Thank you for helping, for sitting with me and Miguel. I know this isn't your job."

"Anything that worries or troubles you is definitely my job. You're special, Kate Everly. The world can't afford to let anything happen to you. *I* can't afford to let anything happen to you."

She searched his face—for what, he wasn't sure. But he sensed she needed something from him, something warm and true and from the depths of him. Any other time that thought would have scared the bejesus out of him. Just now, it seemed like the very reason he was born.

"You have the biggest, most loving heart in the world," he said, pouring conviction into each word. "And you back it up with action. Do you know how rare that is?"

Pain flickered through her expression and he pulled her against him and wrapped her in his arms, wishing he could anchor and protect her.

They sat in the waiting room, holding each other, cradling hope for Miguel and Alejandro between them.

After a while he set her back and went out in search of a vending machine. When he returned, he brought her a soda and an update.

"I checked with his nurse. Pretty much the same."

"Thank you." When she'd had a drink, he settled beside her and pulled her back against him, cradling her in his arms.

"Kate, you're not responsible for what happened to him any more than I am or Alejandro is. The responsibility for that falls on Raul and on him alone. He's the monster. He is the one who used and then brutalized a young boy given into his care by a dying mother."

"But Miguel wouldn't have been in that situation if I hadn't—"

"He was already *in* that situation. He and Alejandro were already defying their uncle to bring dogs to the shelter. It was probably just a matter of time until Raul found out."

"That's no excuse, Nick. I knew it could get him in trouble, and I urged him to help anyway. I'm an adult. I should have been more responsible with him and his safety."

"And if he hadn't helped, ninety dogs would still be caged and starved and beaten," he said. "Life isn't a scale, sweetheart." He stroked her cheek. "You can't balance a possible good deed against all the possible bad things that might result. If you did, you would never do anything good or right."

He realized he was talking to himself as well as her, and that insight rocked him for a moment. He threaded his fingers through hers, and she laid her head against his chest.

"You have to do what you know to be good and right," he continued. "You give it your all and trust that something, somewhere will make the outcome what it should be." Her gaze came up to meet his. He was quoting her own words to her and she seemed surprised.

"Wasn't it a wise young veterinarian who said that she learned early on that we're a conduit for healing, not the source? Well, I think that's not only true of healing, it's true of doing good, as well. We're conduits for good, not its source. We're not responsible for every life we touch. That's too big a burden for any human being to bear."

She reached up to stroke his face. "You're a remarkable man, Nick Stanton."

"Nah," he said with a wry grin. "But I am teachable. And believe me, sweetheart, I've been paying attention. Everything you've said to me, every wise observation and loving pronouncement you have made is stored right here." He tapped his chest above his heart. "And I think it's making me a better man…a better dad…a better human being."

She pulled back to look at him, and he could see she was trying to drink in the full impact of his words. She had given him her heart and he was giving it back to her…just when they both needed it most. He felt her pulse began to pound as he lowered his face to hers and pressed his cheek against her temple.

"We haven't known each other for very long, but somehow I can't imagine my life without you in it." His words washed over her in a delicious, sense-warming wave. "This may not be the best time or the place…but then, it may be the perfect time and place… I love you, Kate. I feel like you're already part of my heart and my family, and I want to marry you. It doesn't have to be right away, but, please, don't make me wait too long."

"Nick Stanton, rescuer of dogs, star of my dreams and defender of my heart… I love you, too."

She gave him her answer in a kiss so hot and full of passion that he feared they might set off a smoke alarm in the hallway.

THE NEXT MORNING, Kate arrived at the hospital to take up her vigil at Miguel's bedside with a bit more hope. The neurologist said his cranial pressure was better and he was holding his own. There were positive signs in his reflexes, and there were no seizures or other complications. The question of lasting damage was still unanswered and probably would remain so until he awoke and they could assess him further.

It wasn't exactly good news, but it was good enough…something to hang their hopes on. When Alejandro arrived with Nance, he didn't seem all that impressed with the doctor's opinion.

"He get better," the older boy pronounced, holding his young cousin's hand through the bed rails. "You get better, Miguel. I show you llamas. Yes, an' ostriches. We feed them today. Miz Nance an' me. She has animals. A donkey, little like a dog. Pigs. Goats. She says we come to help her. Maybe stay with her. But you get better, little one. Wake up an' you see."

Kate studied Nance's face, seeing in it the same mixture of stubbornness and compassion that had shaped her own life. She caught her grandmother's eye with a questioning look, and Nance gave a sharp nod that said it was settled and there was nothing left to discuss. Kate had seen that look many times. She smiled softly and nodded back. She knew what it was like to be rescued by Nance Everly, body and soul. She patted Miguel's arm, thinking he was in for quite an adventure when he woke up.

For the first time, she was thinking in terms of "when" not "if," and knew just who to credit for that positive change in her outlook.

Later that day, when Nick arrived at the hospital, Kate felt like her world had just arrived. He learned of Nance's plans for the Vasquez boys and after a moment, nodded.

"I can see that. It would be beneficial both ways." He offered Alejandro a hand and after a moment of confusion on the youth's part, they shook. "Welcome to your new life, son."

When Nick left to get them something to drink, Alejandro looked at Kate with a touch of surprise. "He shake my hand."

"Yes, he did. That's what a man does to show welcome and respect to another man." She smiled as Alejandro straightened and his face gradually lit from within. She watched him stand and go to Miguel's bedside and take his hand.

"I am here, Miguel."

Two long days passed without much change in Miguel's condition. The swelling in his brain was going down, but he hadn't awakened. Between her clinic and the hospital, Kate was putting in long hours. Nance took Alejandro to see Miguel each day, and they sat for hours with a book at his bedside, while Nance helped Alejandro with his reading. Each evening, Sarah brought Ben for a visit and on one visit, the boy insisted on bringing Miguel a dinosaur from his collection. He put it on the bedside table, but after looking at it there, he didn't seem especially happy.

Nance suggested they take a walk and before long they were back with a can of soda that seemed to have brightened Ben's mood. Kate was focused on Miguel and didn't pay much attention to the change.

The next day, Kate dropped by the hospital over her lunch break to find Nick had already been there, delivering a bouquet of balloons from the guys in his station. They were tied on one of the bed rails. Sarah had brought some flowers, but they weren't allowed in ICU, so she left them at the nurses' station and came back with a lifelike stuffed puppy instead.

Kate studied the toy and smiled. Leave it

to Sarah to find the perfect gift for a young boy who loved dogs more than his own safety.

On the sixth day, Kate met with Miguel's doctors and learned that his pressures were finally back within normal range. They were just waiting for him to wake up.

That evening, Nick was already filling the doorway to Miguel's room when she arrived—a tactic they'd begun to use when more than two people were inside and they didn't want the nurses to see it. She slid her arms around his waist from behind and gave him a hug, laying her head against his broad back.

"I hope that's you, Kate," he said, his voice rumbling against her ear. "Because if it's not, we're in trouble."

"It's me," she said, sliding around him and into his arms, where she got a glimpse of the room. Too many people, again. Alejandro was there with Nance and Ben. They were focused on something—something moving on the bed. A puppy!

They'd smuggled in a puppy, and it was climbing all over Miguel, sniffing and licking and scratching at the sheets to make a nest for itself. She stared for a minute, unable to decide whether it was crazy or genius.

"Are you part of this?" she asked.

"I wasn't. But I am now. Accomplice. Dead to rights."

"It was Ben's idea," Nance said proudly, beaming at her eight-year-old coconspirator.

"He didn't need a dinosaur, he needed something real," Ben explained. "A puppy. He loves puppies, so why not bring one to help him?"

"So I brought a puppy from the shelter and helped sneak it in," Nance said. "Nick's been running interference."

"What happens if it pees on the bed?" Kate said, still undecided whether it was a good thing, but loving the way the miniature schnauzer puppy—one of their rescues—was curling up by Miguel's head on the pillow.

"Then we change the sheets," Nance said, motioning to the pile of linen perched on a linen cart along one wall. "No biggie."

"Yeah, no biggie," Ben echoed, beaming.

"Your grandmother is a subversive element," Nick said, putting an arm about her.

"And it looks like she's turning my son into one, too."

"You okay with that, Mr. Law-and-Order?" Kate looked over her shoulder at him, sinking back into his embrace.

"I think I could get used to it." He chuckled. "Plus, I want to see if it helps. I'm working on a theory."

It took another evening of "puppy therapy" for Miguel to awaken. When he opened his eyes to noise and confusion, the first thing he saw was a scruffy little puppy face next to his, and a cheer rang out, bringing the nurses running.

Nance grabbed Alejandro and danced him around the room. Ben climbed up on the bed to retrieve the puppy, who had begun to yip frantically, and Kate tried to explain to the glowering nurses why they had so many visitors and a contraband canine in the room.

Everyone but Alejandro was kicked out immediately, but not one of them was sorry. Miguel was awake and talking—at least to Alejandro.

By the next day, they were holding puppy therapy in the family waiting room of the regular med-surg floor; Miguel had graduated out of ICU and was getting food and physical therapy to help him regain his strength. Alejandro was overjoyed to see his cousin recovering and told Miguel about all that had happened since that day at Clara Crowder's farm.

Mercifully, Miguel didn't remember much of the trauma that put him in the hospital, but he broke down in tears of gratitude when he heard he wouldn't be going back to his uncle. Nance—who knew people in every part of Lakeview's officialdom—announced that she had discussed the subject of becoming a foster parent to Miguel and Alejandro with a friendly caseworker. With a little luck and some canny persuasion, she expected that Alejandro and Miguel would soon be coming to stay on the farm with her.

Miguel seemed a little confused. Alejandro explained and described the farm, and soon he was smiling and eager to explore Nance's menagerie.

The day he was discharged, Miguel had a crew of hospital staff people saying goodbye and even more people following him and Alejandro to their new home. It turned into a welcome home party, with volunteers from

Harbor, troopers and two and four-legged friends from Kate and Jess's practice.

As the day wore on and things quieted down, Nick and Kate slipped away for a walk among the trees. They ended up in the field where they had first kissed, sitting on the same rocks.

"I've been working on a theory," Nick said, holding her hand. "Well, it's not entirely mine. I borrowed parts of it, and other parts are still in the works."

"Oh? Are you going to fill me in or do I have to coax it out of you?"

"Coaxing isn't necessary, but would be appreciated." He leaned in for a kiss that left her humming with satisfaction. "So, you know how I 'rescued' Soldier and then he rescued us?"

"Funny how that worked out, huh?" She leaned her head on his shoulder. In truth it was more than amusing, it was miraculous.

"Well, I think the same thing happened to Miguel. He helped rescue the dogs, and then one of the puppies helped bring him back to us. I'm seeing a pattern here."

"Yes?" She waited, sensing something important coming.

"There's something special between people and animals—especially dogs."

"I think that's been pretty firmly established," she said with a chuckle. "For, like, a few thousand years."

"Yeah, well, I'm not sure we've really plumbed the depths of the human-canine relationship. I think there's more to it. There's a healing quality that seems to go both ways. And I've done some research on what's happening with vets coming back from deployment with health problems and PTSD. Did you know there are organizations that select and train dogs to help veterans cope with the stresses of returning to civilian life?"

"I've heard of them. I don't have first-hand knowledge. Every now and then, I get some materials in the mail about charities that sponsor companion dogs for vets."

"Clearly there's something about dogs that aids healing and grounds people emotionally…helps them cope. Given what happened with me and Soldier, I'd like to start a chapter of one of those organizations in this area."

She broke into a huge grin. "That's a wonderful idea, Nick. It would be a great way to help vets and shelter dogs at the same time."

"There'll be paperwork and some fund-raising to do. But I could take Soldier with me. He's become a real buddy these last few days. I look forward to coming home...seeing his tail wagging and watching him jump around to greet me. I swear, he grins at me. Sometimes I think he's about to burst because he wants to tell me something. Last night he followed me into my room and slept at the foot of the bed."

"Wow. Should I be jealous?" She laughed and clamped her arms around him, wringing a small wince from him. "Ooooh, sorry."

"Squeeze away, Doc. That's one thing Soldier will never be able to do. And, of course, there's this."

He pulled her into his arms and kissed her to within an inch of her sanity. Minutes later they were rudely interrupted by a pair of pushy dogs seeking attention. Kate laughed and slid off her perch to kneel by Goldie and give the dog that had brought them together a gentle hug. When she looked up, Soldier was sitting nobly at attention while Nick lavished him with affection.

The sight produced a sweet pang in her chest, and she thought to herself, *Gran is right. Good friends do make good medicine. Whether those friends have two legs or four.*

EPILOGUE

EIGHT MONTHS LATER, a sizable group of guests gathered at the Everly farm for the celebration of Kate and Nick's wedding. A number of guests had brought four-legged friends to the ceremony, including Hines, whose much-reduced Moose was basking in attention, and Ben, who led Soldier and Goldie down the aisle as honored guests. That handsome pair of dogs, the wedding program said, were matchmakers extraordinaire...having brought Kate and Nick together...and having been instrumental in their courtship.

Participating as ushers were Miguel and Alejandro Vasquez, who had indeed become Nance Everly's foster kids. She was delighted to have them around to share her house and her beloved animals. The pair had enrolled in school and were making great strides.

Sarah and Nance sat at the front, side by

side. They had become good friends, and Sarah now volunteered at the shelter one day a week. Nance had begun taking cooking lessons from Sarah and, with her granddaughter now getting married, she turned her meddlesome sights on Jess Preston. If ever there was a gal who needed to settle down, she was heard to say, it was Jess.

Ben acted as best man for his dad and beamed through the ceremony that made Kate his stepmom, as well as his friend. He was still playing soccer, but he made plenty of time for stargazing, helping out at the clinic and going fishing with his dad. Goldie did indeed sleep in his room at night. And so did Soldier.

A new face appeared the week of the wedding: Kate's brother. Jace Everly hit town like a hurricane and set half the county's eligible female population aflutter. He had a natural magnetism that charmed everyone but Jess, who found him pushy, overconfident and generally unbearable. She did manage to put up with him during the wedding rehearsal and the walk down the aisle…where she caught him winking at a couple of Kate's female college friends in the third row.

But the best part of the day came when Kate walked down the aisle to join her hands and life with Nick's. He beamed, standing proud and handsome in his trooper's uniform, backed up by Ben and by Jace, who wore his best ranger gear. Kate matched his joy, looking radiant as she walked down the aisle behind Jess and LeeAnn in a long gown of simple silk crepe that hugged her curves, with a spray of flowers tucked into her hair.

Everyone said they made a beautiful couple, standing together, holding hands, pouring love and gratitude into each other's eyes and into each heart present. And when the reverend asked if she would take Nick Stanton to be her lawfully wedded husband, the whole assembly laughed as she said boldly, "You bet I do!"

At last, when they were asked to say something of their own to each other, Nick brought tears to her eyes by finishing his vows with, "You have become my shelter, my love and the place I belong. And I pray you'll find your 'forever home' in my heart."

* * * * *

If you enjoyed this emotional love story
by Betina Krahn,
you'll also love these
Harlequin Heartwarming books:
A SONG FOR RORY
by Cerella Sechrist,
A BAXTER'S REDEMPTION
by Patricia Johns,
WITH NO RESERVATIONS
by Laurie Tomlinson and
FOR LOVE OF A DOG
by Janice Carter.

All available at Harlequin.com.

Get 2 Free Books,

Plus 2 Free Gifts—

just for trying the
Reader Service!

YES! Please send me 2 FREE Love Inspired® Romance novels and my 2 FREE mystery gifts (gifts are worth about $10 retail). After receiving them, if I don't wish to receive any more books, I can return the shipping statement marked "cancel." If I don't cancel, I will receive 6 brand-new novels every month and be billed just $5.24 for the regular-print edition or $5.74 each for the larger-print edition in the U.S., or $5.74 each for the regular-print edition or $6.24 each for the larger-print edition in Canada. That's a saving of at least 13% off the cover price. It's quite a bargain! Shipping and handling is just 50¢ per book in the U.S. and 75¢ per book in Canada.* I understand that accepting the 2 free books and gifts places me under no obligation to buy anything. I can always return a shipment and cancel at any time. The free books and gifts are mine to keep no matter what I decide.

Please check one:
- ☐ Love Inspired Romance Regular-Print (105/305 IDN GLWW)
- ☐ Love Inspired Romance Larger-Print (122/322 IDN GLWW)

Name _____ (PLEASE PRINT)

Address _____ Apt. #

City _____ State/Province _____ Zip/Postal Code

Signature (if under 18, a parent or guardian must sign)

Mail to the **Reader Service:**
IN U.S.A.: P.O. Box 1341, Buffalo, NY 14240-8531
IN CANADA: P.O. Box 603, Fort Erie, Ontario L2A 5X3

Want to try two free books from another line?
Call 1-800-873-8635 today or visit www.ReaderService.com.

*Terms and prices subject to change without notice. Prices do not include applicable taxes. Sales tax applicable in N.Y. Canadian residents will be charged applicable taxes. Offer not valid in Quebec. This offer is limited to one order per household. Books received may not be as shown. Not valid for current subscribers to Love Inspired Romance books. All orders subject to approval. Credit or debit balances in a customer's account(s) may be offset by any other outstanding balance owed by or to the customer. Please allow 4 to 6 weeks for delivery. Offer available while quantities last.

Your Privacy—The Reader Service is committed to protecting your privacy. Our Privacy Policy is available online at www.ReaderService.com or upon request from the Reader Service.

We make a portion of our mailing list available to reputable third parties that offer products we believe may interest you. If you prefer that we not exchange your name with third parties, or if you wish to clarify or modify your communication preferences, please visit us at www.ReaderService.com/consumerchoice or write to us at Reader Service Preference Service, P.O. Box 9062, Buffalo, NY 14240-9062. Include your complete name and address.

LI17R2

Get 2 Free Books,

Plus 2 Free Gifts—

just for trying the Reader Service!

YES! Please send me 2 FREE Love Inspired® Suspense novels and my 2 FREE mystery gifts (gifts are worth about $10 retail). After receiving them, if I don't wish to receive any more books, I can return the shipping statement marked "cancel." If I don't cancel, I will receive 4 brand-new novels every month and be billed just $5.24 each for the regular-print edition or $5.74 each for the larger-print edition in the U.S., or $5.74 each for the regular-print edition or $6.24 each for the larger-print edition in Canada. That's a savings of at least 13% off the cover price. It's quite a bargain! Shipping and handling is just 50¢ per book in the U.S. and 75¢ per book in Canada.* I understand that accepting the 2 free books and gifts places me under no obligation to buy anything. I can always return a shipment and cancel at any time. The free books and gifts are mine to keep no matter what I decide.

Please check one: ☐ Love Inspired Suspense Regular-Print ☐ Love Inspired Suspense Larger-Print
                             (153/353 IDN GLW2)   (107/307 IDN GLW2)

Name	(PLEASE PRINT)

Address	Apt. #

City	State/Prov.	Zip/Postal Code

Signature (if under 18, a parent or guardian must sign)

Mail to the **Reader Service:**
IN U.S.A.: P.O. Box 1341, Buffalo, NY 14240-8531
IN CANADA: P.O. Box 603, Fort Erie, Ontario L2A 5X3

Want to try two free books from another line?
Call 1-800-873-8635 or visit www.ReaderService.com.

* Terms and prices subject to change without notice. Prices do not include applicable taxes. Sales tax applicable in N.Y. Canadian residents will be charged applicable taxes. Offer not valid in Quebec. This offer is limited to one order per household. Books received may not be as shown. Not valid for current subscribers to Love Inspired Suspense books. All orders subject to approval. Credit or debit balances in a customer's account(s) may be offset by any other outstanding balance owed by or to the customer. Please allow 4 to 6 weeks for delivery. Offer available while quantities last.

Your Privacy—The Reader Service is committed to protecting your privacy. Our Privacy Policy is available online at www.ReaderService.com or upon request from the Reader Service.

We make a portion of our mailing list available to reputable third parties that offer products we believe may interest you. If you prefer that we not exchange your name with third parties, or if you wish to clarify or modify your communication preferences, please visit us at www.ReaderService.com/consumerchoice or write to us at Reader Service Preference Service, P.O. Box 9062, Buffalo, NY 14240-9062. Include your complete name and address.

LIS17R2

Get 2 Free Books,
<u>Plus</u> 2 Free Gifts—
just for trying the Reader Service!

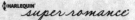

HSRLP17R

Get 2 Free Books,

Plus 2 Free Gifts—

just for trying the Reader Service!

Love Inspired HISTORICAL

READERSERVICE.COM

Manage your account online!

- Review your order history
- Manage your payments
- Update your address

*We've designed the
Reader Service website
just for you.*

Enjoy all the features!

- Discover new series available to you, and read excerpts from any series.
- Respond to mailings and special monthly offers.
- Browse the Bonus Bucks catalog and online-only exculsives.
- Share your feedback.

Visit us at:
ReaderService.com

RS16R

Get 2 Free Books,
Plus 2 Free Gifts—
just for trying the
Reader Service!